Matt McQuaid was the epitome of a Texas lawman. All action, few words.

The Texas lawman was handsome, strong and apparently as hardheaded as Heather was. What more could a woman want?

"You should have asked me about spending the night before you announced that I would."

"I don't like to offer choices when none exist. You need watching over tonight. I'm available."

And that was it. Matter of fact. Cut-and-dried. No "I'm glad to be of service." No wonderful, witty, heroic phrases. Just "I'm available." For some reason, she didn't find his manner offensive. It was almost comforting on one hand, and more than a little seductive on the other.

"Since I'm here for the night, I think I'll turn in. Which bedroom do you want me to use?"

"That's easy," he said, finally smiling. "There's only one."

Dear Reader,

Welcome to the McQuaid family—three brothers who are easy to love and hard to forget. They live their lives the way their father taught them—by THE COWBOY CODE.

This month meet Matt McQuaid, brought to you by Joanna Wayne. Joanna makes her home in steamy Louisiana but feels equally comfortable in the neighbor state of Texas. As a child she loved reading stories of the West and now, as an adult, she visits a ranch owned by friends in south Texas. "The romance of the West is still alive and well," she reports.

You'll want to be sure you don't miss any of these sexy cowboy brothers. If you did, you can still order *McQuaid's Justice* by Carly Bishop and *A Cowboy's Honor* by Laura Gordon by sending $3.99 ($4.50 CAN.) plus 75¢ postage ($1.00 CAN.) to Harlequin Reader Service, 3010 Walden Ave., Buffalo, NY 14269.

Regards,

Debra Matteucci

Senior Editor & Editorial Coordinator
Harlequin Books
300 East 42nd Street
New York, NY 10017

Lone Star Lawman
Joanna Wayne

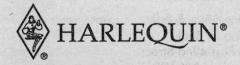

HARLEQUIN®

TORONTO • NEW YORK • LONDON
AMSTERDAM • PARIS • SYDNEY • HAMBURG
STOCKHOLM • ATHENS • TOKYO • MILAN • MADRID
PRAGUE • WARSAW • BUDAPEST • AUCKLAND

With special thanks to my friend, Linda Lewis,
for sharing her wonderful Texas family with me
and traveling with me on great research trips. To my own
family for all the support they've given, and to Wayne,
always, for keeping romance in my life.

ISBN 0-373-22505-9

LONE STAR LAWMAN

Printed in U.S.A.

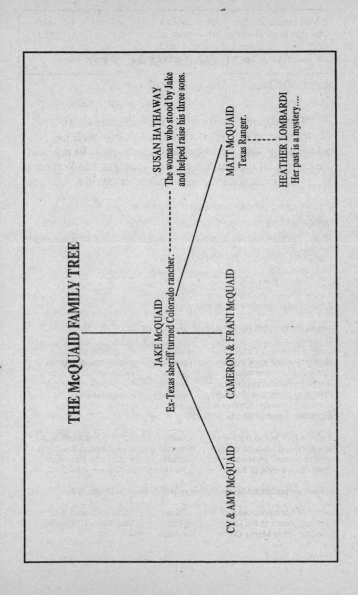

THE McQUAID FAMILY TREE

JAKE McQUAID
Ex-Texas sheriff turned Colorado rancher. - - - - - - - -

SUSAN HATHAWAY
The woman who stood by Jake and helped raise his three sons.

CY & AMY McQUAID

CAMERON & FRANI McQUAID

MATT McQUAID
Texas Ranger.

- - - - - -

HEATHER LOMBARDI
Her past is a mystery....

CAST OF CHARACTERS

Matt McQuaid—The youngest son of Jake McQuaid. He's like his father in many ways though he resents the man who drove his mother away.

Heather Lombardi—She'd never intended her search for her birth mother to tear the town of Dry Creek apart.

Edna and Rube Lawson—Owners of the motel where Heather has rented a room, but what do they really know about the murder that happened right under their noses?

Cass Purdy—She worked at the orphanage where Heather was abandoned, but is her memory accurate after all these years?

Gabby—The town sheriff. Is he part of the past that someone in Dry Creek will kill to keep secret?

Billy Roy Lassiter—He was murdered twenty-five years ago. Is his death connected to the disappearance of Heather's birth mother?

Logan Trenton—One of the wealthiest ranchers in south Texas. He's charming, but can he be trusted?

Sylvia—Logan Trenton's stepdaughter and an old friend of Matt's.

Paul Ridgely and John Billinger—Local ranchers who consider Matt's dad a friend and a legend.

Chapter One

Heather Lombardi jerked upright and gulped a breath of stale air. For a second, she didn't recognize her surroundings, but slowly her sense of place came back to her. She was in a dingy motel room in Dry Creek, Texas, hundreds of miles from her cozy apartment in Atlanta, Georgia.

She blinked, rubbed her eyes, then circled the room with her gaze. Pale moonlight filtered through the window, highlighting the shadowy images that crept across her walls. But in spite of the moonlight, the room was darker than usual. Evidently, the harsh outside light that had glared into her room for the last few nights had burned out.

A square of white caught her eye. She stumbled sleepily to the door and picked it up. Her mind still groggy, she tore open the sealed envelope and hurried back to the bed, flicking on the lamp so she could read the note.

Forget Kathy Warren and get out of town. Now. Leave before your welcome wears out and you find yourself wishing you'd never heard of her or Dry Creek.

It took a minute for the meaning to sink in. When it did, the words were still bewildering. There was no earthly reason why anyone should care if she stayed or left this town. She'd come here on a quest, in search of information about her real mother, the woman who'd given her up for adoption mere days after her birth twenty-five years ago. But so far no one she'd talked to admitted to having ever heard of Kathy Warren.

Heather reread the note, her mind struggling to make sense of the warning. She walked back to the window, pushing hard to force it open. She needed fresh air to clear the last dregs of sleep and help her think rationally. The note was probably some teenaged prank, kids out of school for the summer and bored.

Minutes later, she closed and locked the window and went back to bed, jumping at the sound of the squeaky bedsprings beneath the impact of her hundred and twenty pounds. The truth was she'd like to heed the note. She was tired and more than a little homesick. She missed her apartment, missed her own soft bed, missed chatting with her friends.

But she couldn't give up and go running home. Not yet. Questions that had haunted her for a lifetime were still unanswered.

MATT MCQUAID shoved the white Stetson back on his head and let his booted foot grow heavy on the accelerator. A straight yellow line, miles of smooth Texas highway and two weeks of well-deserved vacation stretched out before him. Fence-mending, windmills to check, and some quality time getting to know his own small spread. At least small by South Texas standards.

He'd saved and bought the place while he was assigned to this area, but he'd been promoted last year, uprooted from his land and plopped down in a city apartment a hundred and thirty miles away.

San Antonio never quite felt like home, but he liked the

job. So, he was left to commute every chance he got and scuff his boots on cement streets when he couldn't.

The Lone M, a plot of mesquite-dotted, drought-hardened dirt that beckoned to him like a pot of spicy chili on a cold Texas night. Not that anyone but him ever called it the Lone M. The other ranchers referred to it simply as "McQuaid's country," an old South Texas usage, defining the land by the man who owned it. Matt didn't mind. Any name you called it, the wind blew free across wide-open spaces, and it was his.

Damn, but life was good.

No bloody crime scenes to be dissected. No district attorneys demanding evidence that didn't exist. Best of all, there would be no reporters in his face ragging him for information for the news media to twist and enlarge to suit their own purposes.

After the hellacious case he'd just wrapped up in San Antonio, nothing could be nicer than two weeks of conversing with nature and cud-chewing critters. Not that he'd ever willingly give up all the aggravation and challenge of being a Texas Ranger. Being a lawman was in his blood, as necessary as air or food.

Fingering the dial of his radio, he worked until a country song blared from the contraption. He rolled down the window of his pickup truck and sang along, enjoying the sting of the dry wind in his face and the sound of his own voice blending with the whining twang of the female singer. Another ballad of love gone bad. Woman trouble, one problem he didn't have now and had no intention of acquiring.

Matt slowed as he entered the town limits of Dry Creek. The sun hovered low on the horizon, making it difficult to see the road, but painting the shabby town in shades of gold and red that glistened off tin roofs and sparkled on iron cattle gaps. A fitting homecoming, he decided.

Matt turned into the drive of Ridgely's Feed and Hardware Store and parked between a tractor and John Billinger's new truck. He'd already stopped for groceries, but he needed to pick up some supplies so he could start work in the morning with the sun. He might as well let the locals know he was home for a couple of weeks while he was at it.

His boots clattered against the wooden boards of the porch and heralded his arrival even before he walked through the open door.

"Well, look who's back, the Texas Ranger who just stuck it to Clemson Creighton like a June bug to a screen door." Billinger's voice boomed across the store as Matt stepped into sight.

"Just doing my job, Billinger. Trying to make sure you Texans get what you pay for."

"Yep." Paul Ridgely spit a long stream of brown goop into a tin can and then stepped from behind the counter. He extended a hand. "Of course, it took a McQuaid to nail him. Those pretty boys up in San Antonio let the man walk around right under their noses for ten years. You done your pa proud, Matt."

Matt took Ridgely's callused hand and shook it firmly. "I'm sure Jake could have done it better and faster." The men laughed but nodded in agreement without guessing at the sarcasm that rode beneath the surface of Matt's words.

It had been almost a quarter of a century since Jake McQuaid had been sheriff around here, but his legend lived on. Who was Matt to disturb the image with suggestions of imperfection in their hero?

"Didn't much get by old Jake McQuaid," Billinger added. "So, you here for Logan Trenton's big shindig next weekend, or do you even aim to stay long enough to do a little honest labor?"

"Two weeks. Plenty of time to get my boots dirty." Matt hadn't known Logan Trenton was throwing a party. Now that he did, he hoped he could escape an invitation. "I'm going to spend my time catching up at the ranch."

"Well, I hope you make enough time to come by the house," Billinger said. "I'm smoking some brisket tomorrow, and the wife would love to have you over. Might even bake up one of those apple pies for you and I'd get a piece of it. She's read another of those tomfool articles on cholesterol and heart attacks and has me eating my apples from around the core now."

"I don't know about your cholesterol, Billinger," Ridgely joked, "but that roll of fat around your middle ain't too appealing. She's probably tired of trying to reach around it."

"Don't you be worrying about my middle. I can handle my woman." He leaned over for a better look out the door. "Of course I don't know if I could handle one like that." He nodded his head in the direction of the door and a view of a compact rental car that had just pulled up in front of the greasy-spoon joint across the parking lot.

All three of the men watched as a shapely young woman climbed out. Her short, straight skirt inched up, revealing just enough thigh to assure the onlookers that her legs were as fine as the rest of her.

"Forget the apple pie," Billinger said, rocking back on his heels. "Just watching that woman walk has my blood pressure soaring. She's too much for me, but I bet the Ranger here could handle a woman like that."

"Don't count on it." Matt studied the woman with the practiced eye of a man who had built a reputation of never missing a detail. Her hair was sandy blond, bouncing about her shoulders as she walked. The blue suit fit her to perfection, simple, but probably expensive, and the shoes on her feet would never make it in a cow pasture. Her skin was creamy smooth and not bronzed by the South Texas sun.

To sum it up, she was as much out of place in Dry Creek as quiche at a Texas barbecue.

"What do you say, Matt? Is that a looker or what?"

"She's not my style," Matt said, pulling his eyes away from her with a severe expression.

"Maybe not, but my guess is you're going to get a chance to get up close and personal before you leave town," Billinger said. "Then you can find out for yourself if she's your style."

"How's that?" Matt asked, hating to admit even to himself that the woman had aroused his curiosity.

"She's been questioning everyone in town. Seems her momma ran out on her when she was just a baby, and now she's looking for her."

"Who was her mother?" Matt asked, in spite of himself.

"A woman by the name of Kathy Warren. Ever heard of her?"

"Nope." Matt turned his attention to a notice of an upcoming auction.

"No one else in town has either," Ridgely said, still standing and staring even though the woman under discussion had already disappeared behind the doors of the café. He scratched a bald spot on the back of his round head. "I think she's barking up the wrong tree. I've lived in Dry Creek all my life, and if a woman good-looking enough to birth a young'un like that had come around even for a little while, I'd dang sure remember her."

"Someone would anyway," Billinger agreed. "This town is short on pretty women and long on memory. All the same, I can't help but feel sorry for Miss Lombardi. It's got to be tough knowing your mom just walked off and never came back. I can see why she'd want to find her.''

Matt let the subject lie. Life was tough, and Miss Lombardi should have learned that by now. Mothers *did* just walk away, and maybe they had their reasons. Or maybe they didn't. Either way the kids they left behind didn't get a vote in the matter. ''Do you still run a store here, Ridgely, or is this just gossip central?'' he asked, pulling his list from his pocket.

''I'll take your money,'' Ridgely said, his deep laughter rumbling through the store as he stole a peek at Matt's list.

''Yeah,'' Billinger threw in, ''but if you were half smart, you'd be next door about now offering to help out a damsel in distress. You might just get lucky and wind up with a real looker like your dad did. They don't make many like Miss Susan, but that Heather Lombardi might run her a close second.''

''You're right. They don't make many like Susan Hathaway.'' Matt gave one last look out the door. ''But I'll leave luck alone tonight and settle for supplies.''

''Yeah, well, I'd say you'll be spending your luck tonight on a full moon with nothing but the wailing of coyotes to keep you company.'' Billinger fingered a can of mosquito repellent someone had left on the counter. ''Personally, if I were in your boots, single, available and some hotshot Texas Ranger, I'd be finding a way to share that moon with Miss Lombardi.''

''Chasing down a long-lost mother? No, thanks. I'm on vacation. I'll stick with rounding up cows. They're a lot less trouble.''

''I agree with Matt,'' Ridgely said, already walking toward the back of the store to get the first item on Matt's list. ''He don't need to go messing around with the likes of Miss Lombardi. Women like that are nothing but trouble.''

The door swung open and a couple of hands from a neighboring spread walked in. Billinger started a new conversation, and Matt caught up with Paul Ridgely. A few minutes later, Matt was loading supplies and some sacks of feed onto the back of his truck. Delicious odors drifted from the café, and his stomach gnawed at his backbone, fussing about the fact that he'd missed lunch.

He glanced at his watch. It was already seven-thirty. If he ate in town, he wouldn't have to bother with cooking tonight. He knew just what he wanted: a big, juicy hamburger, smothered in sautéed onions and dripping with mustard and mayo.

Ridgely and Billinger would notice him walking into the café and make a few salty comments about his chasing after the slick city woman, but he could take their good-natured ribbing.

Heather Lombardi, or whoever the heck she was, held no fascination for him beyond the fact that she was a gorgeous woman. He could look and enjoy without the need to own or even to rent. After all, he knew his limitations and his strengths. And right now, he had life in the palm of his hand, just the way he liked it. He didn't need a thing.

HEATHER NURSED HER CUP of after-dinner coffee and watched as the young señorita poured a tall glass of iced tea for the newest cowboy to enter the café. The girl lingered to flirt and he rewarded her efforts with a crooked smile guaranteed to set a young heart fluttering.

The effect on Heather was somewhat milder, but she had to admit the man was attractive. His face was a mixture of rugged planes and distinct angles, but the overall impression was both masculine and distinctly Texan, that indefinable quality that separated him and his cronies in town from the few urban cowboys she'd met growing up in the big city.

Heather stared at the man, struck by a sudden impulse. Joining strangers at their table wasn't her usual style, but at this point she didn't have much to lose. Another wasted day was coming to a close. She picked up her coffee cup and headed his way before she had a chance to change her mind.

"Mind if I join you for a few minutes?" she asked, sliding into the seat on the opposite side of the table.

"Looks like you already have."

"I can leave again."

"Why would you? I figure you have a reason for being here or you wouldn't have bothered coming over."

He caught her off guard, had her fumbling in her mind for something to say. "Are you always so direct?"

"Pretty much. It saves a lot of trouble." He stuck out a hand. "Matt McQuaid," he said, wrapping his palm around hers and shaking it firmly. "And you must be the famous Ms. Lombardi."

She grimaced. "So, my reputation precedes me. I'm afraid I've made a pest of myself around Dry Creek the last few days."

"I don't think pest is the right word, but you've gotten a little attention."

And not all of it good. Heather slid her fingers into her pocket and touched the note that rested there.

"Is this business or pleasure?" The man's tone bordered on intimidation, but he followed the question with the same easy smile he'd flashed the waitress.

Heather plunged in. "Business."

"Too bad. I thought I was about to be picked up."

A blush burned her cheeks. "Not tonight, cowboy. At

least, not by me, but I would like to ask you a few questions.''

"That would have been my second guess."

His gaze bit into her, a penetrating stare that left her feeling exposed. She took a breath and continued. "I'm trying to find out about a woman named Kathy Warren. I don't know much about her except that she was last seen in Dry Creek twenty-five years ago. She would have probably been in her early twenties at the time."

"I would have been a young kid then. What makes you think *I* might know something?"

"Desperation," she finally answered. "So far I've hit nothing but dead ends in my search, and I noticed that everyone in the café knows you."

His eyes narrowed. "So you just came right over to my table with your questions?"

"I didn't think it would hurt to ask you. Apparently I was wrong." She scooted to the outside edge of the booth.

"No, wait." He took her hand and tugged, keeping her from standing. "I didn't mean to offend you. I'm just not good at small talk."

"So I noticed."

The waitress interrupted, setting a plate of food in front of Matt. He caught Heather's gaze. "Would you like something?" he asked.

She took the offer as an invitation to stay. The sandwich she'd eaten was more than enough to fill her, but dessert would buy her more time with the cowboy. His attitude needed adjustment, but, after all, she wasn't interested in friendship, just facts.

"I'll have a piece of the cherry pie," she said, "with a cup of decaf."

Matt bit into his hamburger as the waitress moved on to the next table. "Tell me about Kathy Warren," he said, when he'd finished the bite of burger and taken a long drag on his iced tea.

"She was my birth mother. She left me at an orphanage in Dimmit County when I was just a few days old."

He ate and chewed, taking his time before continuing the conversation. "And you think your mother ended up around here?"

"A woman from the orphanage said she gave Kathy a ride into Dry Creek and let her off at the bus station. I've searched and searched, but there's no record of her after that night."

"So Kathy Warren rode into the sunset and disappeared, probably just the way she'd planned." He looked her square in the eye. "She gave you up. It happens. So why go against her wishes to have you out of her life at this late date?"

The chill in the cowboy's tone caught Heather off guard. Despite his casual demeanor, he'd seemed friendly enough. But now the temperature at the table seemed to have suddenly changed. "You don't waste a lot of effort on sympathy, do you?"

"I didn't know you were looking for sympathy. I thought you were chasing around Texas looking for your mother. I can think of better ways to waste your time."

"Wrong. I'm not looking for my birth mother. She died years ago. I just thought it would be nice to have some closure, to make contact with members of my biological family. But I shouldn't have bothered you with my problems." She jumped to her feet.

"What about your pie?"

"You eat it. My treat for wasting your precious time." She took a few bills from her purse and threw them onto the table. "Have a pleasant night, Mr. McQuaid, if you're capable of that."

Matt watched her march out of the café, her head high, her back straighter than a fence post. She was angry with him. The fact didn't make him feel particularly good. Actually, it ground in his stomach and stole his appetite away.

But if his unsympathetic comments got Heather Lombardi off her mission of recreating the past, he'd probably done her a favor. Fairy-tale endings were the stuff children's books were made of, not real life.

Still, he had to admit, Billinger might have been right. Heather Lombardi in the moonlight would have made for some interesting memories.

MATT SLOWED HIS TRUCK as a couple of deer stepped from the bushes into the glow of his headlights. Experience had taught him the animals could bolt without warning, dashing into the highway and causing havoc for themselves and the vehicle that hit them. But this time the animals played it smart. They turned and loped back into the gathering darkness.

Matt looked in the direction they'd fled as he passed the spot. No sign of movement, but he caught sight of a car, pulled off into the tangle of brush a few yards from the road. Probably young lovers looking for a bit of privacy.

But maybe not.

Matt cursed the lawman instincts that kept him from driving by without investigating. He slowed and guided the truck into a U-turn. Minutes later, he'd located the spot, or at least close to it. He brought his truck to a stop on the hard dirt shoulder of the road.

The gate the car had probably used was at least fifty yards down the road. Undaunted, Matt grabbed a flashlight, ducked between the rows of barbed wire and tramped through the brush. His beam of light roamed the area in search of the car he'd spotted earlier.

He was about to call out when a loud male voice shattered the quiet. "Somebody's coming. We gotta get out of here."

Someone was clearly up to no good. Of all times for him to be without his gun. Matt had just about convinced himself to go back for it when the beam of illumination from his flashlight found the car he'd seen originally. Proximity and a brighter light added dimension and color to the vehicle. Small, white, identical to the one Heather Lombardi had driven away from the café in only a few minutes before he had.

Adrenaline pumped into Matt's bloodstream, and he took off at a run. An engine roared to life in the distance just as he reached the white car. He looked up, but all he saw was the glow of headlights darting through the brush to the west of him. Cautiously, he turned back to the car, swung the door open and peered inside.

His stomach turned at the sight.

Chapter Two

Heather Lombardi was slumped over the steering wheel. Her jacket was torn and Matt could see blood on one of her hands. He reached inside the car and gripped her upper arm.

"Leave me alone, you ape!" She kicked at him and jerked away from his grasp.

Her voice shook with pain and a fighting spirit that pulled at Matt's control. He ached to pound his fists into whoever had done this to her. He was far more adept at that than tending the wounded.

"Settle down. I'm not going to hurt you."

Her eyes widened in recognition. "Oh, it's you, cowboy." She rubbed a jaw that was already swelling into an ugly mass. "How did you get here?"

"Pure luck. The real question is how did you get here?"

"I had help." She shuddered. "Two nasty men." She looked around nervously.

"Take it easy. You're safe for the time being, and you can fill me in on the details later. Right now, I want to get you out of this car and into my truck."

"No, I'm not going off with you. I don't know you any better than I knew those guys. Just call the cops, or the sheriff, or whatever it is you have out here."

"If that's the way you want it." He backed away from the car. It took her about two seconds and one brief glance into the darkness to change her mind.

"Okay, I'll go with you." She scooted across the seat, groaning all the way.

"Here, let me help you." He tucked an arm under hers and tugged.

Her groans dissolved into a string of mild curses, mostly aimed at the cowards who'd attacked her. Matt helped her out of the car, and she leaned against him, her bruised body weak and shaky.

"Where to?" she managed.

"It's just a few yards to my truck, but I don't think you're going to make it on foot." He swept her into his arms and was amazed at how light she was. He started off through the brush, frightening a jackrabbit and sending it hopping out of his path.

"You don't have to carry me," she protested, though with little conviction.

"I know. I could let you crawl, but I don't have all night."

"Wait! Go back."

"Don't tell me you changed your mind again."

"No, I need my purse."

"Do you think it's still there?"

"Why not? This wasn't a robbery. It was a scare tactic by some of your friendly townsfolk who don't like strangers." She groaned again. "So much for Texas hospitality."

Matt turned and headed back to the truck. "You must be real special," he said, possibilities bucking around in his head like a spooked pony. "I don't remember hearing about any welcoming parties like this around here since..." Memories rushed his mind. He pushed them back. "Not since I was a kid," he finished.

"Yeah, I'm special, all right."

Matt propped her against the fender of her car while he dug in the back seat for her purse. Sure enough, it was there, and didn't appear to have been touched. The plot definitely thickened. He slung the handbag across his shoulder and started to pick Heather up again.

She straightened on her own. "No, thanks, cowboy. My head's all but quit spinning. I can walk, if you'll just share an arm for support."

"Whatever you want." He led her through the brush, guiding her around a prickly cactus. He had a thousand questions, but he'd let her regain her equilibrium before he bombarded her with them. He opened the door of the truck and gave her a boost as she climbed inside. "The nearest hospital is forty-five miles from here. I'll call for an ambulance to meet us in town."

"No, I just need a lift back to my motel room in Dry Creek. Actually, I'm feeling stronger every minute. I think I could drive my own car and not put you to any more trouble."

She leaned her head against the back of the seat and closed her eyes. "Or maybe not. The stupid jerk with the taco breath slapped me so hard I saw double for a minute or two. And one of him was more than enough."

Matt turned the key and started the engine. It purred to perfection, and he pulled onto the road. "Can you identify the men?"

"I don't think so. They wore masks. One of them should have my nail prints imbedded in his stomach, though, and he won't be walking too straight after where my knee caught him."

Matt smiled in spite of himself. Miss Lombardi was clearly tough as well as gorgeous. But he was starting to have his doubts about her story of a search for a long, lost mother. Her appeal to men who beat up women and didn't bother taking their cash suggested that Miss Lombardi might have a few secrets of her own.

"How did you happen to be on this deserted stretch of highway?" he asked, after they'd driven in silence for a few minutes.

"Not by choice. I was kidnapped back in Dry Creek by one of the men. He was waiting in the back seat floor of my car when I left the café."

"You better start locking your doors."

"The drivers of half of the cars in the parking lot had left their windows down to combat the heat. I stupidly followed the example of the natives, especially since there were plenty of people around." She pushed a tangle of hair back from her bruised face. "The man drove me here in my car and then another goon jumped out of the bushes. I thought it was my car they wanted. My second major mistake of the night."

"The second man must have been driving the vehicle they got away in. I heard it start up just before I got to you, but I only caught a quick glimpse. I don't suppose you got a look at it."

"I didn't even hear the engine. My ears were ringing from being slapped around."

Matt beat an irritated fist against the steering wheel. "A simple carjacking turned ugly. Only we don't have carjackings in Dry Creek." He was thinking out loud, but Heather jumped on his statement.

"Do you think I'm lying about this?"

"No. I'm just saying there's a lot more to this than is floating on the surface of the water barrel."

"Yeah, like someone in your town doesn't like visitors."

He drove in silence for the next few minutes, his mind

buzzing and coming up with nothing. Finally, he turned off at a dirt road. Grinding to a stop, he swung open his truck door so he could get out and unlatch the gate.

Heather opened her eyes. "Where in the hell are we now?"

"My place."

"Now, wait a minute. I'm thankful for the rescue, but not so thankful I'm planning on giving up any of my virtue."

"Good. I'd hate to have to settle for entertainment from someone in the shape you're in. But since you're not willing to go to the hospital, you'll have to withstand my first aid. A little liniment and some peroxide for that nasty cut over your eye."

Heather feathered the cut with her fingers. With the rest of her body aching like crazy, she hadn't noticed the bloody cut. "You're not planning on using cow liniment, are you?"

"No, that stuff's too expensive to waste on women."

"Very funny."

Matt took care of the gate duties, and they headed down the road toward the small cabin that had come with the land. "What do you do when you're not searching for long-lost relatives?" he asked.

"I work in the public relations department for a television station."

"So who relates to the public while you roam around Texas?"

"Probably someone vying for my job. I'm on vacation."

She turned to face him, this time without groaning, but her face was more than slightly misshapen, and her right eye was practically swollen shut.

"Are you sure you don't want to see a doctor?" he

asked, grimacing at the sight. "You look like a rodeo clown who didn't escape the bull."

"Thank you. And, yes, I'm sure. Ice and aspirin will be fine. They just slapped me around a little." She squirmed and peeked under a stack of papers that occupied the seat space between them.

"Looking for something?"

"A phone. I'd like to report this incident to the authorities."

"You've already done that."

"I beg your pardon."

"You're talking to the law, not a local authority, but the law all the same. I'm with the Texas Rangers. My office is in San Antonio."

"Oh, jeeez. Rescued by a Texas Ranger. They'll love this story back at home." She stretched her neck, rubbing the back of it with agitated strokes. "You're a long way from the office."

"It's a small world. I'm on vacation, too."

"I don't know about you, but this wasn't part of my itinerary." She shifted and moaned again. "I'll rest at your place for a few minutes, but then we have to go back for my car. It's a rental. The insurance company would frown on my leaving it parked it the middle of nowhere overnight."

"It won't be. I plan to have it picked up by the sheriff and dusted and checked for prints, and I want the crime scene checked for any available evidence."

"Didn't I mention that my attackers wore gloves?"

"No. What kind of gloves?"

"Leather. Not the dressy kind, the kind you might work in. They didn't look new. What do you expect to find, other than prints?"

"I'll take what we can get. A piece of clothing would

be nice or some unusual tire prints from the other car. That, with any information you can give us, might help identify at least one of the perps.''

"I'll help all I can. I want these men caught and prosecuted, although I'm sure they meant for me to be too afraid to report the attack. They said as much.''

"I'm glad you're not. The sheriff and I will both want to hear all the details and the truth about why you're *really* in Dry Creek. Then maybe we can figure out why someone around here, or a couple of someones, wants to get rid of you.''

Heather tracked a spot over her left temple where another pain was throbbing to life. "Do you want the story about how I'm a Mafia princess on the run or the one where I'm wanted for spying in twelve countries?''

"I want the truth.''

"You've already heard it. Sorry, Matt McQuaid, Texas Ranger, but I'm just a woman tracing her roots. But I'd still like to take you up on that liniment and the strongest pain reliever you've got. I have a feeling things are going to get worse before they get better.''

"Funny. I have that same feeling.''

Matt pulled the truck to a stop in the carport and climbed out. He hadn't been at the ranch house in over a month. He couldn't remember how he'd left it, though he doubted it was ready for company. But it couldn't be any worse than the one dilapidated motel in Dry Creek, and besides, as long as Heather was with him, she wouldn't have to worry about a repeat visit from her wrecking crew.

The thought of any man dirty enough to use a woman for a punching bag ground in his gut. He expected her to be all right except for some nasty bruises and sore muscles, but if he hadn't arrived the story might have been tragically different. What they'd told her about not wanting to kill her wouldn't have mattered. He'd seen it happen too many times before. Attacks, fueled by anger and power, that escalated into murder.

Two big men against one petite woman. Dirty cowards any way you looked at it. Now all he had to do was find the scum who were responsible and make sure they paid their full dues. That, and keep Miss Heather Lombardi safe.

The woman would be nothing but trouble. He'd suspected it from the moment he'd watched her sashay into the café. Now he was sure of it. He could kiss his peaceful vacation goodbye.

A BRIEF STRUGGLE with the key and the back door squeaked open. "It's not much, but it's home," Matt said, ushering his guest inside, "at least when I'm lucky enough to get back here."

Heather leaned against the door frame and gave the place a cursory once-over. She'd seen worse. They'd entered the back door, passing through the laundry area and into a small kitchen. Nothing fancy, but cozy, with a wooden table and several chairs. Not all of them matched, but they were sturdy and seemed to fit the ranch house's sparse but functional decor.

There were clean dishes in a drainer at the side of the sink, and some glass canning jars filled with preserves on the counter. Somehow she doubted Ranger Matt had put up the preserves himself. She didn't have him figured out yet, but he was a far cry from the Martha Stewart image.

Manhandling criminals probably fit his persona better. She hoped to get a chance to find out by watching him arrest the hoodlums who had worked her over.

"We'll get you fixed up in no time," he said, guiding her through the kitchen and into a den that reeked of masculinity. Dark leather covered the well-worn chairs and couch, and heads of animals glared at her from their positions on the walls. A pair of boots rested on the hearth, and one lamp and a supply of newspapers and magazines covered the end table.

"Sit here," he said, motioning toward the couch. "I'll get the ice and then tend that cut on your forehead."

She eased to a sitting position, tugging her skirt down as best she could and pulling her blouse together. The top two buttons were missing, and a jagged tear revealed more than a scrap of her bra.

"Do you live alone?" she called over the serenade of cracking ice in the kitchen.

"What gave me away, the dust or the curtainless windows?"

"Neither, but I don't see a wife appearing to check out the injured stray you brought home."

"There's no wife."

He returned a second later with a contraption that resembled a sling, a couple of tubes of antiseptic and a brown bottle of something that probably burned like the jalapeños she'd eaten in her enchiladas at lunch.

He eased to the couch beside her and tilted her face upwards. His hands were big, strong and weathered by the sun, but he surprised her with the gentleness of his touch.

"You must have taken a couple of power punches to this cheek."

"I did. The man who drove my car slapped me across the face. I tried to fight back. I poked a finger in the other man's eyes, and that's when he landed the first blow with his fist."

"What about the rest of your body? Did they hit you in the stomach or chest? If there are internal injuries..." His eyes fell to the tear in her blouse. "They didn't..."

She read the new fury, hot and dark in his eyes. "No,

they didn't rape me. My blouse must have gotten torn in the skirmish." She bent down and rubbed her legs. "I did get kicked in the shins, but I think I got in a pretty good kick myself. You must have shown up about then. One guy was dragging me out of the car. I glimpsed lights in the distance, and they took off running."

"Don't worry. They won't be able to run fast enough or far enough to get away permanently."

"Sure of yourself, aren't you. Do you always get your man?"

"Sooner or later." Matt took the sling and tied it around her head as if she had a toothache. "I made a pouch for the ice. It should slow the swelling in the jaw. I have another one for the eye, but you'll have to hold it in place. Before you do, I need to doctor the cut." He propped a pillow behind her head. "Lean back and try to relax. This will probably burn a little."

"I knew you'd say that. And men use the term *a little* so loosely when the pain doesn't apply to them."

"Okay, it will probably burn a lot." He dabbed the spot with liquid from the bottle.

She flinched, but didn't complain. "Does it need stitches?"

"No, it's not deep, just jagged. I don't know what caused the cut, so we have to make sure it's sterilized."

"A belt buckle, I think. I caught the edge of it against my head when I was clawing and trying to get away."

"I'd say you're a pretty spunky woman to keep fighting when the odds were two to one."

"I didn't know the cavalry was on the way."

"You should have. This *is* Texas, after all."

"Yeah, right." She grimaced as he smoothed some salve across the cut. Her whole face was a mass of tender, painful flesh, but the burning had stopped. "I'll owe you one for this, cowboy."

"No, you don't owe me anything, except enough answers to help us find and arrest the guilty. I called Gabby from the kitchen. He should be here any minute, so I'll hold my questions until then rather than make you do double duty."

"Gabby?"

"The sheriff, and you'll find out soon enough that his nickname is well-earned."

His gaze fell to the torn blouse again, and her hand flew up to hide the exposed cleavage.

"I can get you one of my shirts," he offered.

"I'd appreciate that. And then you can point me to the bathroom."

"Sure."

He disappeared down the hall and returned a few minutes later with a blue broadcloth shirt, Western-style, with snaps instead of buttons.

"The bathroom is the second door on the left. If you need anything, let me know. There are washcloths in the cabinet under the sink."

Heather stood up. Her legs wobbled, and she grabbed the wooden arm of the couch for support. Matt was beside her in an instant, steadying her with a strong arm. She let herself lean against him for a few seconds, absorbing his strength.

"We can still go to the hospital," he said, his gaze scrutinizing her closely, no doubt searching for clues she was in worse shape than she'd admitted.

"Thanks, but no thanks. I'm in no mood to be jabbed, poked and prodded by an emergency room intern, not after what I've been through tonight." She straightened and took a step that was less wobbly. Feeling more secure, she started down the hall, aware of the concern in Matt's eyes as he watched her every move.

He puzzled her. At the restaurant, he'd been distant and cool, but here at his house, he was warm and nurturing. Maybe he performed best in the role of hero. Or maybe, she thought wryly, it was her charm that was winning him over.

She stepped into the bathroom and flicked on the light. Leaning across the sink, she glimpsed her image in the mirror and then recoiled in misery. No wonder the Ranger thought she needed a doctor. She might have suggested an undertaker herself. Gingerly, she guided her fingers to the purple-rimmed eye and the pulpy flesh around it.

It had to be that Matt was at home in the hero role, she decided. She had about as much sexual appeal as the Bride of Frankenstein. She readjusted her icy sling so that she could check out the bruises to her jaw. The sight was equally grotesque.

And all of this just because she'd asked a few questions about Kathy Warren, a woman who'd passed through town twenty-five years ago.

Forget Kathy Warren and get out of town.

She'd been ordered to do that twice now. The second warning had been brutal. But Kathy Warren must have been a very hardheaded woman, because Heather had definitely inherited that trait from someone. She didn't like threats, and she didn't scare easily. Left alone, she might have eventually given up and left town when no one remembered her mother. Now, she'd be staying.

She didn't understand it, but the longing she had lived with for as long as she could remember, the need to know who she really was and where she'd come from, had never been stronger than it was tonight.

HEATHER SAT AT THE kitchen table and focused her one open eye on Gabby as he studied the note she'd handed him. "It was delivered to me at the motel, stuffed under my door while I was sleeping," she explained. "The manager said he hadn't seen anyone around there, but security at that place is nonexistent."

The sheriff refolded the note. "We don't usually have trouble down at the motel. Old Rube don't even have paying guests too often anymore."

"No trouble at the motel. No attacks on women. This town was a regular haven before I came along." She didn't try to hide the sarcasm. She was tired, physically and emotionally, from the events of the night *and* the last half hour of redundant interrogation.

Besides, she didn't like the way the sheriff had been phrasing his questions. She was the victim, not the criminal, but she wasn't at all sure he saw it that way.

"Now don't get all riled, Miss Lombardi. I plan to check everything out. It's just that we don't go fixing fences down here till we know what broke 'em in the first place."

He stood, grabbing his hat from the chair beside him as he did and setting it on his head. "You're a nice woman, and all the talk I've heard around here since you drove into town is how everyone wishes they could help you out. Now all of a sudden, you got someone gunning for you, so to speak. It just don't add up."

"So it must be my fault?"

"I didn't say that."

Matt leaned into the table. "We're not suggesting it's your fault, Heather. We're just trying to make sense of this." He spread his hands as if making a point. "You've come to town looking for a woman who you said passed through here twenty-five years ago. It appears that no one in the area's ever heard of her, and yet you received a note mentioning her by name and warning you to leave town. Now you've been attacked, apparently to put teeth in the warning.''

She shook her head in frustration, and pain shot up her neck, settling in under her swollen eye. "I know it sounds bizarre, but I'm telling the truth.''

"And you're sure this Kathy Warren you're asking about is dead?''

"It was reported to the authorities at the orphanage, my birth mother died a few months after I was abandoned. Shortly after that, I was adopted.'' Frustration was threatening to push her over the edge. She'd said all this before.

Matt scribbled more notes in a small black notebook. "Who reported the death?'' he asked, turning his face toward her.

"I'm not sure. The woman I talked to thought he might have been my mother's brother.''

"Seems like your uncle would've just taken you with him,'' the sheriff said, his eyebrows raised. "Him being family and all.''

"I don't know any of the circumstances. The woman who left me at the orphanage said I was her child but that she couldn't take care of me. She signed away all rights of parenthood.''

Gabby stopped at the door. "Looks like you shoulda left well alone, little lady. I'd think seriously about just clearing out of Dry Creek and letting this die down if I were you.''

"All I'm trying to do is track down my family, discover my roots. That's not unusual.''

"I suppose not. I saw a TV show about that one time,'' Gabby admitted. "Some girl looked for years and then found her mother living two blocks away. But just looking for your mom's family shouldn't cause you to get beat up."

"Thank you," she said. "When you find the men who did it, I suggest you ask them their reasons."

He squared his shoulders. "Oh, I plan to find out exactly what's going on. And if this Kathy Warren was around here, I'll find that out, too."

"I think we've questioned Heather enough for tonight," Matt broke in, moving over to stand behind her chair. "Why don't you call me as soon as you get a fingerprint report off the car?"

Gabby stood and ambled toward the door. "Yeah, I'll do that, though I doubt we find anything, them wearing gloves and all."

"Check it anyway. One of the gloves might have slipped off in the fray."

Gabby scratched his whiskered chin. "I can give you a ride back into town, Miss Lombardi. I'm going that way."

"Miss Lombardi's staying here tonight."

Heather spun around to face Matt. "That won't be necessary. I'm fine now."

"It's necessary. I wouldn't have said it if it weren't."

She stared at him. He was neither smiling nor frowning. He just made the statement and expected her to go along with it. The man was clearly far too used to having the final say, but she wasn't under his control.

She stood and faced him. "What makes it necessary? The attack is over and done with. Surely the men wouldn't dare show up again. Besides, they said they were only supposed to rough me up, and they've already done that."

"Criminals have been known to lie."

As far as Matt was concerned, that was the end of the discussion. She could read the finality in his tone and his eyes. She was tempted to insist that she was capable of making her own decisions about where she spent the night, but the truth of Matt's statement held her back.

She had been no match for the two men, especially the older one. It was as if she could feel the evil inside him when he'd slapped her, and it had been his hand that had ripped her blouse. She trembled, remembering the fear, a black cloud of sickening smoke that had rolled in her stomach and filled her lungs as she tried to fight them off.

She struggled for a calming breath and forced the fear to subside. She needed a clear head. Besides, she was safe here with Matt McQuaid. The Ranger was handsome, strong, and apparently as hardheaded as she was. What more could a woman want?

"How's that jaw?" he asked, closing the door behind the sheriff.

"Sore, like the rest of me. You should have asked me about spending the night before you announced that I would."

"I don't like to offer choices when none exist. You need watching over tonight. I'm available, though it wasn't the way I'd planned to spend my first night home."

And that was it. Matter-of-fact. Cut and dried. No "I'm glad to be of service." No wonderful, witty, heroic phrases. Just "I'm available." Matt McQuaid was the epitome of a Texas lawman. All action, few words.

For some reason, she didn't find his manner as offensive as she should have. It was almost comforting on one hand, and more than a little seductive on the other. Oh, well, when in Rome…

"Since I'm here for the night, I think I'll turn in. Which bedroom do you want me to use?"

"That's easy," he said, finally smiling. "There's only one."

Chapter Three

Matt hesitated and then knocked on the door. In spite of claiming she was too tired to talk, Heather hadn't turned off the bedroom light.

"Come in."

He did and then stared at the waif of a woman propped up on his pillows. His T-shirt, bleached to a snowy white, fell loosely off one slender shoulder, revealing silky, ivory-colored flesh. He fought the surprising twinges of arousal that crept through his muddled mind and weary body.

Just fatigue, he told himself, from weeks spent working night and day, falling into bed only after he'd become so tired he could no longer function intelligently. Weeks of doing what he did best, digging through a cavern of lies and cover-up to discover the ugly truths hidden there.

Now, he would be at it again. The sheriff had just called, and what he'd had to say added more fuel to Matt's suspicions. Heather Lombardi, if that was in fact her name, was beautiful and intriguing, but his hunch was she was only skirting the truth with her story about looking for her mother.

"That was the sheriff on the phone," he said, crossing the room and standing over her bed.

"Does he have my car?"

"Yeah. And a little surprise."

"What kind of surprise?" Her eyebrows rose questioningly, pulling the swollen face into a shape that resembled lumpy oatmeal. Even that didn't diminish her appeal. It was her eyes, Matt decided, that pulled so determinedly at his resolve.

"There was an explosive device attached to the engine of your car."

She jerked to a sitting position. "What are you saying, Matt?"

"When the sheriff and his deputy were checking out your car, they found a device that was set to explode when you keyed the ignition. Fortunately, the bomb didn't detonate. If it had, you would have missed the pleasure of being kidnapped and beaten."

"I don't understand."

"It's simple. Someone tried to blow up your car with you in it."

"I understand that part." Her gray eyes were clouded, her voice shaky. "It's the who and why I can't comprehend. When was the bomb planted? Surely not at the restaurant. There were people around. And the men that kidnapped me didn't mess with the engine."

"Where else did you go today?"

She ran her fingers through her tousled hair. "I was at the motel, at the bank, the library." A sigh escaped her lips. "And I drove out to St. Michael's this afternoon."

"What were you doing out there?"

"I wanted to talk to the priest about Kathy Warren, but he wasn't there."

"How long was the car unattended?"

"About half an hour. I left the car and walked to the cemetery behind the chapel. Maybe that was long enough, though I didn't see or hear anyone." Heather squeezed her eyes shut, but not so tight that a lone tear didn't escape and slide down her cheek.

Matt dabbed at it with a tissue from the box on the bedside table. She opened her eyes and stared at him, shock and fear stripping away the air of independence she usually wore so well.

The room seemed to grow warm, and Matt backed away, suddenly aware of her nearness. Aware of the need to take her in his arms and comfort her. His muscles tightened in response to the unfamiliar urges, and he shoved clenched fists deep into his pockets. "I'm sorry, Heather."

"Me, too." She shook her head. "When the bomb didn't explode, the goons must have decided to come after me themselves. But it doesn't add up. They said they weren't supposed to kill me."

"You'll have to help me find the men. That's the only way we'll get answers."

"Then we're in big trouble. I already told you I can't identify them. They were muscular and dressed in jeans, Western shirts and black boots. That description would fit ninety percent of the men I've met in Dry Creek."

"If witness identification is impossible, we have to look for motive and opportunity," he said, easing down to perch on the edge of the bed.

She scooted over to make room for him. "Someone wants me to leave town. That appears to be motive enough in Dry Creek. As I said before, it's a real friendly town you have here, Ranger McQuaid."

He rubbed the stubble on his chin, making a mental note to shave in the morning, a chore he frequently omitted when he was on vacation at the ranch. But then, he didn't usually have house guests.

"For the most part the people around here are extremely friendly to strangers," he said. "Especially ones who look like you. The men around here are strutting like stud horses at the sight of you. The last thing they want is for you to hightail it out of here.''

"That may be true for most of the people, but someone is ready to kill to get rid of me, and all because I asked a few questions about a woman no one claims to remember.''

Matt stood and walked to the window. "Someone remembers her. It's what they remember about her that concerns me. I'll find out, one way or another, but you could simplify matters by telling me the whole truth.''

"Do you have a hearing problem or just a mental block? I *have* told you the truth.''

She spit the words at him, obviously upset by his implication that she hadn't been totally honest. Or maybe she was simply a good actress. Either way, he had no choice but to push for the truth.

"Someone is willing to kill to see that Kathy Warren's past isn't uncovered. That leads me to think your story has a few holes.''

"The holes aren't my making.'' Heather's eyes blazed, and her bruised chin jutted defiantly. "I don't like your insinuations, Ranger McQuaid, and I don't like the idea of spending the night with a man who's accusing me of lying.''

"I'm not accusing, just asking. And it's a long walk back to town.''

She threw her legs over the side of the bed. "Then I'll sleep in the brush with the coyotes and snakes, in friendlier territory.''

She grabbed her skirt and started to wriggle into it. Matt sidled past her. "Just settle down, Heather. You can't blame me for being suspicious. It's my job.''

"I thought your job was catching criminals, not pretending to be a Good Samaritan just so you can harass the victim in the privacy of your bedroom.''

Her words hit Matt solidly, like a good right to the gut. He put up his hands in surrender. "You're right. I promise, no more questions tonight."

"It's not the questions I mind. It's that I'm wasting time telling you the truth when you're going to believe what you want anyway. A cop by any other name is obviously still a cop."

"I apologize for offending you," he said, taking her admonishing finger and gingerly moving it down to her side. "But not for being a Ranger. Now, go back to bed. Give the coyotes and snakes a break."

She narrowed her eyes. "Okay, but one more accusation and I'm out of here."

Her words were more of a growl, but Matt heard the bedsprings squeak as he headed for the door. He'd have to watch his step with this one. Her temper was clearly as spectacular as her body, and he had no desire to tangle with either. Well, that wasn't exactly true, but he knew his limits. And he damn sure knew his priorities.

Walking to the kitchen, he stopped at the sink and rummaged for a clean glass and the bottle of whiskey he kept stashed in the corner of the kitchen counter. He poured a couple of fingers of the amber liquid, just enough to settle his mind and not enough to dull his senses.

Vacation was over. Two men were celebrating a victory tonight, and he planned to make sure the victory cost them a few years of freedom. He never gave a case less than a hundred percent. It was a matter of pride. And the legacy of Jake McQuaid.

Old resentment jabbed him in the gut. The first time he'd seen Susan Hathaway, she'd been battered just as Heather had tonight. But the beating Susan had suffered had left her near dead. His dad had taken her in and nursed her back to health. She could have walked away then, but she had stayed.

She had been the only mother Matt had ever known, always there for him during his youth. The one who had told him wonderful stories, dried the tears he'd never dared shed in front of his tough-as-nails father, understood how much a child could long for the mother he'd lost.

Susan had been there for Jake McQuaid, too. And how had the town legend thanked her? By taking her to his bed, but not the marriage altar.

"Here's to you, dear old Dad," he said, lifting his glass into the air in a sarcastic toast. To a man who never admitted needing anyone. A man who'd buried one wife, run off another, and cheated the only woman who'd stayed with him out of his name.

He downed the whiskey and set the empty glass on the table. Heather Lombardi wanted to connect with a family she'd never known. How ironic she'd ended up coming to him for help. He couldn't even connect with the family he knew.

HEATHER ROLLED OVER in bed. Her head ached, her toes tingled and every body part in between reacted in some similar, irritating fashion. Stretching, she wiggled her arms and legs. No stabbing, breath-stealing pains shot through her, only the aches and pangs she'd already noted, a good sign that nothing was broken or dislocated. Flinging back the covers, she forced her feet to the floor.

Bright sunlight streamed through a small window, painting streaks of light across the bare planks of a wooden floor, reminding Heather of her whereabouts. The ranch house of Matt McQuaid, the host she didn't begin to understand and wasn't sure she completely trusted. Still, he had saved her last night from who knew what, and he was certainly masculine enough for anyone's taste.

Her gaze scanned the beamed ceilings and wide windows of the room. Like Matt, the place had promise, but the house's promises hadn't been kept for a long time. The walls begged for a coat of paint, and the coverlet on the bed had probably been shiny and new when John Wayne saved Texas from the Mexicans, the version of the Alamo battle non-Texans like Heather knew best.

The scent of bacon hit her nostrils just as she reached the oak dresser and caught a glimpse of her face in the mirror. The sight overpowered the smell, killing any chance of a healthy appetite. Her right cheek was purple and blue, the eye above it open now, but circled by puffy mounds of black.

A knock sounded at the door, swift and hard, no doubt the no-nonsense Ranger. "Come in if you dare," she called.

The door creaked open, and Matt stepped inside. "How do you feel?"

"Better than I look."

"Good." A smile lit up the ebony of his eyes and drew the hard lines of his face into more approachable lines. "Are you hungry?"

"I was, until I made the mistake of looking in the mirror."

"It could have been a lot worse. Besides, there are no mirrors in the kitchen, and the bacon's almost done. How do you like your eggs?"

"Last time I had them, I liked them over easy."

"You sound like that was a long time ago."

"A few years. I'm a bagel-and-cream-cheese fan. I can eat those on the way to the office."

"Yeah, I'm a doughnut man myself, when I have to go

into headquarters, that is. Out here, I like the works, especially since I've already put in a half-day's labor.''

She felt on her arm for her watch. It was missing. ''What time is it?''

''Eight o'clock. Days start early in South Texas. Gabby's already called, but I told him to let you sleep. He'll be here soon though. The bomb find has him fired up and ready to stick somebody in his jail.'' Matt backed out the door. ''Two eggs over easy coming up.''

Heather took quick stock of the rest of her appearance. The borrowed T-shirt hung loose, skimming her breasts and skirting her knees in an uneven drape. All the necessary parts were covered, but she'd have to wash her face and brush her teeth and hair before she could think of facing Matt across the breakfast table.

As for the image of Frankenstein staring back at him, he'd just have to live with it. After all, he'd insisted she stay and then insulted her integrity.

Still, she had to admit that none of the happenings of the last few days made sense. Given only the facts, she might have drawn the same conclusions he had, figuring anyone telling a story like hers had to know more than she was letting on.

But all she knew was that Kathy Warren had been in this town, and someone here knew something about her they didn't want Heather to find out.

But what, and why? To find out, she might need Matt McQuaid's help. That was reason enough to cooperate with him as much as she could. But under no circumstances would she be taken in by his rough, tough Texas charm. She was the victim. He was the law. With that reminder firmly in mind, she left the mirror of horrors and headed down the hall.

BREAKFAST WAS to die for, Tex-Mex at its finest. Eggs peeking from under a smattering of salsa and perched atop a flour tortilla that slid like heaven across the tongue. The bacon was thick and honey-cured and so crisp it broke in her fingers and crackled between her teeth.

"How about another cup of coffee?"

Heather nodded, her mouth too full to talk. Matt refilled both their mugs with the dark brew and set the pot back on the counter before taking the chair opposite hers. Quiet settled over the kitchen, and Heather pushed all troubling thoughts away as she let the satisfying aromas and taste of the meal provide a temporary calm.

Matt watched as Heather chewed the last bite of food.

"Okay, I'm impressed," she said, smiling at him from across the table. "Where did you learn to cook like that?"

"From the woman who raised me and my brothers. She thought all boys should know how to take care of themselves."

"She was a good teacher."

"She was good at a lot of things. Still is, I'm sure, though I haven't seen her in a while."

Heather wiped her mouth and hands on the plain cotton napkin and took a long sip of the coffee. "It sounds like you miss her. Who is she?"

"Susan Hathaway." Matt got up from the table and carried their plates to the sink. "She was a friend of my dad's who lived with us."

"What happened to your mother?"

"It's a long story." He sat back down, this time with a pencil in hand and a black notebook in front of him. "And we have more relevant things to discuss."

"From breakfast to business in a matter of seconds. You don't waste any time, do you?"

"I try not to. Leads, like coffee, are always best hot."

Around headquarters, "sex" took the place of "coffee" in that simile, but Matt decided the tamer version was safer when talking to Heather. He tapped his pencil against the notebook. "I want you to tell me everything that happened last night, beginning with the second you saw the attackers."

"I told you all of that last night."

"You'd just been through a traumatic experience then. This time you might remember more, some scrap of information you failed to mention. It's usually the little things that trip up a criminal. A careless move. A slip of the tongue."

"Do Texas Rangers typically investigate simple cases of battery?"

"You were kidnapped and a homemade bomb was found in your car. That's not a simple battery." He drummed his fingers against his coffee cup. "But this isn't my case, if that's what you're asking, not officially anyway. Even so, if the sheriff requests my assistance, I can get involved."

"Do you think he will request your assistance?"

"After I ask him to."

"Why would you do that? You said yourself, you're on vacation."

Matt's mind staggered under the weight of her question. He'd asked himself the same thing a dozen times since last night. Heather Lombardi was sexy and desirable, even in her bruised and swollen state. Maybe more so. Now there was a certain vulnerability about her that hadn't been there before.

But she wasn't his responsibility, and he didn't usually let his libido do his thinking for him. Heather was not the only reason this case had his attention. "I can't resist a good mystery," he said, when nothing better came to mind.

And that was as close to the truth as anything else he could think of.

"Then you'll help me find out what happened to my birth mother?"

"I didn't say that, but I will find the men who attacked you and tried to blow up your car. They made the mistake of doing their dirty work practically under my nose. I take that personally." Matt swirled the last dregs of his coffee, staring into it as if it had some power to reveal the truth. Finally, he pushed the cup away. "Did anyone use a name during the attack?"

"No. I'd remember if they had. They did refer to someone who wasn't there as 'the boss,' but they never used a name." She propped her elbows on the table and leaned in. "What could have happened twenty-five years ago that would make people this desperate to keep it hidden? Isn't there a time limit on crimes?"

"There's no statute of limitations on murder."

"Murder? Kathy Warren wasn't murdered. She died in a car wreck."

"That wouldn't have prevented her from being involved in a murder. I warned that you might be opening a can of worms that won't be to your liking."

"I can assure you my birth mother took no part in a murder. She wasn't like that."

Matt watched Heather's eyes darken and her swollen lips purse. No doubt she'd created a fantasy about her mother in her mind that she chose to accept as fact. Unfortunately, as an investigating officer, he couldn't afford to play that game. "How do you know what she was like? All you can be sure of is she deserted a helpless baby."

"She was extremely upset that she had to leave me. Cass Purdy told me that much."

"Cass Purdy?" Matt thumbed through his notes. "I don't think you mentioned her before."

"I did, but maybe not by name. She worked at the orphanage when I was there, though she's been gone from there for twenty years. Cass is the one who dropped my mother off at Dry Creek."

"How did you find her?"

"I made phone calls and wrote letters until I located the woman who managed the orphanage fifteen years ago. That's when it closed. She gave me the name of Mrs. Purdy."

"And this Cass Purdy remembers that twenty-five years ago someone named Kathy Warren brought a baby to the orphanage and that she dropped the woman off at the bus stop in Dry Creek. That's quite a memory. How old is this woman now?"

"She's in her seventies, but I believe her."

"Yeah, you're a trusting sort."

"There's nothing wrong with that."

"Not if you can afford to be mistaken. In my line of work, it can cost you your life. Is Mrs. Purdy certain she dropped Kathy Warren off at the bus stop and not at someone's house?"

"Yes. She said my mother was going to New Orleans to meet a friend. It struck her as odd that my mother ended up in Texas with a new baby when she claimed she knew no one in the whole state." Heather pressed the folded edge of the napkin with her finger, ironing away the wrinkles.

"I want to talk to this Cass Purdy myself. Do you have a number where she can be reached?"

"Yes, but there's no need to bother her. I've told you everything she told me."

"Call her, Heather. Tell her we'd like to drive over this afternoon."

"Her number's back in my room at the motel."

"Then we'll get it right after Gabby finishes his questions."

Heather pushed away from the table. "No more questions. I answered at least a hundred last night."

"I know, but I need something more. This won't be fun, but I still need you to relive last night for me. Tell me everything, every word of conversation you can remember, every action. We just need a scrap of a clue to get us started."

"If I had a clue I would have told you already."

HEATHER LEANED BACK in her chair and closed her eyes. Trembling inside, she forced her mind to replay last night's events. The images rumbled and raged, tearing at her control, straining her muscles and sending jabs of pain through her already aching body.

Matt's voice, unexpectedly gentle, broke the silence. "Don't think first, Heather. Share the images with me. Say everything that comes to mind."

"I'll try." She took a deep breath and started talking, letting the memories inside her break through the protective wall she'd unconsciously erected. Her voice grew distant, as if someone else was inside her, ripping out each statement, forcing her to recall the pain, to remember details her mind had refused to accept last night.

"The men were cruel. One of them spoke with a Texas accent, but the other one didn't sound like he was from this area. They were coarse, rough. Every other word was a filthy curse or some vile derogatory term."

"Were both of them like that?"

She nodded, the memories so alive she could smell the men, feel their hands on her. "Yes, but one was worse."

"Go on."

"They were following the 'boss's' orders. Only the older man wasn't afraid of the boss like the other one. He was all over me, ripping my blouse, squeezing my thighs." She could feel him now, groping, trying to pull her from the car. She was going to be sick.

"That's enough, Heather. That's enough for now."

Matt's words shook Heather back to the present. He was behind her, though she hadn't realized he'd left his chair. His fingers dug into her shoulders as his thumbs massaged the corded muscles that ran the length of her neck and knotted at the base of her brain. Opening her eyes, she trembled, leaning against him.

"If you hadn't shown up when you did..." The words died in her throat. "I want those men caught," she whispered. "And I *will* find out about Kathy Warren. If they think they can scare me away, they're wrong."

Matt pulled her to her feet and turned her around to face him. His dark eyes stared into hers, the intensity of his gaze searing clear to her soul. "You are not dealing with these monsters again. The sheriff and I will handle this our way, without your interference."

"I'm sorry, Ranger McQuaid. You may be heading up the investigation, and I appreciate your concern, but you are *not* running me. I will not leave Dry Creek until I know why someone is willing to hurt me rather than have me question my birth mother's presence in this town."

Matt tightened his grip on her, pulling her closer. "I don't know what we've stumbled into, but it's not for the likes of you. Go home. Leave the dirty work to the people who get paid to handle it. We'll contact you when we need you to testify."

"No, I have a right to be here."

"And that right could get you killed. Is that what you want? Would that prove you're a good daughter to a woman who gave you away years ago? Is that what you think you owe her?"

Tears scalded the backs of her eyes. She held them back. Matt had no right to challenge her determination, no right to question loyalty she couldn't defend. "Can't you protect the citizens of your state, Ranger? Is that why you want me to run and hide while you and the sheriff play lawmen?"

She tried to pull away. He held her all the closer.

"Will you let me protect you, Heather?" His voice was husky and dry. "Will you stay here at the ranch so that I can keep you safe?"

She tilted her head and met his gaze. The fire that had colored his eyes seconds ago had dimmed to a smoky haze. She struggled to keep her temper hot, but the burning inside her switched from anger to something warmer, softer, something that caught in her breast and tugged at her heart.

Matt traced the swollen lines of her face with his finger. "I can't let you stay in town alone and risk this happening again. I don't have the manpower to have you watched there every second." His finger lingered on the bruise beneath her eye, his lips so close, she could almost feel them on hers.

She swayed against him. Did she dare stay here, deal with the kind of crazy attraction she was feeling at this minute for a man she barely knew? Did she have a choice? "I'll stay here if you think it's necessary, but I won't leave town until this thing is settled."

"You drive a hard bargain." Brushing a wisp of hair from her cheek, he tucked it behind her ear. "Looks like

I'll have to work fast or get used to sleeping on the couch. Unless of course...''

"No way, cowboy." She pulled away, still struggling for breath and a break in the tension that crackled between them like heat lightning on a summer night. Her attempts were aided by a loud banging on the back door.

The sheriff had arrived.

Chapter Four

Heather quickly pulled on her skirt and the shirt Matt had lent her last night. She might have had breakfast with Matt in a loose-fitting cotton knit, but she wasn't entertaining Gabby and the man Matt had introduced as John Billinger in that getup. Besides, if she was going to be staying at the ranch with Matt, she needed to try to keep gossipy tongues from wagging, for both their sakes.

The three men were standing in front of the hearth when she rejoined them. They stopped talking and turned to gaze at her.

Gabby fingered the soiled brim of the hat he held in his hand, over the round of his protruding belly. "I'm real sorry for all the trouble you've run into, Miss Lombardi. The attack was bad enough, then we find that bomb. I'm just glad the dadburn thing didn't explode with you in the car."

"So am I. Do you have any suspects?"

"Not yet. I've checked the whereabouts of some local teenage boys who've run into trouble with the law before. So far they all have reliable alibis."

Heather moved into the circle of intimidating Texans. Running a finger over her bruised face, she stared from beneath her blackened eyes. "The men who did this weren't teenagers. And attempting to blow up a car with the passenger inside isn't your run-of-the-mill act of vandalism.''

John Billinger rolled back on his heels, his thumbs tucked into his front pockets. He was a tall, thin man, whose face wore the battle scars of long days in the outdoors under a hot sun. "I wouldn't go jumping to conclusions, Miss Lombardi.'' His thick drawl gave her name a dozen syllables. "They may not have been teenagers, but they could have been young men out of control. There's some pretty rowdy wranglers working out at that new dude ranch. I wouldn't put nothing past 'em when they get a drink or two under their belts.''

Gabby stared at John from beneath his wiry brows. "I told you I'd handle this. I only let you come along 'cuz Miss Lombardi was attacked on your land.''

"You didn't *let* me come along. I told you I was coming out here to talk to Matt and give him my two cents' worth. You just offered to let me ride with you.''

Tension simmered between the two men, creating a new series of doubts in Heather's mind. John obviously wasn't too confident of Gabby's ability to find the culprits. Should she distrust the sheriff, or was the running argument between the two men purely personal?

Matt stepped closer to John. "What makes you think the men from the Galloping R might be involved in this?''

"I've seen 'em around town. They pamper the tourists during the day and then let off steam at night. Just last month Paul Ridgely like to have shot one of them for messing with his daughter.''

"Now, John,'' Gabby countered, "you know Donna was as much at fault as the wrangler. That girl could get in trouble at a church social.''

Irritation rattled Heather's nerves. "I don't think arguing

about Donna Ridgely's morals is going to find the men who beat me up and planted a bomb in my car.''

"I agree," Gabby said. "Why don't you and I talk, Miss Lombardi, and John and Matt can do their conversing outside?"

Matt propped a booted foot on the hearth. "I don't think so. John and I can talk later. I want to be with Heather during *all* questioning."

Gabby raked weathered fingers through his thinning hair. "If that's the way you want it."

"That's the way it's going to be." Matt took Heather's arm and steered her toward the kitchen. "We'll sit at the table so we can take notes. John, I'll have to ask you to wait on the porch. Questioning of the victim is confidential at this point."

"Whatever you say, Matt. I'm just trying to help. But I sure wouldn't rule out those drugstore cowboys in their fancy shirts and tight jeans. Ben Wright's not one of us, and he don't do things the way they've always been done in Dry Creek."

"How's that?"

"He throws money around like it grew on trees, wearing them expensive Western suits, and he pays his wranglers extra to dance and flirt with the women who come to the dude ranch."

"None of which is against the law. But don't worry, we're not ruling out anybody." Matt threw John Billinger a look that made the man mutter and scowl as he stamped out the door. Then, kinking his foot around a kitchen chair, Matt dragged it closer to the table. He held it while Heather sat and then straddled one nearby. "I'd like to be asked in on this case, Gabby," he said, as the older man poured himself a cup of coffee.

"I kinda figured that." The sheriff pursed his lips disapprovingly.

"Is that a problem?"

"Not for me. It might be for you or your superiors. This isn't one of the high-profile murders they usually assign you to. And you said yourself, you're only here on vacation."

"I can extend my stay if I need to."

"I see." Gabby's brow knitted into a series of deep groves. "This thing might drag on for months, seeing as how we've got no clues."

"We have clues."

The same surprise Heather felt registered on Gabby's face. "That's news to me," he said, pulling his chair closer. "Fill me in."

Matt's voice was low and steady, as casual as if he were going over a grocery list. "Two men were involved. They were apparently taking orders from someone they simply referred to as 'the boss,' but one of them appeared to have an ax of his own to grind. My guess is he's come into town specifically to put a stop to Heather's nosing into the past of Kathy Warren. That means whatever happened twenty-five years ago stretches beyond Dry Creek. There could be more than one agenda in all of this, and Heather might not be the only one at risk."

Gabby shook his head. "Sounds good when you say it, but them's still slim pickings. You can't build a case on that kind of hogwash."

"I didn't say we had a case. I said we had clues. My suggestion is that we begin the search with ranchers who have at least two men who aren't family working for them. The ranch economy being what it is, that narrows the suspect field down considerably."

Confidence blossomed inside Heather. Evidently Matt

did know what he was doing, and the endless questioning he'd put her through had accomplished something. For the first time since her abduction, she felt they were getting somewhere, that she might actually stop butting her head against the proverbial brick wall.

"I was out at the site of the attack at dawn this morning," Matt continued.

"Yeah." Gabby tapped his fingers on the edge of the table. "What did you expect to find that I didn't?"

"I was hoping for tire prints from the getaway vehicle."

"Not much chance of that. Worst drought we've had in ten years. The ground's hard as asphalt."

"You're right. I didn't find sufficient tire marks, but I did find something." Matt retrieved a plastic bag from the counter and laid it on the table. Peering through the plastic was a man's watch with a broken band. "I want it dusted for prints."

Gabby chuckled. "You do live up to your reputation, Matt McQuaid."

"I try. Now it's your turn, Gabby. I'm sure Miss Lombardi's anxious to get this morning's questioning behind her."

Gabby turned his gaze to Heather. "I reckon you're ready to do more than that. I'm sure you're itching to grab up your things and get out of this town. Can't say that I blame you, but I'm real sorry things turned out this way. We're usually a lot more hospitable around here."

"So I've heard. But I won't be leaving town."

His eyebrows drew together, and he leaned in closer. "You'll be making a mistake if you stay around here, especially until we get these men behind bars. The way it sits now, we don't even know what the hell we're dealing with." He looked to Matt for help.

Matt waved him off. "I told her that. She makes up her

own mind. She's checking out of the motel though. She'll be staying at the ranch with me until we're sure she's out of danger.''

A frown cut deeper into Gabby's leathery face. "Don't you Rangers have rules about getting involved with the victims of a case you're working on?"

"We're talking protection, not personal involvement."

MATT WASN'T ANTAGONISTIC, but his tone left Heather in no doubt that this was just a job to him, and she was sure Gabby was convinced too. *She* was a job to him. The only reason she was at the ranch was that he believed her to be in imminent danger.

At the thought, fear knotted inside her. Last evening, fighting off two strange men, when the risk to her life had been palpable, terror and anger had surged inside her like suffocating clouds of poisonous gas. But now, in the bright light of day, the events of the attack seemed more like a bad dream that had been washed away by the dawn.

Only this wasn't an ordinary bright sunny morning. The pain that swam through her muscles and the ghoulish bruises that disfigured her face were proof of that. And these weren't just acquaintances she was chatting with. One was a Texas Ranger, the other a sheriff—undeniable evidence that her nightmare had substance.

"Miss Lombardi."

The sound of her name jerked her to attention. "I'm sorry, Sheriff. Were you saying something?"

"Just that I hate to put you through more questioning, especially when you seem a bit tired. It must have been tough sleeping after what you went through last night."

"No, I'm fine. I was just lost in my own thoughts for a second. Fire away, and I'll answer as completely as I can."

"Let's start with the note you received."

Heather took a deep breath and plunged in, retelling the story that repetition was burning into her mind. It was an hour before the two men across from her closed their notebooks and came up for air.

HEATHER BREATHED a sigh of relief as Gabby tipped his hat and headed for the door. Matt trailed him out, saying he needed to talk to John if they could find him.

Silence followed on their heels, but the solitude was welcome. Heather walked to the window and gazed out over land that seemed to stretch on forever.

Tufts of grass, tall and yellow-green, were splashed between clumps of scraggy mesquite trees. Yellow and red flowers danced in and between the spines of prickly pear cactus, and a hackberry at the corner of the house offered a few orange berries that a blue jay found to his liking.

Peaceful, but still, the land had a harshness about it, as though it issued the same challenge she'd heard voiced more than once over the last few days. Farming or ranching in south Texas was not for sissies.

Perhaps that was what had toughened the men who lived here, given them the rugged edge they wore with the same pride that Matt showed in his badge. Or maybe the land itself did the choosing, attracted the type of rugged, fierce men who had tamed the West originally and then stayed to see the challenge through.

The romance of the West. A charming idea, but the promise had turned sour for Heather. Every corner she turned slammed her against another barrier, each as barbed and impassable as the fences that crisscrossed the land that lay in front of her.

Matt swung through the back door, pulling her out of her reverie. "I need to make a couple of calls before we visit Cass Purdy. Do you want to come along?"

"Do I have a choice? I thought I was under house arrest."

"I wouldn't have put it quite that way, but you've got the concept. John offered one of his men for a few hours if I need a watchdog, though. He could come over and stay with you if you'd like to rest a while this morning."

"A watchdog. How flattering." She ran her hands down the front of her skirt in an unsuccessful attempt to remove the excess of wrinkles. "Actually, I'd like to go into town and get my things from the motel. This outfit is not the last word in fashion for ranch wear."

A smile touched the edges of Matt's lips and softened the lines around his eyes. "I don't think I've ever heard ranch wear and fashion used in the same sentence before, and definitely not when talking about my ranch." His gaze walked from her ankles to the above-knee skirt. "No one's complaining about your wardrobe, but I imagine you'd find jeans a lot more comfortable. Do you have any?"

"Of course I have jeans." Heather smoothed the wrinkles in her skirt with the palm of her hand. "I don't wear suits on weekends or when I'm not working."

"But you chose them for the wilds of Texas?"

"I thought I might get a little more respect and cooperation if I showed up in Dry Creek asking questions in a business suit rather than casual attire. Wrong again."

Matt propped his backside against the counter, his shadowed eyes belying the ease of his stance. "Your clothes have nothing to do with the reception party someone threw you last night."

"No, I'm sure they don't. Evidently the mention of Kathy Warren is enough to bring out killer instincts in some of the citizens of your fair town."

"Every town has a few buried secrets, most of them better off staying buried."

Heather walked over and stood in front of him, her back straight, her muscles suddenly tense. "I didn't come here to expose the town's dirty laundry. I'm only looking for the truth about one woman."

He waved her off. "Simmer down. I never said you were to blame for any of this. I just made an observation."

MATT WATCHED THE FIRE in Heather's eyes cool to a dusky shade of charcoal. She was quick to anger but just as quick to mellow. Either way, she was too damned attractive for her own good. Or his.

Not that it mattered. He had a crime to solve and then Miss Heather Lombardi could traipse back to Atlanta and the life she'd left behind. There were probably at least a half-dozen young men bemoaning her absence at this very minute. But how many of them had sat across from her at breakfast with her wearing nothing but their T-shirt?

An uneasy pang akin to indigestion settled in his stomach. He ignored it. "So, make up your mind," he said, tapping his fingers on the edge of the counter. "Do you want to tag along into town with me or not?"

"Of course I'm going. Who could refuse a charming invitation like that?"

"I'D LIKE TO STOP at the spot where we left my car last night."

Matt stared straight ahead, his eyes on the road in front of them. "I don't recommend it. There's nothing to see. Gabby took your car in as evidence."

"Still, I'd like to see the spot where the attack took place for myself."

"I don't see the sense of that."

"I don't see the sense of any of this. Whoever planted a bomb in my car intended to kill me. Yet last night one of the men who kidnapped me and beat me up insisted their orders were *not* to kill me."

"It's a mystery, all right."

Heather sighed audibly. "Why do I always feel that having a conversation with you is like getting a confession of guilt from my six-year-old nephew? There isn't any limit on the number of words you can use in a lifetime, you know. You could just spout out a complete thought without waiting for me to coax every detail from you."

"The way you do."

"Damned straight. Now tell me your theory as to what's going on. No word limit."

Matt shook his head in mock disapproval, but laughter rolled inside him and escaped to split his lips in a grin. "Now that you've asked me so politely, I think there could be more than one person who wants you out of town. Someone may be more desperate than the other, or others."

"You didn't mention that to the sheriff. Why not?"

"Right now it's just theory."

"I still don't think you're telling me the whole truth."

"Really. What makes me think you're about to tell me what I left out?"

She twisted in her seat and faced in his direction. "You're curious as to why the sheriff didn't think about the same possibility you did. It's his job to notice things like that. He could be in on all of this. He might already know why people want me out of town, and he might be cooperating with them. He might even be masterminding this whole thing himself."

"Whoaaa. Old Gabby is not a suspect in this. He's just a good-ole-boy sheriff who's not used to dealing with much more than a family argument, a loud Saturday night drunk or a few schoolboys cutting fences. You've been reading too many detective novels.''

"I don't read detective novels. I read news magazines. And romance novels. So if I came to the conclusion that this is not a one-man show, the idea should have occurred to Gabby as well.''

"Point taken, but not necessarily valid.'' Matt slowed and pulled to the side of the road. "We'll have to climb between the barbed wire,'' he said, opening the door of his truck.

"Why? The man who was driving my car last night went through a gate.''

"Yeah, that's John Billinger's gate. It's a few yards ahead, but Gabby had him lock it today. He doesn't want the crime scene tampered with until he's sure he's through with it. He's keeping out everything except cows and jack-rabbits.''

"And us.'' Heather jumped to the ground and bounded around the car and toward the fence, a step behind the sure-footed Ranger. Matt put a foot on one wire and raised the top one with his hands, making a gap big enough for her to crawl through without serious risk to body parts.

Wary, but determined, she wiggled between the rows of wire. Her short skirt slithered up to her panty line. Planting both feet on the ground, she tugged it back into position.

"From now on, I wear jeans,'' she said, heat suffusing her cheeks.

"I'm not complaining.'' He took her arm and led her around a patch of cactus. "I'd recommend boots, though. Open-toed shoes in cow pastures can be dirty business.'' He pointed to a pile of cow chips to emphasize his point.

Heather stepped gingerly around it, and then Matt took her by the elbow and guided her past a thick clump of sage. For a second she was only aware of his hand on her arm, a gentle pressure that created a surge of unfamiliar feelings. Then she marched ahead of him into the open pasture.

There was no sign her car had been here last night, no sign that she'd been trapped in it with two men. Yet, standing here, in the exact spot... Goose bumps prickled her flesh. She shuddered and tilted her head upward.

Matt stared down at her, his eyes hot and liquid. Heather gazed back at him, an alarm sounding in her heart. Matt McQuaid wore the trappings of a cowboy and spoke the words of a lawman, but there was more to him than that. Close to him like this, their eyes locked, she felt it as strongly as she did her own heart beating inside her. Perhaps he had his own ghosts to deal with, just as she had hers.

"I know this is tough," he said. He slipped a reassuring arm around her shoulder, and for a second his fingers tangled in her hair. Unexpected warmth drove away the chill that had settled in her heart the minute she'd arrived on the scene. She was in over her head, but she wasn't alone.

Matt let his hand slide down her arm. "Heather." His voice was strained. "I don't know what's going on, but as long as you're with me, you'll be safe."

Impulsively, she rose to her tiptoes and planted a whisper of a kiss on the drawn lines of his mouth. "Thank you," she said. "I'll hold you to that promise."

She turned and walked back to the truck, head down, watching carefully where she planted her feet. And wondering what in the world had possessed her to make a move on the Ranger.

"WE'LL STOP at the motel first and pick up your things," Matt said, finally breaking the silence that had ridden between them ever since the impromptu kiss.

Heather continued to stare at the passing blur of fence posts. "While we're there, I'd like to change clothes."

"Fine. I'd like to talk to Rube a minute anyway. He's been around town all his life, ran that motel for most of it, and he's usually up on the latest gossip. He's likely to know if there have been any strangers hanging around town."

"I know you said you wanted to go see Cass Purdy. What other stops will we be making today?"

"The Galloping R."

"The dude ranch John Billinger mentioned this morning?"

"That's it."

"Do you think there's something to the accusations he made, that the wranglers who work at the ranch might be involved?"

"Could be."

Her muscles tightened, tugging painfully at the swollen face. "Okay, cowboy. Let's go for a sentence with more than two words this time. Who owns the Galloping R and what's the likelihood they'll be threatened by my asking questions about Kathy Warren?"

Matt shoved his hat back a little farther and gave a two-fingered wave to a passing motorist in a dark green pickup truck. "Ben Wright owns the place," he said, rubbing the back of his neck with his right hand. "It's only been operating as a dude ranch for a couple of years, but Ben's been in town for about ten. He retired from the rodeo circuit and bought up a stretch of land. Tried his hand at raising Brahmans for use in rodeos, but decided that was too much like work."

"He's been here ten years? The way John Billinger talked, I thought he was a newcomer."

"That's the way the long-timers see it around here. If

you haven't been around a generation or two, you're a newcomer.''

"They seem to accept *you* as one of their own."

"I was born in Dry Creek."

"I didn't know that."

"Yeah. We lived here until I was almost eight. My dad had a small ranch on the outskirts of town. He raised a few head of cattle along with being the sheriff."

"Where are your parents now?"

"My dad's in Colorado."

"And your mom?" She was beginning to sound like Matt, speaking in fragments that left more unsaid than spoken.

Matt turned down the side street that led to the motel. "Rube will ask you a lot of questions when you check out. Don't volunteer any information about what happened last night."

"Why not? Is he a suspect?"

"I just don't believe in spreading the facts of a case around like fertilizer."

"Such picturesque speech." She settled into her own thoughts. Matt had avoided her question about his mother, either intentionally or because he'd grown tired of friendly conversation and wanted to get back to business. Either way, the message was clear. Their relationship was purely business, and his private life wasn't open for discussion.

Minutes later, he pulled into a parking space in front of the motel. He followed her up the walk and waited while she unlocked the door and pushed it open. The now-familiar musty odor greeted her—that, and a trail of mud.

"Looks like they forgot to vacuum," Matt said, scraping his own boots on the hewn-fiber mat.

"I don't know where they found mud," she said, eyeing the black gunk suspiciously.

"From in front of your window. Someone left the hose on that plant with the pink flowers."

Heather shook her head. She hadn't noticed. Grabbing a pair of jeans and a yellow cotton shirt from the hangers, she headed toward the bathroom. She'd change first and then pack. The whole process shouldn't take more than fifteen minutes.

Matt leaned on the door frame. "Anything I can do to help?"

She considered asking him to empty the contents of the dresser drawers into her bag but changed her mind. The thought of his rough hands on her intimate apparel, his fingers cradling her panties and bras, made her insides feel weak.

And weakness was not a good idea when dealing with the take-charge Ranger. She was in Dry Creek for only one reason, and it didn't include becoming romantically involved with Matt McQuaid. She needed to keep things strictly business, make sure he didn't read anything more than gratitude into her impulsive kiss this morning. "It'll only take me a minute to change," she said, "but you can ask Rube for a copy of my bill since you're going to see him anyway. That would speed things up a little."

He nodded in agreement and ducked out the door. Taking a second to check the progress of the bruising on her cheeks, she squinted into the mirror. Bad as she looked, it could have been worse. She could be dead.

She sighed and opened the door to the minuscule hole that masqueraded as a bathroom. The blood caught her eye first, a thick crimson stain splattered over the shower curtain and the wash basin.

Blood that soaked the tailored white blouse of the woman who lay at her feet and made sickening patterns on the blue linen suit. The dead woman's legs sprawled like those of a discarded mannequin, her eyes open and bulging.

Heather heard someone scream. Maybe herself. Shaking and weak, she stepped back and against the hard barrier of a man's body.

Chapter Five

"Rube? What are you doing here? What have you done?" She tried to run, but he grabbed her arm.

"Are you all right?"

The answer stuck in Heather's throat. She pointed shakily to the bathroom and the body.

Rube let out a string of curses that dissolved into a hoarse cry. "Oh, no! It's Ariana!"

She watched as the man who owned the motel fell to his knees beside the blood-soaked body of the young woman on the floor. Hands shaking, he felt for a nonexistent pulse and then closed the woman's bulging eyes with a stroke of his fingers.

Heather backed away, grabbing the corner of the dresser for support. Her limbs grew rubbery as the room spun dizzily about her, the walls getting closer and closer until she thought they would swallow her up. Finally, a door slammed behind her, and she forced her mind to function.

Matt crossed the floor in two strides. She longed to run into his arms. Instead she forced her legs to hold her upright and her voice to speak with a minimum of shaking. "There's a body in my bathroom."

"What the…"

"It's Ariana," Rube said, backing from the bathroom to

join them. "The lady who helps out with the cleaning when my wife don't feel so good. Someone's shot her. She's dead." His words were uttered in a lifeless monotone, his mind obviously still tackling the reality of the scene.

Matt stuck his head in the bathroom and followed with his own string of curses. He stepped toward Heather and reached out a hand. She slid hers into his and trembled, her stomach still warring with her equilibrium.

"Are you all right?" he asked, his eyes dark and angry but coated in concern.

"No, but I'll survive," she said as reassuringly as she could.

"Then I need you to go into the main office and call the sheriff," he said.

She picked up the phone. "I can call him from right here."

"No." He took the phone from her hand, slamming it back into the cradle. Rube groaned, and Matt turned back to the bathroom where the man was leaning against the door, his face the color of putty. "Don't touch anything," Matt ordered. "I need a clean crime scene."

"Nothing clean about it," Rube muttered. "It'll take weeks to clean this place."

"That's not the kind of clean I mean. Just don't touch anything." He placed a hand in the small of Heather's back and guided her to the door. "Now go and call Gabby, Heather, and stay out of here until I send for you. This will be ugly."

"She's wearing my clothes."

The comment stopped Matt cold. "What are you talking about?"

"Ariana, the girl who was killed." Lips quivering,

Heather continued. "She's wearing my clothes. The blouse, the suit, even the shoes. They're mine."

Matt said nothing but his big hands drew into tight, threatening fists.

"What do you think it means?" she whispered through a throat that was dry and clogged.

Matt gave no answer. Instead, he all but pushed her out the door. "Go into Rube's office and stay there," he ordered.

His strength was contagious. It stiffened Heather's spine as she raced toward the motel office. Punching in the sheriff's number, she was certain of only one thing. She couldn't be in better hands than those of Ranger Matt McQuaid.

MATT SOAPED HIS HANDS for the second time, in a fruitless effort to wash away the memories of the last two hours. No matter how many times he faced it or how many ways he replayed a murder scene, he could never fully wipe the sights and smells from his mind. And he wasn't through with this one. He'd have to go to the morgue later for the autopsy.

The other Rangers teased him about his meticulous approach, calling him a control freak. Maybe he was, but he liked to make sure nothing was overlooked in dealing with clues that might lead to an arrest and conviction.

The autopsy would have to wait until a fully qualified medical examiner arrived, and the nearest one was sixty miles away. Waiting for him would give Matt enough time for a needed break from crime-scene madness—and Gabby's endless chatter.

He needed to have a talk with Rube and his wife Edna, but first he wanted to check on Heather. She'd been through plenty in the last twenty-four hours, enough to send even a headstrong woman running in the opposite direction.

He almost hoped she was ready to run. She'd opened a passel of trouble with her questions about Kathy Warren. Matt was sure there was more to come. In his experience, once a stampede started it didn't stop till *it* wanted to—unless it came to a cliff first. For her sake, Heather needed to get out of town, go back to Atlanta and leave the investigation to the authorities. For his sake...

The image of Heather across the breakfast table sidled through his mind, his T-shirt sliding to the edge of one shoulder, her hair loose and wild. His chest constricted. For his sake, he should be on his knees praying she left town today, before she took it into her head once again to scoot up so close to him that her lips brushed his. He was not the kind of man for long-term commitment.

But he was a *man*. He'd been achingly aware of that fact ever since Heather Lombardi had come into his life. In his house, in his bed, in his arms.

"Matt."

Heather's voice startled him. He turned to find her standing in the doorway, staring at him.

"I saw the others leaving. Are you finished in here?"

"For now."

"Is it okay if I get my things?"

"Sure, but try not to disturb anything else."

She walked to the closet and reached for the piece of luggage that rested on the top shelf.

He stepped behind her. "Let me help." Her back pressed against his chest, and he fought the ridiculous urge to forget the suitcase, to forget where they were and why and to take her in his arms and taste her lips. Not the tickling tease she'd offered this morning, but a kiss she'd remember all the way home.

As usual, his conservative side won out. This was the wrong place, the wrong time, and he was the wrong man. He tossed the case to the bed and opened it. "Tell me where to start, and I'll help you pack. The sooner you get out of this room the better."

"I have some toiletries in the bathroom cabinet. If you could get those…" She nodded her head toward the murder scene but averted her gaze. "I know the body's been removed, but still…"

Her voice gave the only indication of dread, though Matt was certain her insides still quaked at what she'd witnessed earlier. He'd seen big burly lawmen in training faint or become violently ill when they made their first call to a homicide scene.

"I don't blame you a bit," he said. "Fortunately there's no reason for you to go back in there. I moved all of your things from the bathroom into the bottom drawer of the dresser to keep them clean. Fingerprint dust was flying hot and heavy in there."

"Thanks." Her voice dropped to a near whisper. "For everything. I have a lot of questions, but they can wait." Her gaze traveled the room. "I'd really just like to get out of here as soon as possible."

"I'm sure." He took her hand and pulled her closer. "The danger just doubled, Heather. Now I'm even more convinced you should go home and leave the investigation to us. No one would blame you, not even your mother if she were still here to talk sense into you."

As he'd half expected, she lifted a bruised but determined chin. "I can't go, Matt. Not now. I can't explain it, but I have to find out what happened to my birth mother. I owe her that."

She shuddered, and Matt pulled her into the circle of his arms. Touch seemed to be the only comfort he could offer.

All the words he could think of were too harsh, the hard truths he'd learned through years of living.

Giving birth did not make a woman a mother any more than providing sperm made a man a father. Some women stayed even if the children they held in their arms and cooked and cared for were not their own. He knew one who had, even though the man who shared her bed denied her his name and treated her like a hired hand.

But other women ran out on their husbands and their children. That was life. He let go of Heather and walked over to stare out the dingy window. "Dry Creek is no place for you, Heather. Not now."

"I think it is."

The old floor creaked at her footsteps, and the flowery smell of her lightened the stale air of the room. Matt didn't turn away from the window, but he felt her presence behind him.

"I have my reasons for staying, Matt. They wouldn't make sense to you, but they're important to me."

He turned to face her. "The way I see it, your reasons are to dig up the past. You might be sorry. Unearthing old secrets sometimes has a way of burying pleasant memories."

"I'll take my chances."

"And risk your life doing it?"

"I'm not afraid of the truth, and I trust you to protect me from the evil. Matt McQuaid, Texas Ranger. If the name and title weren't impressive enough, I've seen you in action."

Apprehension swept through him. He gripped her shoulders. Holding her at arm's length, he locked his gaze with hers. "Don't cast me in your fantasy, Heather. I'm no hero from a Hollywood script. I'm just a Ranger. I do my job. You can count on me for that, but nothing more."

"Who said I expected—or wanted—anything more?" Eyes flashing, she broke from his grasp and dissolved the tension of the moment in a flurry of activity.

Heather yanked open a dresser drawer and grabbed a handful of lacy scraps of underwear and shoved them into the back right corner of the suitcase.

"I didn't mean to make you angry, Heather."

"No? What did you mean to do? You certainly weren't trying to reassure me that what I wanted and felt was important."

"I was trying to make life easier on you."

"That's not your job, Ranger."

"You're right. Call your own shots, if that makes you happy." He was never known for his patience, and Heather had a way of riling him almost as fast as she could arouse him. Dealing with her was the last thing he needed right now, but he might as well accept the fact that she was almost as hardheaded as he was.

"Just don't interfere with the investigation," he snapped.

She ignored him, folding a flimsy cotton nightshirt with a vengeance. She was too damn independent, a trait that could get her killed. He grabbed her hand and tugged her closer, tilting her head up with a thumb under her chin. "And don't even think about sneaking away from the ranch without me. If you're staying in Dry Creek, I plan to know where you are every second."

"Fine. Now if you'll pack the things you moved, I'll get the rest of my belongings and we'll be out of here," she said, tossing a couple of paperback books into the open suitcase. "I do want to stop in the manager's bathroom long enough to slip into jeans and a shirt of my own, though. That is if you'll let me out of your sight long enough to change."

"I'll consider it." Matt walked to the door and opened it, dragging in a deep breath. Getting into a fight with Heather wasn't going to keep her safe and it wasn't going to help him come up with answers as to who and what was behind the lunacy that had struck Dry Creek.

He packed the toiletries he'd stashed in the bottom drawer and then lifted the edge of the spread to peek beneath the bed. A white sandal with signs of excessive wear and tear rewarded his efforts. He picked it up and balanced it on his palm. Funny, Heather's feet looked much more petite than the empty shoe.

"Where did you get that?" Heather asked, walking over to examine the sandal.

"Under your bed, but I don't see the mate."

"It's not mine. Whoever stayed here before must have left it."

Matt lifted the shoe from his hand, holding the strap between two fingers. "Fresh mud, and the pattern on the sole matches the tracks we found on your floor."

"Then they must be Ariana's."

"Not likely. We found Ariana's shoes in a pile with her clothes. What size shoe do you wear?"

"A seven."

Matt held the shoe up and found the size inside. "This is a nine. And Ariana's feet were approximately the same size as yours. The pumps she'd taken from your closet fit her perfectly."

"But that would mean another woman was in here, that she walked in after the water was left running outside." Heather dropped to the edge of the bed, confusion knitting her brow above the blackened eye.

"It looks that way," Matt agreed.

"But why was she in here? Unless..." She flung up her

hands in exasperation. "Do you think a woman might have killed Ariana?"

"Anything's possible." Matt went in search of the other white sandal. His quest was almost immediately rewarded. The shoe was lying behind the pine desk, askew, as if someone had kicked it off or thrown it at somebody.

"Let's get out of here," he said, retrieving the sandal. "I need to talk to Rube and Edna and drop these shoes off for prints. After that we'll pay a visit to the Galloping R and see if any of John Billinger's theories are worth investigating."

While Heather changed, Matt called the sheriff with information about the latest find, then returned a call to his office in San Antonio. His assignment to the case wasn't official yet, but it would be any day. Homicides that didn't fit into the traditional household-passion variety were his specialty.

So were those that had gone unsolved for years, cases that had never been closed but had lost the sense of urgency over time. And if his suspicions were correct, this one had roots that went back two decades.

Matt mulled over what he knew. According to Heather, Kathy Warren had disappeared on an autumn night twenty-five years ago, the same year and season when another woman had been beaten and left for dead. Susan. His surrogate mother.

Kathy Warren and Susan Hathaway. Coincidence or connection? Was the tale of two women woven together by some intricate knotting of threads or were they merely isolated stories from the same time period?

His mind toyed and tangled with possibilities. A day ago he'd wanted only peace and quiet—now he yearned for answers with the same passion. He only hoped that finding them didn't destroy the faith Heather had in the mother she'd never met.

That responsibility lay heavy on his mind when Heather reappeared, clad in a pair of snug jeans, her hair pinned in a loose swirl atop her head. She smiled and his heart plunged to his stomach.

He'd have to watch his step every minute. The attraction between them grew with every touch and look, but he couldn't fool himself. No matter how attracted he was to her, when this was over, he'd walk away. It was his heritage.

The legacy of Jake McQuaid.

HEATHER TURNED from the truck window and the rush of unchanging scenery. "Tell me about the Galloping R."

"It's your typical dude ranch."

"That doesn't tell me anything. I've never been to a dude ranch before."

"Neither have I, at least not as a paying guest. The way I understand it, it's a bunch of tourists paying money to do what regular wranglers expect pay for. Except the truth is, there's not a lot of work available for regular wranglers anymore."

"Is that because of technical advances in ranching?"

"Partly. And partly because of a shortage of manpower. The idea of being a cowboy sounds romantic. The reality is different, so as wranglers became harder to find, ranchers turned to other methods, like dogs or helicopters to help in rounding up cattle. They use modern machines to do the work cowboys used to do."

A pickup truck passed them, heading in the opposite direction. Matt made eye contact with the driver and lifted his fingers, but not his hand, from the wheel. A typical cowboy greeting, friendly, but low-key and noncommittal.

Heather was learning a lot about the ways of the modern West.

"Tell me about the reality of cowboy life," she said, not ready for Matt to return to his own thoughts and shut her out again. Besides, she liked the sound of his voice when he wasn't upset. It was low and slow, yet strong and rhythmic, like a western ballad that haunted the soul.

"A cowboy spends most of his time talking to cattle and eating dust. The pay's poor, the work's dirty, and the cattle don't even say thank-you."

"So why does anybody do it?"

"They can't help themselves. The life-style gets in some men's blood, like a drug. Wide-open spaces, the brightest stars in the universe, a mount who never lets you down, and dealing with men who stand by their word." A smile eased the taut lines in his face. "And then there's the quiet."

"Meaning I talk too much?"

"No, but more than I'm used to." His gaze left the road for the briefest of seconds and found and captured hers. "Under other circumstances, I'd enjoy having you around."

Heather's pulse quickened, and a titillating warmth rushed through her. It wasn't much of a compliment by normal standards, but coming from Matt McQuaid, the simple words were like a sonnet.

The puzzle was why what he said or felt mattered enough to make her blood heat and her cheeks flush. Danger, she decided. The imminent threat of danger always heightened the senses. Or maybe it was a natural reaction to a man who'd saved her from being seriously injured, or worse.

Whatever the reason, she couldn't deny the overpowering attraction she felt every time he was near. And, she decided suddenly, she wasn't going to shortchange herself. Every aspect of what was supposed to be a vacation/fact-finding mission had turned sour except for running into Matt McQuaid.

So if being near him aroused her sleeping sensuality, so be it. After all, if the killer who appeared to be stalking her had his way, it might be the last time her sensuality or anything else about her was aroused.

With that chilling thought, the warmth evaporated. They both sat quietly until Matt turned in at a metal sign that heralded the Galloping R, a picture of a bowlegged cowboy toting a pair of six-shooters.

"I'll get the gate," she offered. She pushed open the door and jumped to the ground as soon as the truck came to a full stop. As the gate swung open, an uneasiness swept through her. In minutes, she might be standing face to face with the men who'd attacked her last night, maybe even with the man who'd just put a bullet through the heart of a young woman named Ariana.

She climbed back into the truck and listened with unaccustomed meekness to Matt's instructions about leaving the talking to him as they drove the dusty road to the main building of the Galloping R.

BEN WRIGHT'S OFFICE resembled the set of a forties Western. The walls were rough pine planks, the floor Mexican tile, the ceilings beamed. Only the myriad of photographs hinted that this was a ranch devoted to pleasing tourists instead of raising cattle.

The Kodak moments that lined the wall were all framed glossies of paying guests participating in the Galloping R's offerings. Cookouts by a creek. Laughing children riding horses single file along a well-worn path. A half-dozen smiling wranglers line dancing with a group of gray-haired women in matching shirts.

Matt paced the floor. Heather squirmed in her chair. They had been left to wait while the young woman on duty went to find Ben Wright, and the jiffy she'd promised to be back in had already stretched to five minutes.

They both turned as the door opened.

"I'm sorry, Matt." The receptionist smiled and touched him on the shoulder as she passed.

Heather was sure she had never seen more obvious flirting. The woman's efforts were wasted. Ranger Matt plainly had nothing but business on his mind.

"Does that mean you didn't find Ben?" he asked, scooting to the front of his chair.

"I found him, but he wasn't in the tack room like I thought. I paged him and he called back from the cookout area on the Roy Rogers Trail." She wiggled onto the back edge of the desk and crossed her long legs, swinging them seductively beneath a short denim skirt.

Smiling, she turned briefly to Heather. "All our trails are named after famous cowboys. The Gene Autry Trail…"

"So how do we get to the cookout area?" Matt interrupted, clearly not willing to waste time on promotional small talk.

"It's difficult by car," she said, her winsome gaze returning to Matt, "but it's only a short ride by horse. Ben suggested you get a couple of mounts from the stable and ride up. He said he'd meet you here if you preferred, but he thought you'd enjoy seeing what he'd done to the area. Besides it's a lovely day for a ride."

Matt stood and motioned for Heather to do the same. "We'll ride up," he said, his boots clacking against the tile as he headed for the door.

Heather stopped cold. "I don't ride."

Both of them stared at her as if she'd just professed she didn't salute the American flag. "I live in the city. We drive our cars or take the rail system."

"Well, there are no train tracks on the Roy Rogers Trail." The receptionist laughed at her own joke and winked at Matt. "I could ride up with you, Matt, and Heather could stay here and answer the phone. I'd love the chance to get out of the office for a while."

Matt grabbed his hat from the chair by the door and slid it onto his head. "This is as good a time as any for Heather to learn. I'll have them get her a gentle mount."

Heather followed him out the door. She had misgivings about climbing atop a horse, but at least she, and not the flirty receptionist, would be the one riding off with Matt. After what Billinger said this morning and what she'd seen in the motel room, she had no desire to be left alone at the Galloping R.

A few minutes later, after a close-up look at the animal he'd chosen, she changed her mind. "Can't you find me a smaller horse?"

"I could, but the wrangler on duty said Rosy's the most gentle mare in the stable. They save her for first-time riders and children. Talk to her softly as you approach her and don't be afraid. Horses always sense fear."

"Then I doubt she'll be fooled by my talking softly."

"There's nothing to be afraid of. These horses walk this trail every day, and they've never lost a rider yet. Well, hardly ever." Matt tightened the cinch on the saddle and placed his hand on the horse's head, whispering in the animal's ear that they were taking her for a ride. She neighed in appreciation.

Heather stepped closer. "Rosy acts as if she understood what you said."

"She understands the tone. I could have been quoting the day's cattle prices and she'd have reacted the same way as long as I'd kept my tone nice and easy."

"Okay, Rosy. I'm not afraid." Heather ran her hand down the length of Rosy's long neck. "That's not my heart you hear. It's friendly drums in the distance. You and I are going to follow the paths Trigger trod, and Trigger never threw Roy Rogers."

"You'll be all right, Heather. We'll take it slow, walk until you're ready to go a little faster."

Heather recognized Matt's tone. It was the same soothing one he'd used on Rosy, but it was working. She took a deep breath. After all she'd been through in the last two days, she'd surely survive a ride on a horse.

"I'll help you into the saddle and then show you how to use the reins. Controlling them will let you communicate with Rosy on the trail, let her know what you want her to do."

Matt's mouth was at Heather's ear, his breath warm on her neck. Emotion rose inside her, unsettling, dancing along her nerve endings. "I think we better get started," she managed, her voice weak and lacking conviction.

"Heather."

Her name was a whisper, husky with tamped-down desire. She turned to face Matt, knowing what would follow.

Chapter Six

Matt's mouth claimed Heather's, and he reeled with the sensation. Even as the kiss deepened, he knew it was all wrong, yet he couldn't stop. Heather was in his arms, her breath mingling with his, challenging every aspect of his control.

Finally, it was Heather who pulled away. "I think we'd better go," she whispered, but the strain in her voice gave her away.

She'd been as consumed as he had by the kiss. The thought pleased him and then turned bitter. What the devil was he thinking of? Heather had been through enough the last two days without the lawman who was honor-bound to protect her taking advantage of her. A lawman who had nothing more to offer than a meaningless kiss and an investigation that might tear the heart right out of her.

"I'm sorry, Heather."

She looked him in the eye. "Sorry because you didn't like the kiss...or because you did?"

The challenge was plain. He let it ride. They both knew the answer. Bending down, he wove his hands together to form a step. "Put your right foot here," he instructed, eager to be moving.

He understood action, the same way he understood handling an investigation. Right now, he was itching to get back to both and to forget the desire that had rung his bells a few seconds ago.

Heather threw her arm around his shoulder and planted a foot into his hand. She swung her leg over the horse's flank and scooted into place on the saddle.

"Slip your feet into the stirrups. I may need to adjust the length."

"It's a long way to the ground," she said. Her voice fell in an uneven rhythm.

"You're doing fine. Just don't look down." He adjusted the stirrups and placed the reins in her hand. Their fingers brushed, and once again he knew he was in big trouble. He'd forget how to breathe before he forgot how it felt to kiss her, and long before he reached the stage where he didn't want to do it again.

Resolutely controlling his emotions, he demonstrated the use of the reins. In no time she had the simple skill down pat. He mounted the horse he'd picked out for himself and led the way out of the corral and down a winding path that led to Crockett Creek, which turned out to be a creek in name only. It was a trickle at best. He talked of the scenery, as they eased into Heather's first nervous moments of the ride.

The sun was at their back, the wind in their faces. It would have been Matt's idea of a perfect day if it weren't for the fact that a killer was on the loose, and the beautiful woman riding behind him had likely been the intended victim.

The woman who had been shot in her hotel room had been close to Heather's age, nearly the same size and dressed in her clothes. Was it a case of mistaken identity, or had the killer forced Ariana to parade around in Heather's clothes before he killed her?

The sickness of the image turned his stomach, but it was no sicker than he'd seen more than once in real life. And then there were the sandals. His mind swam in the stream of possibilities, but his eyes stayed on the trail, mindful of anything that might spook Heather's horse and cause her trouble. She was knee-deep in that already.

"I COULD GET used to this," Heather admitted before they'd covered the first mile, "especially with a horse like Rosy."

"Does that mean you're ready to take her to a canter?"

"I didn't say that."

Matt gave his horse a little more freedom, easing into a slightly faster pace that wouldn't frighten Heather. She and Rosy kept up easily, and the smile of satisfaction on Heather's face was proof enough she was handling the new speed with ease.

His mind drifted back to the motel and stayed locked in mire and details until they rounded a clump of sweet gum trees and were met by the sound of hammering—and loud male voices.

"Looks like you found the place," Ben boomed, as the sound of hooves alerted him to their presence. He left his spot in the shade and came lumbering toward them.

"We couldn't miss it," Matt said. "Once the horses set foot on the trail, they kept to it just the way you've trained them."

"It's a good thing. Some of those tourists get lost finding their mouths with a full fork."

Matt studied the group. The hammering was coming from a spot near a man-made pond where two wranglers were assembling a row of wooden picnic tables.

"You brought a guest." Ben smiled and walked over to offer Heather a hand in dismounting. "Nice of you to brighten our day with a beautiful woman.'' He flashed her a toothy smile. ''Miss Lombardi, isn't it?''

Matt climbed from his horse and tethered the animal while Ben tended Rosy. ''We've had some trouble, Ben. I guess you've probably heard about some of it by now.'' He didn't waste time on small talk. It wasn't his strong suit, as Heather had so bluntly pointed out to him on more than one occasion.

''If you're talking about what happened to Miss Lombardi, I heard about it,'' Ben said, hitching up his jeans. ''That kind of thing makes a man want to buckle on his .38 and go gunning for the skunks, the way we would have done in the old days.'' He took a long, hard look at Heather's face. ''Now that I see for myself what the bastards did, I'm even more inclined to go after them myself.''

''Forget the .38,'' Matt said. ''If you really want to help, give me some information.''

Ben's eyes narrowed into slits. ''Of course. What kind of information would that be, Matt?''

''Which of your wranglers were unaccounted for last night?''

''My help's all over twenty-one. I don't do bed checks.'' He shifted his weight from one foot to another and ground the toe of his boot into a tuft of grass. ''Have you got a reason to suspect someone from my ranch was involved in this?''

''You know me, Ben. I don't need reasons. I'm an equal-opportunity Ranger. I suspect everyone.''

''Then you better spread your suspicions around. It might not have even been local guys who did the dirty work. Somebody driving through town might be responsible.''

''Any reason for you to think that?''

"We haven't had trouble like this before. I don't see any reason why it would start now."

"You're right." Matt said, his voice still friendly. "Still, I'd like the names of every wrangler who can't prove he was at the Galloping R between six and ten last night. I have to start somewhere."

"Does that mean you have nothing to go on?" Ben asked. He stepped closer, swatting at a gnat that was cruising the top of his earlobe.

"It means I don't have a suspect in custody."

"I'll be glad as the next fellow when you do. Tourists getting beat up doesn't help my business any. When do you want this list?"

"Yesterday."

Ben chuckled awkwardly. Matt waited a moment before he threw in the next bit of news. "The attack's not the only trouble. We had a young woman murdered this morning at the motel. You might have known her. Ariana Walker. She worked for Rube from time to time."

Heather watched and listened as Matt told of the horror of the last few hours in the same calm, steady voice he'd used to question Ben about his employees. His gaze never touched her, zeroing in on Ben. She recognized the tactic, but was amazed by his proficiency at it.

The talk circled around the murder and back to her attack. Heather stepped away, roaming down to the area where the wranglers were at work. For all she knew one of the men wielding a hammer could be responsible for her black eyes and bruises, but she was safe here, with Matt so close by. And if she was lucky, she might recognize a voice or notice one of her scratch marks on someone's face or arms.

"Howdy, ma'am." The wrangler closest to her laid

down his hammer, tipping his cowboy hat as she approached.

"Howdy, yourself. You look like you know what you're doing. You've put a table together in the short time I've been talking to your boss."

"I know what I'm doing, but I'm not doing what I like. I hired on to handle the horses, but I learned quick. When you work for Ben Wright, you do what needs to be done to keep the paying guests happy."

"And picnic tables will keep them happy?"

"Cookouts." He shook his head disdainfully. "Me, I'd take my grub inside in the air conditioning, but tourists thrive on heat and bugs."

"Have you worked at the Galloping R long?"

"Going on my second year. I'm saving money to buy a small spread of my own up in the hill country. At the rate I'm going, I won't get there until I'm too old to run cattle on it."

Heather looked up as another wrangler left his pile of lumber and ambled over to join them. She stepped backwards, her breath quick and shallow. The cowboy's hat was pulled low, but it didn't hide a cut over his right eye or the bruise that discolored his jaw.

She'd fought for her life last night, swinging her fists and clawing with her nails, but could she have delivered this kind of damage to one of her attackers?

Footsteps rustled the grass behind her, and she whirled around. Matt stepped behind her. "Looks like you fellows got a hot day for table building."

"It's not too bad." The guy with the bruise responded to Matt's statement, then turned to walk away.

Matt stepped in front of him. "Looks like you had a bad *night*, too. What does the other fellow look like?"

The wrangler snickered. "Right now, he looks fine, but his day is coming."

"Who'd you tie into it with?"

"This ain't a matter for the law." The cowboy cocked his head defiantly.

Matt stepped into the wrangler's space and flashed his badge. "Miss Lombardi here was attacked last night, and a woman was killed today in town. Right now *everything's* a matter for the law. If you don't like jail cells, I suggest you start talking."

"Tell him what happened, George," the other wrangler prodded. "The jerk that did that to you isn't worth going to jail for."

George used a finger to shove the brim of the hat off the cut. "Some guy got rowdy two nights ago out at the roadhouse, started harassing one of the waitresses. I told him to lay off, and when I went to get in my pickup truck, he jumped me. He came at me from behind, the coward's way."

"Do you know the coward's name?"

"Nope. Never laid eyes on him before the other night, but I'll know him when I see him again. Only this time I'll be ready for him."

"Describe him for me."

Heather sat on one of the picnic benches while Matt made notes in his ever-ready pocket notebook. She listened to the description, but nothing clicked. A scrawny fellow in jeans and a Western shirt, blond, middle-aged. Once again, the description fit a couple of dozen guys she'd seen in the last week. Even if it hadn't, she wouldn't have been able to match it to one of her attackers. Her assailants had worn masks.

Matt exchanged a few more comments with the wranglers and then took Heather's arm and led her back to their horses. Once again, he helped her climb into the saddle, but this time the contact was cool and impersonal.

Ben walked over and stopped beside them. "Have you talked to Logan Trenton lately?"

"No, should I have?"

"He keeps his ear pretty close to the ground. He might know something. Besides, I'm not the only fellow around here who has help. You might want to question him about his hired hands, or is he too rich to get this kind of treatment?"

"I'm not going to waste my breath answering that question."

"I guess you'll be going to his big shindig Friday night though."

Matt was already turning his horse around. "It's hard to say where I might be on Friday. I guess it all depends on how long it takes me to find a murderer."

Heather waited until they were out of Ben's earshot before she began her questions. "Do you think Ben Wright could be the boss my attackers were talking about?"

"It's hard to say." He brought his horse alongside hers. "I'll find whoever's responsible, Heather. I just wish that was my biggest worry right now."

His answer surprised her. She studied his profile, straight in the saddle, his dark hair poking from beneath his hat. His skin was bronzed from the sun, his angles hard, his muscles taut.

He was a man of many facets. Last night when he'd tended her wounds, she'd glimpsed a hint of tenderness. Today, when they'd found Ariana's body, she'd felt his fury. And now she sensed something deep inside him that drove him, something that reached beyond his macho sense of duty to the badge he wore.

"What else are you worried about?" she asked.

He faced her, his gaze penetrating. "You," he said. "I'm worried about keeping you safe."

"I'm staying with you at your ranch. Surely I'll be safe there. Who in their right mind would touch a woman sleeping under the roof of a Texas Ranger?"

"That's the other thing I'm worried about."

"I don't understand."

"I'm worried how in the hell I'm going to stay in *my* right mind with you sleeping under my roof."

She didn't have time to answer before he broke into a faster speed and put a few yards between them.

HEATHER PACED THE FLOOR of Matt's ranch house, from the dining room to the kitchen and back to the bedroom. Matt had left her at the ranch while he drove to the autopsy site, and there was nothing she hated worse than being shut out of things.

He hadn't left her alone. She was a prisoner, well treated, but a prisoner all the same. Her assigned guard was Tommy Joe, one of Gabby's overzealous deputies who took his duties very seriously. For the first hour he'd dogged her every footstep, following her from one room to the next.

Finally she'd convinced him that in a house this small, he would hear her if she so much as whimpered, let alone called out. Now he was in the living room, reading an outdated copy of *Texas Monthly*.

She checked to make sure he hadn't shot himself with the gun he kept fingering and then went to the kitchen for a glass of the lemonade she'd made earlier. The sun was resting on the horizon, but the heat of the day lingered, defeating the efforts of Matt's window cooling unit.

Glass in hand, she shoved through the screen door, reassuring Tommy Joe that she would go no farther than the porch swing. It wasn't that she didn't appreciate Matt's concern about her safety. She did. She only wished she was doing more than waiting around while he did the leg work.

She'd had such high hopes for this vacation. She'd managed to save up so that she had three weeks off, but if something didn't break soon, she'd have to go back to work knowing no more than she had when she'd left Atlanta. As it was, the pile of work waiting for her return was probably already a small mountain. Still, she'd take every day she had coming to her. This was too important not to give it her best shot. After a lifetime of wondering, this was the first time she'd had both the time and the resources to actively search for her birth mother. She had so many questions. There were lots of valid reasons for a woman to give her baby away. And no matter what Kathy's reasons were, Heather didn't blame her.

It was just that she'd always wondered about her birth mother, wondered who she was, why she'd had to give up her baby. Heather couldn't explain it in any way that didn't sound hokey. She only knew that she felt a need to connect with the unknown part of her past, knew that she wouldn't be complete until she did.

Lost in thought, she didn't hear the truck approaching until the door slammed shut and Matt climbed out. Tommy Joe bounded out the front door and down the steps, probably eager to tell Matt what a lousy prisoner she'd been.

The two of them talked for a minute, but even straining, she couldn't make out the gist of the conversation. A few minutes later, the deputy waved to her and climbed into his own truck. He was probably as glad to be rid of her as she was him. He'd clearly wanted a clinging virgin to watch over.

She was neither.

The sun sank a little lower in the sky, painting streaks of orange across the paling blue as Matt stamped up the steps and onto the porch. Shadows fell across his face, but they didn't hide the worry that was etched into every line. Still he managed a forced smile as he caught sight of her. "Got any more of that stuff?" he asked, eyeing her lemonade glass.

"Half a pitcher, unless my bodyguard finished it off." She jumped to her feet. "Would you like for me to get you some?"

"I'd love a glass, but only if you'll come back and sit beside me in the swing while I drink it."

"Don't worry. I'll be back. I want to hear everything you've learned since you deserted me here today."

"Be glad that I left you behind. An autopsy is not something you want to experience firsthand unless you have to. And the only other thing you missed was another talk with Rubc. Gabby had him into his office for questioning."

"I thought this was going to be your case."

"It is. As of…" He pushed his shirtsleeve up and glanced at his watch. "As of forty-five minutes ago. But Gabby will still be involved. In most cases, we Rangers only assist the locals."

"Did you get anything new from Rube?"

"Only that he'd seen a strange car in town yesterday, a blue Camaro, late model, with some guy behind the wheel he hadn't seen around Dry Creek before. The car had New Mexico plates."

Matt dropped into the swing, hooking his hands behind his neck. A lump caught in Heather's throat. The seductive, tempting cowboy she'd met at the café last night had disappeared, replaced by a man who showed distinct signs of overwork and stress.

She left him there and went for the lemonade. When she

returned, his eyes were closed and his head was slumped forward. She hesitated by the swing, hating to wake him. Finally, a horse neighed in the distance, and he opened his eyes.

Stopping the sway of the swing with his foot, he reached for her hand and pulled her down beside him. "Thanks," he said, taking the lemonade. His fingers lingered against hers a little longer than necessary.

The unexpected caress touched her, comforting but at the same time unsettling. She'd only known Matt twenty-four hours, and yet she was living in his house, bringing him lemonade at the close of a long and frustrating day, sitting beside him in a creaky porch swing.

The tug to her heart now was even more frightening than the attraction that smoldered between them, heating every look, every touch. It had to be the dramatic situation they'd been hurled into. If she read anything else into their relationship, she'd be fooling herself and making it more difficult for them to work together.

She waited until Matt had downed half the lemonade and the muscles in his arms and neck had started to relax before asking her first question. "Did the autopsy show anything unusual?"

He stared into the gathering dusk. "Nothing we didn't expect to find. Ariana was shot at close range, and it was definitely not suicide. The bullet was from a .44 Magnum. Rube says he doesn't own a gun like that. There were no contusions or scratches to the body except those from the bullet wound."

"So she didn't struggle with the killer."

"Exactly. Which means it could have been someone she knew or that she was taken by surprise. We're not even sure why she was in your room. She didn't have her cleaning supplies with her."

"Maybe she heard someone in the room and went to check it out."

"Possibly, but at some point and for some unknown reason, she decided to try on your clothes."

"Could it be that she just wanted to see how she'd look in a nice suit? Women frequently try on clothes for fun when they're shopping."

"Yeah," Matt stretched his long legs in front of him. "Or maybe someone else decided he'd like to see how she looked in your clothes."

Heather tried to imagine the scene. Ariana in the musty motel room with a man, a stranger or maybe a lover. Ariana slipping out of her own cotton skirt and faded work shirt and perusing the choices, choosing a silky cream blouse and a blue linen suit. The man waiting until she was fully dressed and probably preening before the mirror. Then he'd put a bullet into her heart and had stolen her life away.

Or maybe Ariana hadn't been preening at all. She could have been shivering with fear. The images clawed inside Heather. She took a deep breath and forced these thoughts away. She needed facts and reason.

"Was anyone close enough that they could have heard Ariana if she'd called for help?" Heather pulled a foot into the swing and tucked it under her leg.

"Rube said he was in the office most of the morning, plenty close enough to hear a scream. He didn't hear a thing."

"He sure got to me fast when *I* screamed."

"I asked about that. He said he'd seen you go in and was on his way over to see how you were doing. He'd already heard about your accident."

"New travels fast in Dry Creek. What about Rube's wife? Did she hear or see anything?"

Matt tapped his fingers against the glass. "She claims she'd taken medicine for a migraine and had fallen into a dead sleep."

"I detect a little doubt on your part."

Matt finished his lemonade and set the glass on the floor under the swing. "She seemed a little nervous when I talked to her at the motel after the shooting. Shaky, but not out of it as she would have been if Rube had roused her from a drugged sleep."

"Couldn't the shock of hearing about Ariana have caused that reaction?"

Matt slipped an arm over the back of the swing and wound a finger in Heather's hair. "Are you looking for a job with the department?" The humor in his voice was strained. "I'm supposed to be the know-it-all Ranger, and you're supposed to stare at me with those big, gray eyes, admiring my brilliance."

"I would, but I can't see well enough to stare from under the swelling."

Matt traced the tender area around her eye and down her right cheek. "Does it still hurt?"

"Only when I laugh."

"Then I don't guess you'll be needing any painkillers tonight."

"Not likely." She felt Matt's hand come to rest on her shoulder. As always, his touch jolted her senses. No matter how grim the discussion, it never totally overshadowed the effect of his nearness. She'd have to work all the harder at staying focused.

"Do you think Ariana could have known something about Kathy Warren, that whoever was determined I not ask questions about her thought Ariana might talk?"

"I can't imagine what the connection would be. Ariana

would have been five years old at the time your mother was said to be in Dry Creek.''

Heather's mind flashed back to the body in the bloody bathroom. "So she was thirty. So young to die.''

"Way too young.'' His mouth twisted into a frown. "Are you *sure* it would have been twenty-five years ago this fall that Kathy Warren was supposed to have been in Dry Creek?''

"That's what I was told. I'll be twenty-five the fifth of October, and I was only a few days old when she dropped me off.''

"A year of trouble in Dry Creek.'' His muscles tensed. "One woman beaten and left for dead, and another one who apparently left secrets that still haunt the town today.''

"I'm not following you.''

Matt leaned forward and propped his elbows on his knees. "I was just starting school that year, finally big enough to tag along with my half-brothers when they went hunting. It was about this time of the night, not quite dark but late enough—we were supposed to be home.''

A coyote howled in the distance, and Heather shivered, but didn't interrupt. For once Matt was opening up, talking in more than clipped sentences that delivered cold facts.

"We heard a moan,'' he continued, staring into space. "I thought it was a wild animal and started to run, but my brothers went over to investigate. They found a woman, bloody and bruised. She was barely breathing, but she opened her eyes and looked at us. We went and got the pickup truck—my oldest brother was too young to have a license, but he knew how to drive. We put her in the back and took her home, never once realizing that we could have killed her in the process.''

"Did she live?''

He nodded and leaned back in the swing. "She did. She

always said our finding her was a miracle. My brothers and I agreed, but we thought the miracle was for us. She turned out to be the best cook in the county and the best nurse for stomach aches, poison ivy and bruised pride a boy ever had.''

His eyes lit up, softening the rugged lines in his face and easing the defiant jut of his jaw. ''And the best all-around substitute mom in the state of Texas.''

''The Susan who taught you to cook?''

''That was her. Susan Hathaway.''

''You mean she stayed with you? What a wonderful story.''

''She stuck with us like a poor uncle come dinnertime, as my grandfather liked to say.''

''Did you find out why she'd been beaten?''

''No. She recovered slowly, but never remembered anything about the attack.''

''Were the men who did it to her prosecuted?''

''They were never arrested. It was the one crime my dad never solved. Strange, don't you think, for a sheriff not to follow up on a crime that hit so close to home?''

''What does he say about it?''

''Jake McQuaid? He doesn't explain himself to anyone.'' The bitterness in Matt's tone left no doubt that he had *not* paid his father a compliment.

Heather scooted closer, envisioning Matt at seven, motherless, frightened at animal sounds. She stole her hand into his, reconciling the strength of him now with the boy of the past.

''So you have a long history of saving women who've been attacked,'' she said. ''No wonder you're so good at it.''

He turned to face her. She couldn't read the message in

his eyes. They were dark as the night had become, piercing, but mysterious.

"I'm just thankful it wasn't your body I found today, Heather." His voice was low and husky.

Heather's insides quaked, emotion swelling inside her. How could a man she barely knew have such a devastating effect on her? "We should go in," she whispered.

"I know."

Their eyes met, kindling a crackling surge of desire that left her breathless. And then she was in his arms, his lips on hers. Lost in the kiss, she forgot everything except the passion soaring inside her.

She wasn't sure how many times the phone rang before they were aware of its jingling coming from inside. "I have to get that," Matt said, pulling away. "It could be about the case."

She nodded, and he headed across the porch and into the house. Wrapping her arms around her chest, she thought only of Matt, unwilling to lose the magic of the moment. But the magic died on her kiss-swollen lips the moment he reappeared.

"I'm afraid to ask," she said, "but what's happened now?"

"That was Rube. We don't have to wait for fingerprints. The white sandals belong to his wife."

Chapter Seven

"What does that mean?" Heather asked. "Why were her shoes in my room? Did Rube's wife see the killer? Is she involved in this?"

Matt shook his head. "Don't you have to come up for air?"

"Not when something like this hits. Why didn't she say those were her sandals while we were there this morning?"

"All I know is that Rube wants me to come over and see Edna. He said she's hysterical and won't tell him anything except that the white sandals are hers."

"I'm going with you."

"Right." He stepped to the edge of the swing and offered a hand. "You're going with me as far as John Billinger's house. You can stay with him and his family until I get back."

"No!" She jumped from the swing. "Look at me, Matt. I'm the one who got my face beat in. I'm the one who found Ariana's body. All of this started because I asked a few questions. You are *not* cutting me out of the good parts of this investigation. I've earned my right to be there."

"There are no 'good parts.'" He turned and headed down the front steps. "And you are not part of the investigating team."

She passed him at a near-run, opened the passenger door to the truck and climbed in. "I refuse to be left out of this. Don't even think of stopping at Billinger's place."

Staring straight ahead, she braced herself for an argument that didn't come. He simply revved the engine and backed out of the narrow drive and onto the dirt road without one look in her direction.

Matt's muscles tensed as silence smoldered between them. Things were galloping out of hand, and it was all his fault. His job was to protect innocent citizens and apprehend the guilty, not to seduce victims.

Yet twice now he'd given in to the overwhelming attraction he felt any time Heather was near, losing his control like some love-struck schoolboy. Nothing like this had ever happened to Matt McQuaid. Now the boundary lines between duty and personal feelings were jagged instead of clean and straight. Now every decision he made had dangerous repercussions.

"Why is it you feel the need to go back to the scene of the murder?" he asked, when his irritation with himself and Heather had cooled to just below the boiling point.

She crossed her arms, stuck her nose in the air and jutted her chin out like a strutting cock. "I didn't start any of this, but since I'm in the middle of it, I need to know what's going on and why. Ariana's dead. I could be next."

"You told me you trusted me to see that you aren't."

She twisted in her seat, finally turning to face him. "I don't want to argue, Matt. It won't get us anywhere. Besides, I'm not as good at these rapid mood changes as you are. One minute you can't keep your hands and lips off me. The next you're all but shoving me out of your way."

Seemingly of its own volition, Matt's mind swept back to the kiss. Losing control like that was unforgivable in this situation and as foreign to his life-style as champagne and caviar. ''I shouldn't have kissed you, Heather. It won't happen again.''

''Won't it?''

Matt's insides knotted. He knew what she was thinking, that his willpower hadn't been worth two cents so far. She was probably used to that reaction from men and expected more of the same. If he had anything to offer, she might get what she expected, but he was who he was, a man who'd never learned the art of making relationships work. Not even a woman like her could change that.

''I was out of order, Heather, a simple mistake. Don't go reading anything into it. I'm the kind of man you'd throw back if you caught me.''

''I don't have a line out, Matt.'' She undid her seat belt as they neared the gate.

He slowed to a stop. ''I didn't mean it that way. The kiss was my fault, not yours. But it will go better for both of us if we keep our relationship strictly business.''

She opened her door, but paused, capturing his gaze. ''All business? Fine with me. Only how are we going to ignore the fact that every time we get within touching distance or even are alone in the same room, the sizzle of hormones is louder than that bacon you fried up for breakfast?''

She was out of the truck before Matt could respond. He was fresh out of arguments anyway, especially when the hormones she talked about were raging inside him even now. But he was sure he could tamp down his feelings, tuck them away so deep inside him he almost forgot they existed. He'd done it all his life and for far less reason than he had now.

A coyote howled in the distance and an owl hooted overhead. Both creatures who knew how deceptive and dangerous nights in South Texas could be. There was a killer on the loose, with elusive ties to Heather. He'd have to work fast to untangle the knots and discover what was going on.

Her life depended on it.

It DIDN'T TAKE a Texas Ranger to figure out that Rube's wife was lying. Heather knew it from the moment the woman opened her drawn mouth. But it wasn't the lies that made Heather's blood run cold. It was the fear that crouched in Edna's eyes and turned her warm-toned complexion to pasty Swiss cheese.

"What time were you in room 4, the room that was rented to Heather Lombardi?" Gabby repeated a question that had been asked before.

Edna recrossed her legs and wrung the tissue in her hands. "I don't know, sometime after breakfast. I went in to see if Ariana had cleaned. She hadn't. And she wasn't there either. I told you that already."

Matt eased between Gabby and Edna, his relaxed manner contrasting with Gabby's accusing one. "We're not blaming you for anything, Edna. We just need to know the truth so we can find the killer."

She nodded, but kept her gaze directed at the scarred wooden floor.

"How do you think your shoes got in Heather's room?" he asked.

"I don't know. All I know is I had on these old tennis shoes today." She stuck her feet in front of her as if that should settle the question. "The sandals might have been on the porch. I wear them outside when I'm working in the garden."

"That's quite a green thumb you have, Edna, to coax flowers out of this dry clay," Matt commented. "The flowers around the front of the building look great. You must water them all the time.''

Edna's lips split into a smile. "Every day. We have a deep well, you know. Ariana always said I had the prettiest flowers in the whole town."

"You and Ariana must have gotten to be pretty good friends, what with her working here from time to time. Did you ever see her with anyone around the motel? A boyfriend, maybe?" Matt asked.

Edna's breasts heaved beneath the cotton shirt that hung outside a pair of denim shorts. "I don't know who Ariana sees. She's a grown woman."

"She *was*," Matt said. His tone was insistent. "Now we need to find out who killed her. Just try to remember. Have you seen any unfamiliar men around here on the days Ariana was working?"

"She's told you everything she knows," Rube complained, wrapping an arm around his wife's shoulders. "Can't you let it go at that? Both of you know she's not a killer."

"We didn't say she was, Rube." Matt kept his voice calm and friendly. "Answer the question, Edna. Have you seen anyone hanging around with Ariana?"

"No." She squirmed in her seat and scooted closer to Rube. "I didn't see anyone today either. I don't know anybody who would want to kill a sweet girl like that. I keep telling you that. Why don't you believe me?"

Heather breathed a sigh of relief as Matt said he'd hold off on further questioning. They had been at this over an hour, and Edna showed no signs of changing her story and blurting out the truth, whatever that might be.

Matt explained to Rube that neither he nor Edna should leave town and warned them not to talk to anybody but himself or Gabby about the crime. Rube agreed and led Edna away.

Gabby watched them go, hitching up his jeans so that they could work their way back down and under his belly. "You can't count on nobody to cooperate with the law anymore," he muttered, stamping towards the door.

Matt took Heather's arm and they followed the sheriff outside. The night air had grown cooler, and she breathed in the tart freshness of it. They were almost to their vehicles before Gabby made his assessment.

"That got us exactly nowhere."

"I'd say a little further than that," Matt corrected. "We know Edna's awfully upset."

Gabby snorted. "As jumpy as spit on a hot skillet. She's scared, that's what she is, and upset about poor Ariana. They'd gotten to be friends."

Heather lifted her hair from her neck to let the breeze cool her skin. "I think she's lying."

Both men turned, eyebrows arched, as if they'd forgotten she was there. Matt leaned against the front fender of his truck. "You think she's lying about having had the shoes on?"

"I think she's lying about everything. She knows something, but she's afraid to open her mouth. Every time you asked her a question, she looked to her husband before she answered. Maybe she saw the man who killed Ariana, and he threatened to kill her too if she squealed on him."

"If that's the case, why would he threaten her?" Gabby asked. "Why didn't he just shoot Edna while he was at it?"

Heather didn't back down. "Maybe he didn't want to kill her. Maybe they're friends, or relatives."

Gabby shook his head. "This ain't the big city. We don't go around accusing our neighbors of murder around here,

Miss Lombardi, unless we got strong evidence. Rube ain't got a mean bone in his body, and Edna's good as gold. She'd have no cause to lie to us.''

Heather saved her breath and let Matt and Gabby make their parting comments. Now that the questioning was over, she wondered why she had insisted on coming. She was tired and hungry and more frustrated than ever.

Finally, Gabby crawled in his truck and backed out of the dirt drive. Matt stepped behind her. ''Are you too tired for a walk?''

''So that you can tell me more about how I shouldn't think any citizen of Dry Creek could lie, much less commit a crime?''

''No.'' Matt kicked at the dirt with the toe of his boot. ''I agree with you. Edna was lying, no doubt about it. But she was scared, too.''

''So what are you going to do about it?''

''Give her a little time to stew. I had Gabby put a guard on this place tonight, though he argued there was no need for it. I want to know who comes around to talk to her after we've gone. And I want to make sure she's not the next target for shooting practice.'' Matt took Heather's arm and guided her away from the truck and down a dirt path that ran the edge of the highway.

''I don't get it,'' she said. ''If you and I could both tell Edna was lying, why didn't Gabby see it? It's as if he chooses what he wants to believe and ignores the other evidence.''

''That's a problem when you're policing people you've known all your life. Familiarity sometimes gets in between the investigator and the suspects and witnesses, and makes objectivity impossible.''

They walked past the motel to the front of a restaurant that had closed for the night. The windows were dark, the wood of the building old and battered, the roof a slanting line of tin.

A shiver snaked down her spine. She could swear someone was watching them. The town did this to her, made her feel the presence of ghosts. Perhaps they were the remnants of her own life, the past she didn't know. "Does this walk have a purpose?" she asked, increasing her pace.

"This is the spot where Kathy Warren would have caught a bus if she actually did leave Dry Creek that October night."

Heather stopped and looked around. "This is a restaurant."

"It is now." Matt tugged her toward a creaking sign. "I asked a few questions today. Twenty-five years ago this building was a hotel that also served as a bus stop."

"It's not big enough."

"The back part burned in '79. The hotel had closed a couple of years before, and the bus stop had moved down by Grady's Mercantile."

Heather dropped to a bench that sat by the front door. "My mother might have waited in this very spot for a bus to take her away from me."

She trembled, and Matt dropped down beside her, taking her hands in his. She swayed closer, suddenly craving his warmth. "I wonder if it was dark and deserted like this. I wonder if she was afraid, if she felt all alone, if she thought about me."

Matt gathered Heather beneath the curve of his arm. He knew what she wanted to hear, but he couldn't say it. "There's no reason to think she was afraid. She was doing what she chose to do."

"But she was young, barely more than a teenager. Mrs. Purdy told me that. She didn't want to leave me. She made them promise over and over to take good care of her little Heather.''

''Is she the one who named you?''

''Yes. My adoptive parents kept the name my birth mother had given me. Mom said they wanted to do something for the woman who'd given me to them.''

The coils tightened in Matt's stomach as his own memories merged with Heather's. Only he had no illusions left.

''Your mother left, Heather. Either she couldn't deal with a baby or she was running away from something, or someone. We may find out which, but chances are you aren't going to like what we find.''

''So you've said before, but you can't know that.''

''You're right. All I know for sure is that she left you a hell of a legacy—people smashing in your face and planting bombs in your car. And there's a good chance that the bullet that killed Ariana today was meant for you. I shudder to think what waits around the next corner, all thanks to Kathy Warren.''

Heather pulled away from him. ''She gave me life, Matt. Part of her lives on inside me. And good or bad, I want to know the truth about her.''

''I hope so, Heather, because we've gone too far to back down now. The murder today made certain of that.'' Matt stood and extended a hand to Heather. She ignored it, standing on her own and stalking back towards the truck. He'd upset her again. No surprise.

As his Ranger captain had always said, he lacked the fine art of tact, always blurting out the truth when a white lie would be much more palatable. But what good did it do to coat a hard reality with sugar? It would still be bitter when the shell melted away.

Tomorrow they'd pay a visit to Mrs. Purdy and then he'd spend the afternoon digging up the past, his own as well as Heather's. And if it turned out the two were tied together in some bizarre web of murder, there might be all hell to pay—for him, too.

His father had been sheriff of Dry Creek twenty-five years ago, and he had not found Susan's attackers. As Matt had told Heather, it was the only major crime in his district he'd let go unsolved…

Matt had his theories on the subject. He hoped this investigation proved him wrong. No matter what personal wounds festered between him and his father, he didn't want to be the man who tarnished the legend of Jake McQuaid.

"YOU MUST BE STARVING," Matt said, pushing through the back screen door of his ranch house and standing aside for Heather to pass. "It's nearly ten, and we haven't had dinner."

"I thought maybe starvation was part of the protection plan."

"No, but it's pretty standard procedure for a Ranger chasing after a murderer. Eat on the run, or do without."

Heather opened the refrigerator. "There's milk and bread." She pulled opened the crisper and peeked inside. "And makings for a salad. I'll throw one together."

"That'll do for starters."

"A salad's a meal."

"Sure, for a jackrabbit. I take mine as an appetizer before a steak, grade A beef, not long off the hoof."

"How carnivorous. I guess the steak you're salivating for used to wander about on your ranch."

"Of course. I raise beef cattle. Damn good ones. I'll fire up the grill."

He pulled a pair of fresh-thawed filets still wrapped in freezer white from the refrigerator, and she realized he'd planned ahead. Steaks for two, an intimate dinner. The prospect dissolved her fatigue. Only she wasn't really a guest. Her presence had been forced upon Matt, all in the line of duty.

"What's that you're using on the steaks?" she asked when he came back in the kitchen after firing the grill and started brushing a dark liquid over the meat.

"The Hathaway special marinade."

"Not the McQuaid special? After listening to the locals talk, I'd expect the McQuaids to be best at everything."

"My dad was well-liked by his cronies."

"You're too modest." Heather poked the lettuce under the faucet and let the water splash over the crisp leaves. "Jake McQuaid is a regular folk hero around here. Rube and I had a long conversation this morning while you were with Gabby and the body. He told me how Jake McQuaid had cleaned up the town and put a stop to the fights and shooting that went on every weekend. He said there were men still behind bars that Jake McQuaid put there when no one else would take them on."

"That's the way I've always heard it." Matt poked in the refrigerator. "Would you like a beer?"

"Are you having one?"

"At least one. It's been a long day. I might even have a bottle of wine somewhere if you'd rather have that."

"No, a beer would be fine."

He opened the can and poured hers into a tall glass. He left his own in the can, taking a long drink before he took two plates from the shelf and set them on the table.

"You don't seem quite as impressed with your father's accomplishments as the men around town," she said, not willing to drop the subject.

"He's my father. Living with a legend's a little harder than just knowing one." Matt came up behind her, reaching around her to open the drawer that housed the eating utensils. He took out forks and knives and moved away.

A casual move in a cozy kitchen, but her heart raced erratically. Her breath came quick and shallow while she threw together the fresh greens and chopped a tomato. She mixed her own dressing, a light oil-and-vinegar, avoiding the rich bottled one she found in the refrigerator.

By the time Matt reappeared in the kitchen with the steaks, her pulse had almost returned to normal. He pulled out a chair for her, and she slid into it, suddenly ravenous and not feeling the least bit carnivorous.

"You make a great salad," he said, after he'd swallowed the first bite. "I could get spoiled having you around."

"But then you'd have to put up with conversation with your meal."

"On second thought, maybe I could just get your recipe," he teased.

She stuck her tongue out at him and then rewarded his devastating smile with a few minutes of silence. Besides, it wasn't polite to talk with your mouth full, and for once her hunger took precedence over her curiosity.

The steak was cooked to perfection, brown on the outside, a touch of pink in the middle, succulent juices escaping from every bite, and so tender it seemed to melt in her mouth. She moaned in appreciation.

"I take it the steak is to your liking."

"It's wonderful. I'll swap recipes with you. My salad dressing for your Hathaway marinade."

"It wouldn't be the same. You'll just have to show up at my door again when you want steaks this good."

"Only if you promise your neighbors won't throw another welcoming party."

"I'd never have taken you for a party pooper." He forked another bite of steak.

Heather chewed contentedly, and part of the weight seemed to lift from her shoulders. It must be the beer and the food taking effect. It certainly couldn't be the situation, although even Matt was making a stab at small talk.

"I have to admit it's kind of nice having a beautiful woman across the table from me oohing and aahing over my steaks."

"So why haven't you married?" she asked, and then wondered where the question had come from. "You don't have to answer if that subject is too personal for the body-guard/protector relationship."

Matt looked up from his plate. "You're not thinking of proposing, are you?"

"So you *do* have a sense of humor."

"I try not to but it slips out every now and then." He wiped his mouth on the napkin. When he met her gaze, the teasing smile had vanished. "I've thought about marriage, even got engaged once."

"What happened?"

"The lady in question wised up in time to save both of us a lot of misery. She said I didn't need her enough, that I was married to my job and my cows."

"Didn't you fight for her, try to convince her she was wrong?"

Matt's gaze caught and held Heather's. "She wasn't wrong. And I had no argument for what she said."

"Where is she now?"

"Married to the guy who was supposed to be my best man. They have a baby, and they're very happy. Strangely enough, I'm happy for them. He's still my best friend."

"Maybe you two weren't right for each other, but that doesn't mean you wouldn't be perfect for someone else. Surely you wouldn't let one bad experience frighten you away from marriage and a family."

"I know my limitations, and I don't go looking for trouble." He finished his beer and went to the refrigerator for another, signaling the conversation about marriage had ended. "Want another?" he asked, holding up a can.

"I still have half of the last one."

"It's warm by now. I'll get you a cold one."

"Why not? A good meal and two beers, and I should sleep like a baby."

He returned with the beers and settled back into his steak. Heather pushed her plate aside. She'd had enough food, but not nearly enough answers. One woman had walked away from Matt, blaming his inability to meet her needs on his job and his cows.

Heather's guess was it was something more than the job and cattle that ruled Matt, something that made him afraid of intimacy and commitment, made him keep people a safe distance from his heart.

He'd said he wouldn't kiss her again. She wondered how he'd react if she got up from the table right now and walked over and kissed him full on the mouth. Her insides quivered as titillating images danced across her mind.

"You're awfully quiet," Matt said after he'd chewed and swallowed the last bite of his steak and finished off his beer. "You must be exhausted after the day you've had. Why don't you get ready for bed, and I'll clean up in here."

"I'm not that tired."

Matt started to the sink with their plates. Heather got up to help. Idle hands, paired with the thoughts she'd been entertaining, could definitely lead to trouble. And her cup of problems was already spilling over the top.

THE THREE MEN HUDDLED behind the barn, away from prying eyes and ears.

The short, stocky one glared at the man who'd called the meeting. "I told you I didn't want to be mixed up in murder. I told you that up front."

"You should have thought of that twenty-five years ago."

"I did. You promised then we weren't going to kill anyone. Just rough Billy Roy up and get his attention—that's what you told me and that's the only reason I went along with you."

The tall, lanky guy stepped between the other two. "Forget Billy Roy. Why'd you go and kill Ariana? She didn't know anything."

"I didn't kill Ariana. *You* shot her."

"No, I didn't—why would I?" He wiped his clammy hands on his jeans. "It's Heather Lombardi and Matt McQuaid who are causing all the trouble."

"If you didn't kill Ariana, who did?" The short man was sweating buckets in spite of the cool, dry night air.

"Probably someone who thought she needed killing, but it has nothing to do with us. It was just damn poor timing. Now Matt McQuaid's not about to let things alone down here." The man raked his fingers through his graying hair. He'd kept his two accomplices quiet for years, but they were getting awfully nervous now. He'd have to do something fast.

"Keep your cool, and keep your mouths shut for a little while longer. I promise you we are not going to jail for the murder of Billy Roy Lassiter or for anything else."

"How can you guarantee that?"

"The same way I take care of everything else. I'm not afraid to do what needs to be done."

HEATHER SAT bolt upright, startled awake from a dreamless sleep. She glanced at the clock by her bed—it was

2:30 a.m., but there was light shining beneath her door. Evidently Matt was up. Maybe the killer had struck again.

Slinging her legs over the side of the bed, she ran her toes around until they found her slippers. She didn't bother with a robe.

The noise stopped her before she reached the door. A sharp, shattering crack, like a gunshot outside her window. Oh, no, not again!

"Matt! Matt!"

But only the echo of her own voice answered her call.

Chapter Eight

The back door stood open, and the wind shuffled the edges of the newspaper on the kitchen table. Heart pounding, Heather rushed to the door and stared into the night. Slowly her eyes adjusted to the darkness. The shadows and angles materialized into the swing, the porch railing, the pickup truck. But no Matt.

Something rustled the grass, and she zeroed in on the spot, focusing on one lone figure crouched beneath a tangle of brush. Moonlight glinted off something in his hand.

If the figure was Matt, why was he crouched in the bushes, and what had he shot? Not a person, she begged silently. *Please don't let it be a person.*

Heather's heart slammed against her chest, her dread so real it stole her breath away. She couldn't handle another senseless death, another body. She'd never bargained for any of this when she'd come to Dry Creek.

"Matt, is that you?"

He stood up and stepped into full view. "It's me, Heather. Go back inside."

But something was wrong. He was clutching his arm, and holding a gun. She rushed down the steps to meet him. "What's wrong with your arm?" Before he could answer, she saw the blood dripping down his sleeve. Her stomach rolled wildly. ''You've been shot.''

''No, it's just a scratch.'' He walked past her.

''How did it happen? What were you doing out here in the middle of the night?''

''The horses were acting up, neighing and kicking around in the corral. I figured it was a varmint spooking them, so I went out to check.''

''Was someone there?''

''I didn't see anyone, but somebody had left my ax stuck between the shelf and the supports with the blade pointing out. My arm caught the edge of it.'' Matt tore the shirt from his body and held his arm over the sink. Adjusting the faucet, he maneuvered his arm under the spray.

''I'll call 911.''

''Don't even think about it.''

''You're hurt, Matt. You have to see a doctor.''

''Not for this. The doctor would shoot me himself if I woke him up for something as minor as this. I'll stop by Dr. Cappey's office tomorrow and have him take a look at it. I need to talk to him anyway.''

''Isn't Dr. Cappey the vet?''

''Yeah. If he's good enough for my critters, he's good enough for a scratch. Don't worry,'' he added, obviously reading the concern in her face. ''My shots are all up to date.''

''Here, let me help you.'' She took a towel from the freshly folded stack in the laundry room and wrapped one around his arm to catch the drips of water. The bleeding had all but stopped, but the wound was an angry red.

''I'll get the antiseptic and the dressing,'' she said, hurrying to the bathroom. Fortunately Matt had an adequate supply of first aid equipment. She'd seen it this morning while getting some more medicine for her own cut, which paled in comparison to Matt's.

She rummaged and found some peroxide and bandages and a disinfecting ointment. When she got back to the kitchen, Matt was at the table poring over a page of notes.

"You said someone left the ax blade sticking out. Who besides you would have been in your tack room?"

"Could have been any number of people. I have help out here checking on things when I'm tied up in San Antonio. The young guys get careless, but that's no excuse. I can't imagine why the ax would have been in the tack room to start with."

"Did you find out what was spooking the horses?"

"No, it doesn't have to be much to get them jumpy."

"But I heard a shot."

"Something slithered in the grass when I stepped on it. I wasn't in a snake-friendly state of mind."

A rattlesnake. Even the possibility sent new shivers flying up Heather's spine. If she had to choose, she'd take a killer with legs any day. She pulled her chair next to Matt's and unscrewed the top from the bottle of peroxide.

"This will only hurt a *little*," she said, mimicking Matt's tone and words from a night ago. Only one night ago…it seemed like weeks. So much had happened.

She'd been in Dry Creek for five days. The first four had been uneventful except for the note, but from the minute Matt McQuaid had walked into her life, the action had been nonstop, and none of it good.

Well, none of it except what passed between the two of them when they were alone. She propped his arm on the folded towel and poured a dash of peroxide over the wound. It bubbled like a witch's brew, but Matt didn't even wince.

"You treat this like nothing, which makes me think

you've seen far worse. Were you ever shot in the line of duty?''

"Depends on what you call duty. My brother Cameron shot me once, accidentally of course. I was six, and he was playing with a BB gun. It hit me in the backside.''

"A BB couldn't have hurt as bad as this cut.''

"Not far from it. The thing stung like crazy, and I howled like I was dying. It scared Cam so bad he didn't touch any kind of gun again for years. Now, he's probably the best shot in Colorado.''

"I meant, have you ever been shot with a real bullet?''

"I took one of those, too. I was shot in the chest about five years ago while making a routine traffic stop, back when I was with highway patrol. I learned real quick not to turn my back on anyone.''

Heather dabbed the wound with ointment and wrapped it in a clean bandage, taping the edges down. "You were lucky,'' she said. "You're around to tell about it.'' Her gaze ran to Matt's bare chest and the scar that tried to hide beneath the mass of dark, curly hairs.

Her fingers rolled across the scar, catching in the hairs. Every inch of him was male, strong, masculine, sinewy, yet everyone was vulnerable to something. If the bullet had been a few centimeters to the left, it could have wiped out his life in a split second, the same way Ariana's life had been stolen from her.

Matt's hand closed around hers. She looked up and met his gaze. The fire was there, hot and burning, feeding the desire that washed through her.

As if reading her mind, he lowered his mouth to hers. His lips devoured her, roughly, hungrily, as if he couldn't stop himself. She didn't even try to stop. She wanted to taste him, to swallow his desire, bathe in his need of her.

"I shouldn't...''

She ended his protest with her mouth. She had learned something in her baptism of fire in Dry Creek. *Shouldn'ts, wouldn'ts, couldn'ts* were for ordinary times. Not for nights when the preciousness of life stood in stark contrast to the reality of death.

Matt's hands splayed across her back, his fingers digging into her flesh while he pulled her closer. Finally, he pushed away. "If we don't stop now, I won't be able to."

"Would that be so terrible?"

"It could be. For you." He stood and walked away from her, his shoulders catching the glare from the overhead light. "I have nothing to offer you except protection and help in finding out how you're involved in the madness that's overtaken Dry Creek. If you start expecting more from me, you'll only be disappointed."

She longed to go to him, to wrap her arms around him and tell him she could handle the problems of tomorrow better if she found some fulfillment tonight. But making love to him would only make her want him more.

"Why don't you go back to bed and try to get some sleep?" he coaxed. "We'll need to get an early start to visit Cass Purdy in the morning."

"If you're sure you're all right."

"I'm not fine, but my arm is. I wish a scratch was my biggest problem."

She turned and walked to the door that led to the hall.

"Heather." She stopped.

"Thanks."

"For what?"

"For dressing the cut."

"That was the least I could do, especially since I've ruined your vacation."

"That's not your doing. Kathy Warren must have been some woman to cause this kind of trouble twenty-five years after her death. And who knows what tomorrow will bring?''

"Facts, I hope.''

"Yeah. Sleep well,'' he said, "and, just for the rec-ord—''

"Yes?'' She turned and caught his gaze. His eyes burned with the intensity that underlay every thing he did.

"I'm not sorry I broke my promise not to kiss you again. I'd have hated to go through life knowing I missed a kiss like that.''

Warmth stirred inside her. Just when she thought she had him all figured out, the Ranger had thrown her a curve. "You may go through life missing a lot more,'' she said. "Let me know if you're ever brave enough to find out.''

With that, she padded down the hall and back to her bed. Danger all around them, as thick as Texas stew, and still her emotions rocked with the attraction she felt for Matt McQuaid. Go figure.

CASS PURDY WAS WAITING for them at the door when they arrived. Heather did the introductions, and Cass ushered them into a tiny living room that was stuffed with the keep-sakes of seventy years of living.

Pictures of her family filled small tables and stood in zigzag fashion across the bookshelves that flanked the fire-place. A stack of magazines filled a basket at the edge of the sofa, and a vase of silk roses rested in the center of the round coffee table.

"You two look as though you've been in a cockfight,'' Cass said, eyeing their bruises and bandages.

"It was a…'' Matt and Heather both answered at once. Heather stopped and let him finish.

"Heather had an accident in her car. Nothing serious. Mine's just a scratch I picked up on the ranch.''

He lied with apparent ease, a fact that sat uneasily in Heather's mind.

"I thought you said you were a Texas Ranger," Cass said, eyeing him suspiciously.

"I am." Matt fished his badge out of his pocket and held it out for Cass to see. "But I also own a small ranch near Dry Creek. I don't get to stay on it much, but running my few head of cattle's a nice break from chasing the bad guys."

"I imagine it would be. It's awfully nice of you to help Heather find her birth mother's family." Cass pushed her wire-framed glasses back up her nose. "Her mother was a nice lady. I didn't get much of a chance to know her, but I'm a good judge of character."

"I'm sure you are," Matt agreed. "What kinds of things did Heather's mother do that convinced you she was nice?"

"Well, she sure was upset over having to leave her baby. If she hadn't gotten killed so soon after that, I expect she'd have changed her mind altogether and come back for Heather long before the Lombardis had a chance to adopt her."

"She must have been a very special lady for you to remember her so well. Either that or something else about her must have stuck in your mind. Twenty-five years is a long time."

Cass chuckled. "Not so long when you're seventy. Besides I remember the old days just fine. It's what happened yesterday I have trouble with. I've already forgotten to offer you folks something to drink. How about some coffee?"

Heather shifted so as not to sink into the worn chair. "We wouldn't want you to go to any trouble."

"Land sakes, it's no trouble being hospitable no more

often than I have callers. Besides, the coffee's already made.''

"Then let me help you," Heather offered.

Matt waited while the women went into the kitchen. No matter how Cass dismissed it, he thought it was strange she'd remember one particular woman so well. She must have come in contact with hundreds of babies and their deserting mothers during that time. So how had one stuck in her mind?

The reliability of Cass Purdy as a informant was suspect, though Heather certainly didn't see it that way. Cass was feeding her exactly what she wanted to hear, that her mother had loved her and hadn't wanted to abandon her.

He couldn't blame Heather. He'd fed himself the same diet of lies and wishes for more years than he cared to think about. Only both their moms had walked away, ready to start a new life without them. Mother love. It wasn't for everyone.

Matt tapped his fingers on the arm of the sofa, waiting impatiently until Heather and Cass returned with steaming cups of coffee and a plate of tea cakes. "Tell me everything you remember about the night Heather was dropped off at the orphanage," he said, after they'd settled back with their coffee.

Cass picked up her knitting and stabbed the needles through the yarn as she talked. "Kathy showed up at the door looking like a scared rabbit. Most of the women did, but there was something different about her. Everyone noticed it."

Matt leaned forward. "How was she different?"

Cass squeezed her lips together and wrinkled her brow. "The way she talked for one thing, kind of refined, and she didn't say 'y'all' or drawl her words. She was blond, petite, pretty, but too thin to have just delivered a baby. It made me think she didn't take care of herself during the pregnancy.''

"How old was Heather when she brought her to the orphanage?''

"I don't rightly recall, under two weeks, I expect. She was a tiny little thing.''

"I was five days old," Heather said, breaking into the conversation. "That was what my adoptive parents told me when I was old enough to understand. They were always honest with me, in a very loving way.''

Matt scribbled a few notes and turned back to Mrs. Purdy. "And you are sure that Kathy Warren was actually Heather's birth mother?''

"Oh, the baby was hers all right. She held on to Heather like it was tearing the heart out of her to let her go. I gave her a ride that night myself when she left. That's probably how I remember so many details. You learn a lot about a person in a slow ride down a lonesome highway.''

"And that was the night you brought Kathy Warren to the bus stop in Dry Creek," Heather added. "You said she was going to catch a bus to New Orleans.''

"New Orleans." Cass rubbed a spot over her right ear. "Yes, I do think it was New Orleans. I can't be sure about that, but I do remember she wanted me to drop her off at the bus station. She cried when she got out and made me promise to take care of her baby girl.''

"And you're sure you let her out at the bus station in Dry Creek?''

"Oh, I'm positive of that. I was driving on into Del Rio to my daughter's house. My granddaughter was born that night. She's only a few days younger than Heather. Maybe that's why I bonded so well with little Heather.''

"And Kathy Warren never returned?''

"She didn't get much of a chance to. A few months

later, this nice young man came by. I think he said he was Kathy's brother." She took a sip of her coffee. "Or he might have said uncle. It's hard for me to remember that part exactly. I only heard about him."

"So you didn't actually see the man who said Heather's mother had been killed?"

"No, but I heard all about his visit from the other employees at the orphanage. He made quite a hit with them."

"How's that?"

"He was young, good-looking and very well-mannered. He said Heather's mother had been killed in a car wreck. It just broke my heart. That's how sad I was, knowing little Heather would never see her real mother again."

Matt stole a glance at Heather. She was quiet and seemed pensive, but her eyes were dry. He doubted they'd been so the first time she'd heard this story. Cass Purdy had a way of squeezing every ounce of melodrama out of the account. He moved up to the front of his chair and looked her squarely in the eyes.

"I know it's been a long time, Mrs. Purdy, but it would really help us a lot if you could remember." Matt waited until he had Mrs. Purdy's full attention. "Did Kathy say anything about why she wanted to catch the bus in Dry Creek instead of one of the other towns along the way?"

"No, she didn't plan to go to Dry Creek, not at first. She was going to ride all the way to Del Rio with me and catch a bus there." Mrs. Purdy screwed her face as if struggling to remember. "We talked some. I asked a few questions about her life, but she didn't seem to want to talk about herself. All of a sudden she told me to let her out. She said Dry Creek would do as well as any place because every place we passed through looked the same."

"So my mother just happened to pick Dry Creek at the spur of the moment. She couldn't have known a soul in town, much less been involved in any wrongdoing." Heather reached over and took Cass's hands in hers. "Thank you, Mrs. Purdy. That's important for me to know."

"I told that to the friend of yours who was here the other day."

Matt jerked to attention, alarms blaring in his brain. "Which friend was that?"

"I don't remember... I think he said his name was Bob Smith, something like that. He came by here about three days ago asking questions about Kathy Warren's daughter. He'd gotten my name from Mrs. Hawkins, same as Heather did."

Heather's voice caught on a hurried breath. "You mean someone has been to see you this week? Exactly what did you tell him?"

"That you were in Dry Creek looking for some sign of your mom's family. He looked mighty pleased when he heard that. I figured he rushed right over and looked you up."

"No, but he could be part of my mother's family. They might be looking for me the same way I'm looking for them. I'll have to go back to the motel in Dry Creek and wait for him."

Matt swallowed a curse.

All he needed now was a description of the man, and then they would get out of here and back to Dry Creek fast. His guess was the man was no longer looking for Heather. He'd already found her. And though he had no idea why, there was a good chance it had been this stranger's calling card that had been left in shades of purple across Heather's face.

Now they needed to find the man.

"I'M REALLY EXCITED, Matt." Heather pulled down the mirror over the dashboard and applied a coat of pink lipstick. She smacked her lips together and smiled at her image. "If the man went to all the trouble to track down the daughter of Kathy Warren, he must be related to me in some way. It might be the uncle who told the orphanage my mother was dead. It might even be my real father."

"For your sake, I hope that's true, but I wouldn't count on too much if I were you."

"You're such a pessimist."

"I like to think of myself as a realist."

"Same thing. If this person who's looking for me is related to my mother or father, he might be able to answer all of our questions about what happened to her after she left Dry Creek. He might know the story behind why someone is so upset by my asking a few questions."

"The timing seems a little too coincidental for my liking. Some strange man turns up at Cass Purdy's looking for you a few days before two men attack you in your car."

"Mrs. Purdy said he was a nice man, and that he wasn't from around here. He tracked me through the former administrator of the orphanage, the same way I found Cass. He's obviously not connected with the trouble in Dry Creek."

"I'd never jump to that conclusion, and you can forget that ridiculous notion you threw out about going back to stay at the motel."

"I knew you'd say that." She touched the bruise around her eye, stretching to get a mirror view from all angles. "I look almost human again."

"Which is no reason to take chances."

"I know. After I thought about it, I realized that anyone

in Dry Creek can probably tell the man where I'm staying."

"No doubt about it." Matt lowered his foot on the accelerator, inching his speed a few miles over the limit. "Tell me about your adopted family, Heather. Were you unhappy with them? Is that what drives you to search for a family that let you be given away?"

"Absolutely not. My adopted parents were wonderful. My mom was a secretary and very funny. She could make me laugh no matter how upset I thought I was. And my dad was super—a little strict, but very loving. They were honest with me from the time I was old enough to understand adoption. If they were still alive, they'd back my search one hundred percent. They'd know no one would ever take their places."

"How long have they been dead?"

"My dad had a heart attack my senior year in high school. He died instantly. My mom had cancer. She fought it as long as she could. She passed away two years ago."

"I'm sorry."

"So am I. I'd like for them to have met you. Actually, they'd probably have flown down here the minute they heard about my attack. My mom would be telling you how to conduct this investigation. She was never at a loss for words."

"Who'd ever have guessed?"

Heather hit him playfully on the shoulder and then nestled closer. A familiar ache settled in the area of his groin. The longer he was around her, the more she filled his mind and tore at his control.

If he gave her half a chance, she'd burrow into his heart so deeply he'd never be able to walk away when this was over. He'd start imagining they could have a life together, fool himself into believing he could make her happy over the long haul.

He'd be wrong. The spitting image of Jake McQuaid in every way. That's what everyone said about him, even Susan Hathaway, and she knew both of them better than anyone else did. She might be the only woman who could love either of them enough to put up with them.

She'd stayed with his dad through thick and thin, but Jake had never been the man she deserved. To this day he wasn't. He'd let her down, let Matt's mother down, too, but in a different way. The rest of the world might call him a legend.

Matt couldn't even call him a real man.

"Hey, this isn't the way to Dry Creek. You should have turned back there."

"I told you we're going to spend the rest of the afternoon looking up old records."

"I assumed you meant at the sheriff's office in town."

"No, we're going to my office in San Antonio. The local records have been transferred into a computer base. They'll be a lot easier to access in that form. Plus, I can check out everything where I have all the resources I need to cross-reference incidents and dates."

"You should have told me. I'd have worn something besides these jeans."

"You look all right."

"Thanks for that gushing compliment."

He snaked his arm over the back of the seat. Her hair brushed against his arm, and his heart plunged. "Actually, you look great," he added, "bruises and all."

She stared up at him, her eyebrows arched in surprise. "Why, Ranger McQuaid, I do believe that's the nicest thing you've said to me since we met."

"I told you, I'm not much at small talk."

"To a woman, a compliment is never small."

They rode in silence after that. It was one of the few conversations they'd had that hadn't ended in a confrontation or a kiss, and he was not up to either.

HEATHER RUBBED the small of her back with her right hand and stretched as far as she could manage in the high-backed swivel chair. They'd been going over records for hours. It seemed more like days, especially since they hadn't stopped for lunch. Matt apparently wasn't joking when he'd said starvation was part of the plan when he was on a case.

"There's no record of a Kathy Warren in Dry Creek or any other town in Texas in the months preceding her dropping you off at the orphanage."

"Meaning if she was around, she stayed out of trouble with the law?"

"Meaning I can't even find her listed as having applied for a driver's license or any kind of welfare or medical aid."

"Do you have access to all of those records in this one office?"

"No, I have other people running searches for me in various state databases. People are usually easy enough to find if you can pinpoint the area. Kathy Warren doesn't fit the mold. She either kept a very low profile or she gave birth to you somewhere else and then brought you to Texas."

"She might not have wanted her family to know she was having a baby."

"That's a real possibility."

"But someone in her family must have found out. That person came and told the people at the orphanage that Kathy had been killed in a car accident."

"Maybe she confessed on her deathbed. If she knew she wasn't going to make it, there would have been no point in keeping secrets." Matt stood and paced the room. "The only proof we have that Kathy Warren existed was that she dropped you off at the orphanage one night in October."

"Were there any crimes reported in Dry Creek that night?"

"Not in the records. In fact there are no records at all for October of that year."

"Isn't it strange for a town to have no records for an entire month?"

"Yeah, especially since I know of one crime that happened that month that was never solved."

"Susan Hathaway, the woman you and your brothers found. So where do we go from here?"

Matt shrugged. "Back to Dry Creek to talk to Logan Trenton. If anyone knows what happened to those records, it should be him. He was deputy under my dad and replaced him as sheriff when we moved to Colorado."

"Can we eat first? I'm starved."

Matt's beeper rang at his waist. He read the number from the display and grabbed the phone from the desk. "As soon as I return this call."

Heather drank a cup of water from the dispenser and willed her stomach to refrain from growling while Matt completed the call. "Good news, I take it," she said, noting his smile as he hung up the receiver."

"It could be. Rube just called Gabby. Edna's ready to talk."

"Did she say she saw the man who killed Ariana?"

"She hasn't said anything yet. Her talking has strings attached."

"What kind of strings?"

Matt grabbed his hat. "She'll only speak if you are present."

"Me? Did she say why?"

"Yeah. She says the man who killed Ariana is a friend of yours."

Chapter Nine

Matt had decided the interview would go better in his living room than in either Gabby's office or the motel. An unthreatening environment that was removed from the scene of the crime was what he wanted. He'd accomplished his goal, Heather decided.

So far the meeting had the ambience of an impromptu gathering of good friends. The men had chatted about the rising price of feed and the poor beef market before Rube and Gabby had walked out to the tack room to look at a saddle Matt was thinking about selling.

She wondered if Rube realized that every aspect of the session had been orchestrated by Matt and agreed on by Gabby before he and Edna had arrived.

It was the familiarity Matt had talked about, the problem with investigating and questioning people you had known all your life. And, of course, neither Edna nor Rube was an actual suspect in Ariana's death. Heather wondered how different the method of questioning would be if they had been. Somehow she couldn't see Matt engaged in the bad-cop intimidation routine so popular on TV and in the movies.

"Would you like some more coffee, Edna?"

"No, Matt. I'm ready to talk."

Heather sat up a little straighter in the rocker opposite the couch where Edna huddled against a plaid pillow.

"I should have told you everything yesterday," Edna continued, "but I was afraid. I still am." Her voice shook. "Somebody capable of killing Ariana in cold blood like that. I mean you don't know what they might do to you if you cause them trouble."

Matt patted her hand. "No one's going to hurt you, Edna."

She kept her head down but raised her eyes to meet Heather's. "I'm sorry, Heather, but your friend is a real mean man."

Heather wrapped her arms about her chest as a sudden chill settled over the room. "Why do you think the man is my friend?"

"He told me he was, but I'm not sure I believe him. But he knows who you are. You may not be safe as long as he's around."

Matt leaned in close to Edna. "The sooner we catch the guy, the safer everyone will be. Just tell us what you saw."

"I was outside watering the plant by the window."

"What time was that?" Matt asked.

"About nine. I had a headache and I'd asked Rube to call Ariana over to clean Heather's room and do the laundry. I just wanted to put the water hose to my bougainvillea before it got too hot."

"Then what happened?" Matt's voice was gentle, coaxing, the same tone he'd used to settle Heather's horse at the dude ranch.

"I heard noises coming from Miss Heather's room, but I didn't see her car anywhere. I didn't know then that the sheriff had it." She paused, her fingers clutched around the strap of her handbag. "I knocked on the door and called out, but no one answered."

"Were you alone at the time?"

"Yes. I hadn't seen Ariana, and Rube was in the office fiddling with that computer of his." She sucked in a deep breath. "I tried the knob, and the door was open, so I just walked in. I thought maybe one of the dogs had gotten in there and was tearing things up. That old cur of Rube's has been known to do that."

"But it wasn't a dog, was it?" This time Heather asked the question. Edna's hesitancy was driving her nuts. She wanted the facts spoken fast and laid out neatly.

"No. At first I didn't see anyone, but I noticed my shoes were getting mud on the carpet. I took them off and dropped them right inside the door. When I looked up the man was standing there watching me." Edna trembled and sank lower into the couch. "I've never seen such eyes, so cold, so evil."

"What did he do when he saw you?" Matt asked, keeping Edna on track.

"He asked me who I was. He talked rough-like, and he had a strange accent."

"Strange in what way? Did he seem like he was from another country?"

"No, but I don't think he's from around here."

Heather scooted to the edge of her seat. "Did he say he was looking for me?"

"Yes. He said he was looking for a woman named Heather Lombardi. He knew you didn't live in Dry Creek, but he said he'd heard you were visiting here."

"Did he say *why* he wanted to see me?"

"He said you were old friends, that he was here to reunite you with your past."

The fear pummeling Heather's insides mixed with hope. Edna could be wrong. The man might not have anything to do with the murder. He could be someone from her birth mother's family.

"Tell me about him," Heather begged. "What did he look like?"

"He was a thin man, rough looking as if he'd led a hard life. I'd say he was close to fifty, starting to lose his hair. What he had left was blond, but thin and set way back on his forehead. I don't remember much else, except that he was a mean-looking fellow. I thought so the minute I laid eyes on him."

Heather fought back a shudder. Edna's description was almost exactly the same as Cass Purdy's. Only Mrs. Purdy hadn't seen the man as evil. Worse, the wrangler who'd been at the dude ranch had described a middle-aged man with blond hair. Paranoia again. There was no way they could all be describing the same man.

Matt took over the questioning. "What else did the man say to you?"

"He wanted to know where he could find Miss Lombardi, only he called her Heather." Edna turned to face her. "He said not to tell you he was looking for you. He wanted it to be a surprise."

"Did he give his name?" Heather asked.

"No. He didn't really say anything else until I said I didn't know where you were. I told him he had to get out of your room. He told me he was leaving, but he'd be back."

"Did he leave then?"

"He was about to, but about that time a wasp came flying in and buzzed around his head. He swatted at it, hit it, too, but it didn't die. That's when he picked up my sandal and started beating it into the rug. He smashed that bug until it was nothing but mush. He tossed the other shoe aside and left."

"So you *were* wearing the sandals?"

"I'm sorry, Matt. I was just so afraid yesterday. I saw what he did to that wasp, and what he did to Ariana. I don't want him to come looking for me. And Rube..."

"What about Rube?"

"He doesn't want me mixed up in this. He's scared, too, Matt. He won't say it, of course, but I can tell. He's nervous, chewing his nails, jumping down my throat if I try to talk to him about anything. That's not like him. You know that."

"I know, Edna. We're doing all we can to find the killer, and Gabby's going to have one of his deputies stay at the motel for a few days."

"I appreciate that."

"You still need to be careful, but I don't think the man will be back. He's probably on the run."

"I hope so. I hated lying to you. Then after I did, I couldn't live with myself."

Heather only half listened to the rest of the questioning. It was a rehash of what she'd already heard, and her mind was spinning with possibilities. The truth was Edna hadn't seen this man with Ariana. It could have been anyone who killed the cleaning lady, a jealous boyfriend, an angry relative, a stranger passing through town. Edna honestly believed it was the man she saw in Heather's room, the one who had asked about her, but that didn't make it so. Killing a wasp—no matter how brutal the technique—didn't make a man a murderer.

There was no reason to believe a member of her birth family could be involved in Dry Creek's secrets when Kathy Warren had only been in this town by accident. Even Matt would have to see that.

Heather stayed lost in her own thoughts while the question-and-answer session droned on. Matt wrapped up the session about the time her right foot went to sleep in protest. A minute later, Rube and Gabby rejoined them. The men visited for a while at the kitchen table, sipping the lemonade Heather served them and munching on some store bought cookies.

Heather and Edna walked out to the porch and sat in the swing. Gabby's dog left his spot by his master's pickup truck and came over to sit at their feet, moving only when the need to scratch overcame his lethargy.

"I'm sorry things have been so hard on you, but I'm glad to know it's not one of Dry Creek's people that is responsible." Edna slipped her hand over Heather's. "You're a sweet lady, smart, too. You're real good for Matt. It's time that boy settled down with someone like you."

Heather jumped to attention. "Matt and I aren't living together. I mean we are, but we're not *together*. He had me move out here so that he could protect me."

"Maybe so, but I know what I see. Matt likes you a lot, and you could do a whole lot worse. He's a good boy, from good stock, at least on his dad's side. His mother wasn't much of a woman. She ran off and left her husband and her son. I've got no use for a woman like that."

"She may have had her reasons."

"What kind of reasons would make a woman leave her own child?"

"I don't know, but there are some. And for all we know, leaving might be a hundred times harder than staying."

"I never thought about it quite that way."

"I have. I've thought about it a lot."

"I guess you have," Edna said, "seeing as how you were left at that orphanage." She ran her hand behind her neck and gathered the wisps of hair that had escaped the knot at the back of her head. "I always wanted a daughter like you, but Rube and I just had boys. If I *were* your mom I'd tell you two things, Miss Lombardi.''

"Call me Heather. And go ahead and tell me. One can never have too many mothers.''

Edna took Heather's hand and squeezed it. ''I'd tell you to stay safe. There's evil out there, and it's looking for you.''

"I'm trying hard to do that.''

"And I'd tell you to get a hold of that man in there and don't let go. A good man like Matt McQuaid doesn't come along every day of the week. Look at my Rube. We've been married thirty years, and I'm just as in love with him as I was the day I met him. I may not get all gooey-eyed, but I love him all the same.''

"Why, Edna, are you suggesting I seduce the Ranger who brought me out here to protect me?''

"I'm suggesting you do what you have to. If you don't, some other woman will, and she won't be half as good for him as you are. Don't ask me how I know that, I just do.''

An easy sense of camaraderie had settled over them by the time the men came barreling out the screen door. For a second Heather almost forgot that somewhere in Dry Creek there was a killer walking the streets. Almost forgot that two nights ago she had been attacked by two strangers. Almost forgot someone had tried to blow her and her car into little pieces.

Almost, but not quite.

"ARE YOU GOING to go through those files all night?'' Heather plopped down on one of the musty boxes Matt had crated over from the back room at Gabby's office.

"Probably, unless I find what I'm looking for first. Do you have a better idea?''

"I thought we might take a ride before dark. You have those beautiful horses just going to waste."

Matt peered over the file he'd been scrutinizing. "You must be bored if you're asking to ride a horse."

"When in Rome, or in this case, when in Texas. Besides, I kind of liked riding the other day after I got used to it. Of course, I'd want a gentle horse like the one I had at the dude ranch."

"Where's your spirit of adventure?"

"Worn out. Another victim of Dry Creek's warm hospitality."

"In that case, I have just the horse for you. Maverick. A pretty chestnut. He's big, but he's got more sense than most men I know. He won't fight you for control, unless you make him."

"How big?"

"Big enough you don't want to go flying over his head, but he won't let you. Why don't you go have a look at him while I finish this file? But do your looking from outside the corral. And don't wander off anywhere else. I don't want you out of yelling distance."

"Yes sir." Heather gave a mock salute and headed out the door. She still hadn't had a chance to shop for boots, but she had traded her sandals for her tennis shoes. When she shopped, she might even buy a hat. One like Matt's, except with a smaller brim.

Not that she'd ever wear the boots or hat again once she went home. Home to Atlanta. The thought seemed strange. As long as she'd stayed in the motel, Dry Creek had seemed like a foreign country. But she'd been at the Lone M five days now, and she was getting way too familiar with the ways of Ranger Matt McQuaid.

Sitting across the breakfast table from him. Seeing him fresh from the shower, his hair wet and dripping down his sun-bronzed face. Knowing he was a few steps away when she crawled into bed at night. And always dealing with the smoky desire his nearness kindled inside her.

She took a shaky breath and stepped onto the bottom rung of the corral. A chestnut came trotting over. So did a large horse that was more brown than red and a prancing horse with white legs that looked like he'd dressed in boots.

"Hello, baby," she said crooning to the booted horse who was nuzzling her hand. She scratched his face the way she'd seen Matt do the other day at the dude ranch. "Are you ready for a ride or do you just want a little attention?"

The wind picked up, waving the grass and whirling sand. Heather stepped back. She had the crazy feeling that she wasn't alone, that someone was nearby, watching her. Was it some sound she'd heard, or only groundless fear that twisted in her stomach?

Her first impulse was to run back to Matt, to fly into his arms and let him hold her until the shaking stopped. But what would she tell him—that she felt eyes that weren't there? She sucked a deep breath of air into her burning lungs. She'd almost convinced herself she was safe and alone when footsteps rustled the grass behind her.

She spun around. "Matt, it's you."

"I didn't mean to frighten you."

"I'm just jumpy these days."

"With plenty of reason. Our ride may help. There's a creek past the south pasture, fed by a spring. The water's cool and clear, and overhung with branches of the biggest oak tree in these parts."

"You do love this ranch, don't you?"

"Have you ever met a rancher who wasn't partial to his own spread?"

"Up until a week ago, I'd never met a rancher."

"And now that you have?" Matt swung open the gate and Heather followed him inside, watching where she stepped.

"I'd say you're a fascinating breed. Other than that, the vote is still out."

"Good answer. You don't want to get too sassy with the wrangler who's saddling your ride."

"Is that from the cowboy book of lore?"

"No, it's from the gospel according to Matt McQuaid."

"Right after the chapter about why you don't need a woman."

"I never said I didn't *need* a woman." He pulled a saddle from the rack. "I *said* I'd make a lousy husband."

"And I think you're a coward, Matt McQuaid, afraid the woman you chose would run out on you and leave you here to explain your predicament to all of the McQuaid admirers."

"Oh, it's not the explaining I'd mind. But you're right about the fear. I'd be scared to death of letting a woman like you crawl into my bed, set me on fire and then go running back to the bright lights of the big city. I don't relish the idea of putting out that kind of flame with cold showers and lonesome nights."

He saddled two horses, then called her over to mount the chestnut. She stopped in front of Matt, and he wrapped his arms around her waist, pulling her close and nestling his mouth in her hair. "But even a coward gives in to temptation occasionally. So you better keep that bedroom door locked at night."

With that, he boosted her up and into the saddle. Her heart raced, but this time it wasn't the size of the horse but the mystique of the cowboy that had her gasping for breath. Edna's words echoed tauntingly in her mind. A good man like Matt McQuaid doesn't come along every day of the week.

It was time to act, to stop playing it safe. Tonight she'd make sure Matt knew the latch on the bedroom door was off.

Chapter Ten

Heather lay in her bed, staring at the shadowed ceiling. The afternoon ride had left her breathless, dizzy with excitement and hungry for more. This time, at Matt's coaxing, she'd grown comfortable in the saddle and taken Maverick through all the stages. A slow walk, a fast walk, a lope, and for a few glorious minutes, a full gallop.

She'd seen the land from the back of a magnificent animal, feeling as if she owned the world. No matter that her world was riddled with problems and spiked with danger. The romance of the West was creeping into her blood, invigorating her with its spirit.

But she knew part of the thrill this afternoon had been due to her riding companion. For once, Matt had shed the tough armor that usually kept her at arm's length. When they'd dismounted by the creek, he'd pointed out every plant, cut off a bite of pear from a cactus and given her a taste of it, even playfully splashed cold water on her when she'd teased him.

For a few glorious minutes, they'd behaved like new lovers, frolicking in the late-afternoon splendor of a perfect day. But all that had changed the minute they'd walked back into the house. Matt had dug into the stacks of files with a vengeance, as if he expected them to disintegrate in front of him if he didn't scrutinize every one before he moved from the spot.

She'd puttered in the kitchen and come up with pasta, flavored with ground beef, carrots, onions and sweet peas. But dinner had been quiet. Matt had avoided eye contact and answered her questions in his typical one-word style.

He'd given no reason for the abrupt change in their relationship, leaving Heather to conjure up her own theories. The man was either scared to death of involvement, or else there was someone else in his life back in San Antonio.

So now she was lying here wide-awake, the victim of her own poor judgment. She'd known it wasn't wise to get emotionally involved with Matt, but her heart had jumped ahead of her, seeing the side of him it wanted to see.

She wasn't sure if she was falling in love with him. All she knew was that she ached to crawl into his arms, that she longed to have him here beside her, sharing the rustic wooden bed. Knew that her insides trembled just remembering the taste of his lips on hers, the feel of his breath on the back of her neck, the sound of his voice, all husky with desire, when he'd whispered in her ear at the corral.

Heather kicked away the sheet that bound her legs. She refused to lie here like a virgin in heat. Matt wanted her every bit as much as she wanted him. No matter how he tried to deny the sizzle between them, it burned its way into every second of their time together.

If she was wrong about that, he could tell her so, get it all out in the open. She slung her feet to the floor and marched across the room, wrapping her fingers around the knob, only to have it turn in her hands without her moving it.

She stepped back as the door swung toward her. "Matt."

He didn't answer, but his hands were shaking as he

locked them behind her and drew her close. Her surprise heightened to hunger as he claimed her lips, and Heather rose up on tiptoe, pushing her body against his.

"I was just coming out to talk to you," she murmured, when he pulled his lips away and leaned against the door.

"What about?"

"This." She caught his bottom lip with her teeth, nibbling and then sucking until she was lost in another kiss. She was clutching and grasping, digging her fingers into his flesh, her body so hot, she couldn't think. Weak with desire, she fell against his chest.

"What about this?" Matt asked, his hands kneading her shoulders, his thumbs riding her neck, to her earlobes and back down again in mesmerizing motions. "That you wanted it or that you didn't?"

"That I wanted you. That I had to know if you wanted me the same way."

His lips found hers again, kissing her until she gasped for breath. "Is this answer enough?"

"It's getting there."

He swept her into his arms and carried her to the bed, laying her atop the rumpled sheet. "I've wanted you since the night I found you in the brush, spunky as hell in spite of having just taken a beating."

"That's a rough way to catch a man."

"You could have saved yourself the trouble. One look at you across the breakfast table in that T-shirt of mine would have done the trick."

His lips found hers again, quick but thorough, and then left them to seek new places, each new touch driving her wild. Below her ear, down her neck, just above the ribbon that held her gown together. He caught the ends of the tie and tugged the front open.

"Without desperate measures," she reminded him,

though her breath was so jagged she could barely whisper, "I'd never have gotten to your breakfast table. You practically pushed me away in the restaurant where we met."

A moan swallowed the last of her words, as her body responded to Matt's mouth sliding down her stomach, his hands still cradling her breasts, kneading her nipples, coaxing them to attention.

"I knew you were trouble even then," he whispered, his breath hot on her flesh. "I just didn't know how much, or how sweet the danger." Words got lost in the passion, reason swallowed up in shivers of anticipation as his fingers dipped inside her.

Heather writhed under his touch. Her body ruled now, soaking up pleasure as if it might never come again, knowing it had never been like this before. Finally, she cried out in ecstasy, the passion so intense she could hold nothing back.

Seconds later, when the first glorious waves of climax had passed, she started her own exploration—kissing, stroking, reveling in Matt's maleness. "What about you?" she whispered, her voice rough with desire and her heart racing in the aftermath.

"I'm still here." He took her hand, guiding it to him. She wrapped her fingers around him, and he shuddered.

"Take me, Matt. I want to feel you inside me."

"I thought you'd never ask."

HE TOOK HER THEN, his own head swimming as his blood rushed and his body caught and matched the rhythm of Heather's movements. He'd never wanted a woman like this, never even suspected that he could. It seemed now as though every second of every day since he'd met her had been leading to this moment.

His willpower over the edge, he exploded inside her before he was ready, a shaking, overwhelming experience that left him weak and disoriented. But still he knew the moment had been all the sweeter because Heather had sky-rocketed with him.

He rolled to his side and held her close and wished the world could always be this wonderful. But even now, doubts were edging out his contentment. He forced them aside as Heather snuggled against him.

Every man should have one night like this, and he wouldn't be robbed of his.

"HOW WOULD YOU LIKE to go to a party tomorrow night?"

Heather looked up from her nearly empty plate of pancakes. Matt had been up and on the phone by the time she opened her eyes this morning. Stomach growling, she'd hopped out of bed and scrounged in the kitchen for flour, milk, oil and eggs while he finished his conversation. She'd never known making love could make one so ravenous.

"What kind of party?"

"Logan Trenton doesn't need an excuse to throw a party, but his reason this time is that his stepdaughter just received her Ph.D. Word is this will be a shindig of magnificent proportions."

"Does that mean music and dancing?"

Matt grimaced. "There'll be some boot scooting. Unfortunately. But there will also be good food, and most important, the chance to talk to a lot of local people at once. This investigation is going dry faster than a watering hole in August, but someone in this town knows something. You can bet a prize steer on that."

Heather considered the prospect of attending a party with Matt. He'd be off talking cattle with every male in the place, of course, digging for clues in the process.

Meanwhile, she'd be odd woman out in a group of people who had all known each other from birth.

She slid a bite of pancake through a river of cane syrup. "Why don't you go without me? I didn't bring clothes for a *shindig of magnificent proportions*."

"You'd outshine everyone else even if you went in your jeans."

She beamed at his compliment. It was the first time this morning he'd given any sign that last night had happened, that he was actually aware of her as more than an inconvenient aspect of his job.

"Or…" He slid his chair back from the table. "We can stop at Ridgely's feed store this afternoon and you can do some shopping."

"A feed sack? No thanks."

"That wasn't exactly what I had in mind, but if the bag were skimpy enough, it might work." He smiled with his lips, though not his eyes. Heather recognized the signs now. Something worrisome was brewing behind his façade of pleasantries. He finished off his milk and took his empty dishes to the sink.

"Actually, Ridgely's wife has a clothing shop in the front of his feed store," he continued, as if there had been no pause in the conversation. "Lots of the ladies around here shop there. You could pick up some boots while we're at it."

"And a hat." The idea was growing on her. The party would provide another chance for her do what she'd come to Dry Creek for, to question people about Kathy Warren. That simple task was getting lost in the search for Ariana's killer, and so far they had no proof the two mysteries were even related.

"Will Rube and Edna be at the party?"

"Probably not. Now that Logan's playing with the financial big boys, he doesn't fraternize as much with his cronies from the old days.''

''Do we know for certain now that it wasn't any of the guys from the dude ranch who kidnapped me the other night?''

''I'm not sure of anything, but they all had alibis, supported by their friends.''

''Friends might lie.''

''Exactly. That's why I had a check run on every last one of them.'' Matt picked up a fistful of faxes from the counter and dropped them to the table beside her. ''Gabby brought these by this morning while you were still sleeping. They came in during the night from Ranger headquarters in San Antonio.''

''What did you find?''

''Dan Granger, age twenty-one, was arrested in Dallas last year for passing a couple of bad checks. Merle Fitch, age thirty-five, has a battery charge against him. He got into a fight with a man in a bar outside of Carrizo Springs. Apparently, they both wanted to sleep with the same woman. In both cases, the charges were dropped.''

''And there's nothing else?''

''Everyone else is squeaky clean, just wholesome young boys wanting to grow up to be cowboys.''

''What about fingerprints?''

''We found a set in the motel and on the sandals that we couldn't identify. We're checking them out now. The watch had been out in the elements a while, so it was apparently not from the night of the attack. John says it looks like one he lost last summer. The car was clean, as we expected it to be.''

Frustration dragged at Heather's spirits. ''And I guess it's the same no-luck pattern with the files you've been scrutinizing.''

Matt's face screwed into hard worry lines. "Not quite. I've found a pattern of missing files. Two weeks' worth of reports from right around the time your mother was reportedly in Dry Creek, and scattered missing files for months before and after that period."

"You didn't mention that last night."

"No, I wanted to wait until I'd gone through every box of files that Gabby had found in the attic. I finished that about daybreak and ran a computer analysis with the dates of the missing files. The pattern emerged. Before and after that year, there are no missing files."

"And the missing files are from the period of time when your father was sheriff?" The reason for his concern took shape in her mind.

"The inimitable Jake McQuaid. The man who never left a crime unsolved, at least never a record of one." He spit the last words out, as if he hated the taste of them in his mouth.

"But you don't *know* that there was a crime involving Kathy Warren."

"No, but I know there was one involving Susan Hathaway. Somebody beat her to a bloody pulp and left her for dead on the side of the road. If my brothers and I hadn't shown up when we did, she wouldn't have lasted the night. That's a crime, no matter who's sheriff. And there's no mention of it in any record I could find."

"Your dad *must* have tried to find out who did that to her."

"I'm sure he did." He stuffed his hands into the back pockets of his jeans, his eyes dark and impenetrable. "Unless he already knew. Unless there was some reason he decided to cover it up."

Heather leaned against the counter, watching him in consternation. "You shouldn't think like that about your father, Matt, not without good reason. It's not healthy."

"A man can't help how he thinks."

"That's not true." She moved toward Matt, but he turned away. She stepped behind him and put her hands on his shoulders, massaging the tight muscles. "Whatever's between you and your dad is eating you alive. You have to let it go before it destroys you."

"You know all of that in six days?" The sarcasm in his voice punctured her resolve.

"Maybe not. Maybe I don't know you at all, Matt McQuaid. I know the man standing in front of me right now is not the man I made love with last night."

He turned back to her, his eyes colder than she'd ever seen them, grim and brooding. The lines in his face were deep and drawn. "About last night…"

She put up her hands. "No, don't start that routine where you tell me you're sorry and it won't happen again. I don't buy it. Making love to me was right. It's this pretending you don't need anybody, not even your own family, that's wrong. So, your dad was human and not the perfect legend everyone thinks. Get over it. At least you *have* a dad."

She was shaking now, fighting back tears. She didn't care. With all she'd been through in the last few days, she didn't need this kind of garbage from the man who'd moved heaven and earth for her a few hours ago.

"I'm sorry, Heather. I didn't mean to drag you into this." He grabbed his hat from a hook by the door. "Be ready in thirty minutes. We're going into town."

The need to cry subsided as she washed the last of the dishes. She couldn't solve Matt's problems. He'd nurtured them too long, clung to them as a baby might a favorite blanket, taking a strange kind of comfort from his simmering resentment.

And he'd never even explained exactly why he resented his dad so much. But if Heather had to guess, she'd bet it had to do with Susan Hathaway.

Susan Hathaway and her mother, both with histories that touched Dry Creek at the same time, a period when criminal records had never existed or else had disappeared. There had to be a tie there somewhere, but what would they have to do to uncover it?

She headed to the bathroom for a quick shower, the gentle ache in her thighs the only reminder that last night had been the most wonderful of her life.

MATT MADE A LIST of necessary chores for his neighbor's son to take care of that day, things he'd originally planned to do himself while on vacation in Dry Creek. Instead he was spending his days working a puzzle where all the edges were jagged and nothing slid into place.

His nights... They were his biggest problem. Last night, to be specific. Heather saw this as a simple problem of a rift between father and son. Hell, if that was all it was, it wouldn't have been a big deal. He'd have gotten on with his life, forgetting he even had a father. Until Heather had fallen into his life, he practically had anyway.

The problem was not bad blood that stood between them but the blood that ran through their veins. He was like Jake McQuaid in too many ways, in all the ways that counted. His brothers Cy and Cameron were the lucky ones. They were different, always had been.

A human thread ran through them that had bypassed Jake and Matt. They had felt the same way he did about their father once, at least they'd claimed to, but they had never crawled inside themselves the way he and Jake did, didn't have trouble showing emotion, talking out their concerns.

Maybe that's because their mom had died. She hadn't chosen to leave them the way Matt's mom had, walking away from her son just so she didn't have to put up with the dark moods of Jake McQuaid or the sterile life he gave her.

Not that Matt remembered that. He'd figured it out from the little bit his dad and brothers had told him when they thought he was old enough to understand. The truth was he had no memory of his mom at all, and he blamed Jake McQuaid for that. Jake had robbed him of ever having known the woman who gave him birth.

Funny, how the old resentments had returned with such force now that Heather Lombardi had dropped into his life. Maybe it was the enthusiasm she felt for a past she didn't know that triggered his feelings of regret. But nothing changed the truth. He'd spent a lifetime as a loner, never able to connect completely with anyone, never able to take the risks true intimacy involved.

He couldn't give Heather what she needed emotionally any more than Jake McQuaid had been able to do that for the women in his life. The difference was that he was smart enough to know it. Heather thought she wanted him now, but that would change quick enough when the newness wore off, when she was faced with life day in and day out with a man who had nothing of himself to give.

He backed the truck from the carport, turning it around while he waited for Heather. Last night had given her the wrong impression of what he was about. He was nobody's hero. Nobody to fall in love with.

She pushed through the screen door, her curly hair pulled back into a ponytail and bouncing behind her. Her shirt was a soft yellow that draped over her perfect breasts. Her short denim skirt buttoned in the front and split open just enough to reveal a flash of thigh.

His heart plummeted to his stomach. Letting himself get mixed up with her was about as smart as squatting with your spurs on. Dumber actually. He'd feel the pain for a whole lot longer.

He reached over and opened her door and she climbed in.

"Where are we off to this time?" she asked.

"Logan Trenton's."

"I thought you'd already talked to him and he'd told you Gabby had all the records."

"I'd like to pick his brains before the party, see what he remembers from twenty-five years ago. As far as I'm concerned, the fact that the records from that time are missing is pretty convincing evidence that *something* was going on back then."

"I still don't see how a woman passing through town could have gotten mixed up in the trouble."

"She might have been in on it all along. We don't know where your mom was living before she dropped you off at the orphanage or what she did before that."

"If Logan Trenton knew anything, isn't it likely he was in on the cover-up? You said he was your father's deputy during that time."

"I've thought of that. My hope is either he was and he's ready to talk now or else he knows something he doesn't know he knows. Some bit of information that means nothing to him but will unlock a clue for me, if I get him to talk about it."

"Maybe he'd speak more freely if I wasn't around. Drop me off in town. I can visit with Edna or shop. You could pick me up when you finish."

"Sure, I'll drop you off at the motel, and, if it's convenient, the killer can drop by. After all, he was there a few days ago. He won't have any trouble finding the place.''

''Then drop me off at the library. I can look through old newspaper files. Something may turn up there.''

''Not in our library. We're too small. We have a few books and the capability of getting whatever you want from the state system if you have a few days to wait.''

''Then drop me at Paul Ridgely's feed store. No killer is just going to march into a shop with a bunch of cowboys hanging around, all of them with a gun of some kind in their pickup truck.''

Matt kept his gaze glued straight ahead. ''Are you so eager to be away from me?''

''No, I'm just not cut out for the role of helpless female. I need to be doing something. At least at Ridgely's I might be able to ask a few questions myself, talk to some people I haven't met before.''

''Okay. I'll drop you off at the feed store and ask Paul to keep an eye on you. He's as tough as anyone in town.'' He turned and captured Heather's gaze. ''Ask all the questions you want, but don't leave the store.''

''Yes sir, Ranger.''

Matt slowed the truck. There was a blue Camaro pulled to the side of the road in front of them, the hood up. ''Looks like someone's in trouble.''

''A late-model blue Camaro with a New Mexico license plate. Matt, that's the same kind of car Rube said he saw driving around town the day before Ariana was killed.''

Matt pulled off the road, coming to a stop behind the car. ''You're getting good at this.'' He opened his door. ''Wait here. I need to check this out.''

''Be careful.''

''Always.'' Matt touched his hand to the gun at his waist as he approached the car. There was no sign of movement.

He circled the vehicle, peering through the windows. There were a couple of old blankets in the back seat and some dirty clothes on the floor, but not a sign of the driver.

Turning his eyes toward a nearby area where the brush grew thick enough to hide a man, he touched his hand to the motor. Cool as a cucumber. He made a second trip around the car, examining the ground around the vehicle.

Pulling the driver's side door open, he reached inside the car and punched the trunk latch. As he did, he heard his truck door slamming behind him, and turned to find Heather striding toward him.

"I thought I told you to stay put."

"You did, but there's no one around here. I could see that."

She followed him to the back of the car and stood beside him while he yanked the trunk open. A string of curses escaped before he even thought about curtailing them.

Heather inched closer. "The man must have robbed a gun store."

"With the intent to equip a small army. There's enough assault rifles in here to conquer a Third-World country."

"What do you think it means?"

"That there's a dangerous lunatic on foot somewhere around Dry Creek." He went back to the truck and grabbed his cellular phone, punching in the number to get a license-plate check.

It took less than three minutes to determine that the car was a stolen one. Matt's next call was to Gabby.

"What's up, Matt? You just caught me. I was about to run out to Ben Wright's to check out a complaint on one of his wranglers who got a little rowdy at Cushman's Bar last night."

"This takes precedence. I just came upon a deserted vehicle on the side of the highway about a mile past the entrance to Billinger's place as you're coming into town. A blue Camaro, stolen, with a small arsenal in the trunk. We need it checked for prints, and we need the border guys out here with their dogs to do an intensive drug search.''

''What kind of guns are we talking?''

''Five assault rifles and a sawed-off shotgun, nothing you'd need for hunting legitimate game.''

''Which means the man probably has an automatic pistol or two in his pocket or strapped to his leg, possibly a *.44 Magnum.*''

''Don't go jumping to conclusions, Gabby.''

''No, but I don't want to find any buzzards circling. I'll get a bulletin on the radio not to pick up any hitchhikers in this area.''

''My guess is somebody already has.''

''Okay, I'm on my way, Matt. I'll have the deputy here alert the state highway boys.''

Matt broke the connection and turned to Heather. ''I want you to stay in the truck with the doors locked until I get back. If you see anyone approach, lean on the horn and I'll tear back down here.''

''Where are you going?''

''To check out the surrounding area, especially that cluster of thick brush to the left of the windmill.''

Adrenaline shot through Heather, fed by a fear that was raging out of control. ''You can't go out there alone.''

''I'm a Ranger. This is what I get paid to do.''

''Then wait for back-up.''

''Haven't you ever heard the old quote, 'One riot, one Ranger'? Well, this is one criminal, one Ranger. The odds are all with me.''

''You don't know there's only one.''

''Yes, I do. From the appearance of the ground, only

one person left the car, and that was from the driver's side.''

"The ground may be too hard for prints on the passenger side.''

"Footprints aren't the only sign a man's walked a path. There's bent and broken blades of grass, overturned stones, slight impressions in the dirt. I've tracked men along the border before with a lot less to go on than there is here.''

"Do the tracks you see lead in that direction?'' she asked, motioning toward the brush.

"No, I wish they did. They appear to lead from the car door to the front of the vehicle and then to the road, but I'd like to look around a little more anyway.''

Heather's breath caught, burning dry in her lungs. She leaned against the back of the car to support legs that had suddenly grown wobbly beneath her. "If someone gave the man a ride, and he's the man who killed Ariana... Oh, Matt, we have to do something. Someone else could be in danger.''

He nodded, his lips drawn, his eyes stormy. "So get in the truck and lock the door.''

Heather did, all but holding her breath until she saw Matt heading safely back in her direction. The sigh of relief was short-lived, as terrible visions began to flash through her mind.

Was the man who'd deserted the Camaro the same man who had put a bullet through Ariana's chest? Was he the man who was looking for her? Were death and murderous strangers the legacy of Kathy Warren?

No. She couldn't think that way. There was no proof her birth mother was tied to this man *or* to Ariana. Still, she didn't put up an argument when Matt told her he wouldn't be dropping her off at Ridgely's store. She'd be going to Logan Trenton's ranch with him.

THE OVERALL-CLAD FARMER eyed the man he'd picked up on the side of road. "I don't know where you're going, unless it's to Trenton's country. His is the only place this far out of town."

"Yeah, Trenton, that's it. He's a friend of mine. He'll give me a ride back into town and help me get the parts for my car."

"Yep. I wouldn't leave my car on the road too long if I was you, though. Used to be a man didn't take nothing that wasn't rightfully his, but times have changed."

"You're right. You never know what kind of man is on the road or what they're after."

"Yep." The farmer fished a toothpick from his pocket and poked at his teeth. "I don't ordinarily pick up hitch-hikers myself, but I hate to see a guy stranded with car trouble the way you were. I've been in that spot myself. In fact, one time I was—"

The man cut him off. "You got a smoke?"

"No, I gave up cigarettes years ago. Where are you from, anyway? You aren't from around these parts."

"Out west."

The farmer slowed to a stop at the dirt road. "It's a good ways from the gate to the house. I'd take you all the way myself, but I'm running way late for my doctor's appointment up in San Antonio."

"Yeah, don't worry. I'll get where I'm going." He jumped from the truck without bothering with a thank-you for the ride.

Strange fellow, the farmer decided, as he watched him leave the road, crawl between the rows of barbed wire and trudge into the brush. Still, if he was a friend of Logan's, he was probably all right.

He revved his engine and pulled his truck back onto the road. He had a long, lonesome drive in front of him. He should have gotten his radio fixed. Then he could have at least had some music to keep him company.

Chapter Eleven

Logan Trenton swung open the door as soon as Matt and Heather knocked, and ushered them into a massive den, paneled in pine and studded with the heads of game he'd snared in remote parts of the globe. The room made a statement of masculinity and power. So did the man.

Heather studied him during the introductions. He was tall, his Western shirt and string tie impeccable, his white Stetson spotless, his voice commanding. Gray touched his hair at the temples, adding distinction to his sun- and wind-roughened face, and his smile was polished and quick, though it never quite spread to his eyes. He had more the air of a politician than a South Texas rancher. And Heather definitely couldn't see him as ever having been a small-town sheriff.

He took her hand, holding it firmly in his instead of shaking it, and she felt his eyes move over her body, sizing her up. "It's nice to finally meet you, Miss Lombardi. I've heard so much about you."

"Yes, I seem to be the talk of the town."

"Well, we're all very sorry about that. I hate to even think what kind of men would attack a defenseless lady. I've told Matt and Gabby that I'd be more than happy to share my resources, an extra man or two, my small plane, anything I have if it would help in finding and arresting the two men who were responsible.''

Matt fingered his hat. ''We appreciate that, Logan. Right now, all I need are some answers.''

''So you said.'' He offered a patronizing smile. ''I hope this doesn't take too long. I've got to be in Uvalde by noon on some business.''

''I suggest we get started then.''

Matt started across the polished wood floor of the gigantic den toward the couch. Logan and Heather were left to follow.

''Matt McQuaid.''

They all turned as a striking young woman in jeans and an embroidered western shirt popped into the room. She fell into Matt's arms, then pulled away to give him a once-over.

''I'd heard you were in town, but I didn't know you were coming out to the ranch today. You look great.'' Her voice was deep, her Texas drawl abbreviated, as if she'd been away for quite a while.

Matt gave her an approving smile. ''Not nearly as good as you. I'd say the last few years have agreed with you.'' Matt took Heather's hand and tugged her closer. ''Forgive my manners. Heather, this is Logan's stepdaughter, Sylvia.''

Heather extended her hand and finished the introductions herself. ''Heather Lombardi. And I hear congratulations are in order.''

''That's right. It took me long enough, but as of next week, I'll be *Dr.* Sylvia McCullough, child psychologist.''

''That sounds like an interesting career choice.''

''I'm a natural at it. I've analyzed myself for long enough. I tried it with Matt, as well, but he's resistant to exploring his feelings. Like most of the men around here, he pretends his skin is cowhide, too thick for anything to get through.''

''I've noticed.''

Matt grimaced.

Logan laid an arm around his stepdaughter's shoulders, and Heather couldn't help noticing how quickly she jerked away. But if her stepfather noticed the reaction, he didn't let on. ''We tough-skinned men need to talk business, Sylvia. I'm going to take Matt back to my office. Why don't you take Miss Lombardi out to the stables and show her your graduation present?''

''Please, call me Heather,'' she said.

Sylvia stepped away from Logan and nearer to Heather. ''Word is you're in Dry Creek to try and locate your birth mother.''

''Yes, so far without luck. Her name was Kathy Warren. I don't suppose *you've* ever heard of her?''

''Not offhand. You can tell me more about it on our way to the stables.''

Heather shot Matt a questioning look. He'd been specific that she was not to go off by herself.

He hesitated, his thumbs hooked in the front pockets of his jeans, his gaze somber. ''I don't suppose it could hurt to go to the stables with Sylvia. There'll be wranglers around,'' he said, though he didn't sound enthusiastic about it. He turned to Sylvia. ''But don't be long. I still have more stops to make today.''

''No, we won't be long.'' She tossed her head back and her long, straight black hair fell about her shoulders. She was a little older than Heather, closer to Matt's age. Heather couldn't help but wonder if there had been more than friendship between her and Matt in the past.

Who could blame either of them if there had been?

They said their goodbyes, and Sylvia led the way as they

left the men and went out through the back door, the same way Heather and Matt had come in. Even with a killer roaming the streets, Dry Creek was a back-door neighborly kind of town.

"We'll take my four-wheel-drive. That way we can take the short cut and not stick to the road," Sylvia announced, marching toward a red Jeep with the doors and windows removed.

"How far is it to the stables?"

"Not more than a mile the way we're going. It's a couple if you take the main ranch road."

"How big *is* this ranch?"

"The San Jose is 150,000 acres." She jerked the vehicle into gear. "When I hit thirty-five, half of it will belong to me."

"Sounds like a nice trust fund."

"It is. My grandfather saw to that before he died. It was a good thing, because Mom left her half to Logan and he's not a man given to sharing." Sylvia took her eyes from the bumpy dirt path and stared at Heather. "Looks like someone worked you over pretty good."

"Don't tell me you haven't heard the details. You'd be the only one in Dry Creek if you've missed out."

"I've heard a little. I quit asking questions about Dry Creek as soon as I turned eighteen and got the hell out of town. I've been back very seldom since." She slowed for a heifer that had wandered across their path. "If I'd known Logan was going to throw a prodigal-daughter graduation party, I would have stayed away a while longer."

"I imagine he's glad to have you home."

"No, it scares him to death to think I might want to come back and take control of my half of the McCullough estate."

"Do you?"

"No, not as long as I have to share the land with Logan. When he's dead, I may reconsider. Or maybe not. I've made a new life."

They rode in silence for a few minutes. In spite of all Heather had been through herself in the last few days, she felt sorry for the troubled woman who rode beside her. She had wealth, beauty and a new career ahead of her, but she obviously harbored a few family resentments. No wonder she and Matt were friends.

Heather ducked and leaned toward the center of the Jeep as they passed a little too close to the branches of a scrubby mesquite tree. "Were you and Matt childhood friends?"

"We were in the same grade. We became better friends when he came back to Texas to go to college." Sylvia swerved to avoid a rut in the worn path she was driving. "We were never anything more, though, in case you were wondering. Too much alike, I think, to be more than buddies."

"Then you went to the same college?"

"Yes, the University of Texas. Matt stayed and got his degree. I dropped out after my sophomore year and spent some time finding myself, so to speak, before I went back and picked up a few degrees."

"Sounds like you did a good job of finding yourself."

They made a sharp turn to the right along a fence line. Heather felt the first tinge of alarm as they approached a narrow bridge without any sign of side rails. One wrong move and they'd plunge into the water below. "Don't tell me we're going to drive across that thing," she protested.

"Relax, it's been here for as long as I can remember. The hands use it all the time to move equipment a lot heavier than my little Jeep." Sylvia barely slowed as they hit the bumpy wooden ties.

Heather held her breath, crossing her fingers for luck.

She wouldn't have trusted the structure to support a small dog, but somehow they made it to the other side and level ground.

Sylvia drove a few yards farther, swerved right and then stopped.

"This doesn't look like the stables."

"No, it's the family cemetery. I'd like to stop for a minute, if that's okay with you. Today would have been my mother's birthday."

"No problem. I'll wait in the car."

"Get out and look around. You might find some of the stones interesting, and I won't be long."

Heather followed Sylvia through the gate. Sylvia was right. The names and dates on the tombstones told their own stories, mostly of hard lives that took people before their time.

Carrie McCullough, born June 1, 1861, died August 8, 1862. *Our precious baby girl."*

Jack McCullough, born April 14, 1898, died December 16, 1944.

Billy Roy Lassiter.

Heather studied the tombstone. Billy Roy Lassiter would have been about the same age as Kathy Warren and he'd died the same month of the same year. The day of the month was missing. Heather read and reread the strange inscription.

Killed at the hands of his fellow man.

"Did you find something interesting?" Sylvia asked, walking up behind her.

"As a matter of fact I did. Do you know anything about Billy Roy Lassiter's death?"

Sylvia ground a toe into the ground, staring at her boot as if it were worthy of deep study. "I know he was murdered." She raised her head, her gaze finally connecting with Heather's. "And I know some folks think Jake McQuaid's responsible."

A cottony lump caught in Heather's throat. Digging up buried truths. Matt had warned her about that. Maybe he had always been afraid the truths she uncovered would rock and sink his own world.

"That's a pretty serious accusation."

"I'm not accusing, just stating a fact." Sylvia started walking again, and Heather followed her, feet dragging, her emotions churning.

"The crime was conveniently never solved." Sylvia bit at her lower lip. "Did Matt tell you about the woman he and his brothers found beaten and left for dead?"

"Yes. Susan Hathaway."

"Some folks think Jake McQuaid beat and killed Billy Roy in retaliation for what happened to Susan. My mother was one of those people."

Heather's mind fought for reason. "How would you know this? You were no more than a child at the time."

Sadness drew the corners of Sylvia's eyes into deep grooves. "I know because I heard my mother and Logan arguing the day after the man's body was found. They thought I was asleep, but my mother's screaming woke me. She accused Logan of helping Jake kill Billy Roy."

"And then what happened?"

"Nothing. My mother died a few months later when her horse threw her. She was an excellent rider, but something spooked her mount, and he reared back, throwing her to the ground in front of him. His front feet caught her before she could roll away. At least that's the way it looked when one of the wranglers found her body."

"I'm sorry." The words snagged painfully in Heather's throat, the hurt as much for herself as it was for Sylvia— and for Matt, and everyone else who'd ever lost a mother.

"It's okay. It happened a long time ago, and I've dealt with it and let it go. It's the good memories I try to hold on to now."

"Have you ever mentioned this to Matt?"

"No. I didn't want him to quit being my friend when we were youngsters. And, to tell you the truth, I hadn't thought of Billy Roy Lassiter for years, not until you called his name."

Heather started back to the car, and then jerked to a stop. Something had moved in the distance. She'd caught a glimpse of it in her peripheral vision. A quick darting. Perhaps a bird, a jackrabbit, a deer.

It was the events of the past few days that had her jumping out of her skin at every movement. That and the fact that she and Sylvia were in an isolated cemetery, so far away that no one would hear them if they cried for help.

She stared into a patch of thorny, head-high brush standing between them and a ragged persimmon tree. This time the darting movement was clear and unmistakable. Someone was out there, watching them, like a coyote waiting for his moment to spring on the helpless prey.

The hair on her neck stood on end. "Sylvia." Her voice was soft, meant not to carry beyond their immediate surroundings.

Sylvia eyed her suspiciously "What's wrong? You look as if you've seen a ghost. You're not going to faint on me, are you?"

"No, but I think there's someone in the bushes watching us."

"No one would be out here without a horse or a car. We're too far from the house."

The taste of fear settled like acid in Heather's stomach. She could feel a man's hands on her, feel a fist plowing into her face, almost as real as it had been the other night in her car. "Let's just get to the Jeep, fast."

The urgency in her voice must have gotten through to Sylvia. Both of them broke into a run, not slowing until they'd reached the Jeep. Sylvia's hand shook as she poked her key at the ignition, scraping metal before sliding into the hole. The engine sputtered and died, and Heather swallowed the curse that tore at her throat.

Sylvia didn't bother. "Damn! What a time for car trouble. Look again, Heather, see if you really see someone."

She didn't get the chance. This time the noise was from the west, and there was no mistaking the approaching horse and rider. Sylvia quit turning the key.

The cowboy tipped his hat. "You ladies lost?"

"No. I never get lost on my own land, but we could use your help. Heather thought she saw a man watching us from those bushes over there." She pointed.

The cowboy pulled on the reins, making a full circle with his horse, his gaze scanning the surrounding area before turning back to them. "More likely a momma cow making sure you're not out here to bother her calf, but I'll ride over and check out the scrub."

Sylvia turned the key, and this time the engine purred to life. "Are you ready to go to the stables, Heather?"

"I'd rather go back to the house. I promised Matt I wouldn't be too long."

"Then back to the house it is." She inched the jeep forward, then stalled as the cowboy rode back in their direction, smiling broadly.

"I scared up a bevy of quail. No sign of anything else." A broad grin cracked his lips.

"I guess I was mistaken," Heather said, sure she hadn't been, but afraid to push the issue with a man she knew nothing about. She was dwelling in a world of strangers where the unexpected was all she could count on. A world where secrets were deadly, and where the only man she trusted was a man she might be about to destroy.

The thought tore at her heart. Matt might bear grudges against his father, but that was a long way from believing he was a murderer. She could almost see the headlines now: Texas Ranger Arrests Own Father for Twenty-five-year-old Murder.

And all because a woman named Kathy Warren had passed through this town one dark night years ago.

And because Heather had fallen into Matt's life. A stroke of luck for her, but it might turn into a heartbreaking stroke of tragedy for him. And the last thing she wanted to do was bring pain to Matt McQuaid.

The Jeep bounced and rocked as Sylvia lowered her foot on the accelerator. "Will you tell Matt what we talked about today?"

"I don't have a choice, not since Ariana's been murdered. The killing has to stop somewhere."

"No, I guess you don't. I hope he understands why I had to tell you about his father." Sylvia hit the accelerator a little harder. "For what it's worth, I hope I'm wrong about Jake."

"So do I, Sylvia. So do I."

HEATHER WAITED until they were in the truck before mentioning her trip to the cemetery and sharing the information about Billy Roy Lassiter's grave. She avoided mentioning Sylvia's suspicions that Jake McQuaid might be involved in his death. Somehow the short ride to Ridgely's store didn't seem the opportune time to suggest Matt's father might be a murderer.

Just as well the topic hadn't been approached, Heather decided, sliding her right foot into the boot that Ridgely's wife had pulled from the shelf. Matt was already distracted and agitated after his talk with Logan, a talk he claimed had gotten him nowhere.

"Tug hard on those pull tabs to make sure your feet are all the way in," Matt instructed. "Then walk around in them. The leather should ride the top of your feet, but not cut into them."

She followed his instructions, pulling up on her jeans as she walked to get a better look at the plain black leather boots that Matt referred to as ropers. Her toes rocked against the new leather, and her heels settled against the solid backs.

"They're not as comfortable as my tennis shoes, but I think they fit."

"Hmmmpf." Paul's wife stuck her hands on her ample hips. "Boots aren't meant for walking or comfort. They're for riding horses. Or else they're for show." She lifted her ankle-length full skirt so that Matt and Heather could capture the full effect of the fancy boots she wore. "Aren't these a pair of doozies? I just got them in today."

"Very nice," Heather admitted, "but not quite what I need at the Lone M."

"No, these beauties are for prancing and dancing, and I plan to wear them half out at Logan Trenton's big blowout. Paul Ridgely hasn't taken me dancing in a month of Sundays. I'll be making him pay for that tomorrow night."

"What are you wearing besides the gorgeous boots?" Heather asked, drawn into Mrs. Ridgely's excitement in spite of herself.

"A full skirt, flowered, and an embroidered blouse. It makes me look even fatter than usual, but I don't care. I like a skirt twirling about my legs when I dance."

"You're far from fat."

"Not nearly as far as I was at your age. But it's fine

with me and fine with Paul, and we're the only ones who matter. He says he likes a woman he can hold on to.'' Her easy laughter rippled through the small shop.

Heather made another circle around the stool and then paused in front of a floor mirror. ''This will be my first pair of Western boots.''

''Then you better be careful, Matt.'' Mrs. Ridgely gave him a conspiratorial wink. ''Nothing gets in a woman's blood faster than Western boots and Texas cowboys.''

Heather turned to hide the blush that heated her cheeks.

''You know,'' Mrs. Ridgely said, walking over to stand in front of her. ''I just got in an outfit that would look terrific on you, make you look like a real Texas gal. Come on over and take a look.''

''Let me take these boots off first.'' Heather dropped back onto the low stool. She slid her hands under the tops and shoved.

''That's not exactly how you do that.'' Matt knelt in front of her. ''Let me help.''

One hand grasped the leather just below her ankle, one caught her leg above the boot line. The crazy sensation attacked her again, hot and sweet, rolling inside her and making her dizzy with unexpected desire. His gaze caught hers and held, invisible steam rising between them, stealing her breath away. The boot clunked to the floor beneath her foot. Matt backed away, flushed and fumbling. ''You can get the other one,'' he said. ''Now that you know how.''

His voice was gravelly and unsteady. He shoved his hands into his pockets and stalked away, not stopping until he reached the far back corner of the store and a circle of men.

Mrs. Ridgely stared at Matt's back and then at Heather, no doubt noticing the flush in her cheeks. She smiled and nodded. ''So, the rough, tough son of Jake McQuaid isn't a robot lawman without a heart after all. And you, Heather Lombardi, must be some woman to make him show it. Many a girl around here's tried without a smidgen of luck.''

"I have no idea what you mean."

"You might be a nice lady, but you're lying through your teeth right now. Come on over here and try on that outfit I was telling you about. You might as well go all the way and brand him while he's weak and willing.''

Heather followed Mrs. Ridgely across the shop, but she knew something the friendly woman didn't. There was nothing weak about Matt McQuaid.

THE SOFT SQUEAKING of the porch swing worked like a lullaby, and Heather's eyelids drooped until only a slit of afternoon sunlight filtered through. Matt had gotten back to the ranch about fifteen minutes ago, after being gone all afternoon. He'd left her guarded by the deputy while he went back into town.

But his beeper had been buzzing as he walked up the steps, and he'd been on the phone with Gabby ever since. She'd had no opportunity to speak of Sylvia's accusation against Jake McQuaid. And until she did, she couldn't get a minute's peace.

She looked up as the front door creaked open. "What was Gabby's problem?" she asked, moving over to make room for him on the swing beside her. Instead he settled on the top step and leaned against the porch column.

"He collected some prints from the car we found deserted on the highway, but he doesn't have a name as yet. They're running a fingerprint scan up at headquarters as we speak.''

"Are there any leads in Ariana's death?"

"Nothing new. But at least we've had another crime-

free day in Dry Creek. No bodies. No attacks. No threats.''
Matt set his hat on the porch beside him and stretched out,
his long legs reaching all the way across the top step.

"And no clue as to what happened to the missing records?''

"Not unless you buy Logan's speculation that Gabby let
rats get into them in that attic above his office and then
threw the damaged files away.''

"Evidently you don't believe that theory.''

"Seems strange the rats would choose the exact records
I'm looking for, especially if we're talking about four-
legged rats.''

Heather ran her fingers up and down the linked chain
that held the swing. "Matt, I need to talk to you.''

"I thought we *were* talking.''

She swallowed past a lump in her throat. "Sylvia mentioned something today that I think you should know
about.''

The phone rang, and Matt started to get up from the
step.

"I'll get it,'' Heather said, beating him to the draw. She
couldn't sit on the porch and wait in silence now that she'd
broached the subject with Matt. Better to be the one doing
something.

She caught the phone on the third ring. "Hello.''

"I need to talk to Matty. Is he there?''

Matty. The name was spoken like an endearment, but
the female voice was shrouded in concern. Heather trembled, suddenly ill at ease and shaky. "Matt's here. I'll get
him for you. Who shall I say is calling?''

"Susan Hathaway. I need to talk to him about his father.'' She hesitated. "But don't tell him that.''

"No, I won't.'' Anxiety was playing havoc with
Heather's nerves as she handed Matt the phone.

Chapter Twelve

Matt took the phone from Susan. "Matt McQuaid."

"Matty. It's Susan."

His fingers tightened around the receiver. "Is something wrong?"

"No, I wanted to hear your voice, to find out how you're doing. It's been so long since you've called."

"Yeah. I've been busy." The lie was bitter on his tongue. Not that he hadn't been busy, but it had little to do with the fact that he hadn't called. "How are you?"

"Older, slower. A few more wrinkles. Other than that I'm the same."

He tried to imagine Susan as old, but he could only ever picture her as the young woman he and his brothers had found in the ditch. The beautiful lady who'd moved into their lives like an angel dropped from the sky. He'd never see her any other way.

"Have you talked to Cy or Cameron lately?"

"They're both well, absorbed in their own families and careers, but they drop by when they can. They'd love to see you." Her voice shook slightly. "We *all* would."

All. She meant his father, of course, though they both knew that wasn't true. Matt had been a thorn in his father's side for as long as he could remember, a reminder of the wife Jake had needed, but never loved.

But Susan would always stand by and defend Jake McQuaid. She didn't need vows or legalities to be faithful and loyal. It was who she was.

"How is Jake?"

"Not as well as he should be. The doctor's warned him to take it easy, to watch his blood pressure. He doesn't listen to him or to me."

"That's Jake."

"That's your *father*. He'll turn sixty-five in two weeks."

"I'm sure you're planning a party. Wish him all the best for me."

"You need to do that yourself, Matt. I want you to come home for his birthday."

"I can't." He swallowed, his throat drier than south Texas earth. "I'm in the middle of a case."

Silence hung on the line, accusing, pleading. It was difficult to refuse Susan anything, but more difficult to return home and play the role of loving, respectful son, especially now.

"Think about it, Matty. If you won't do it for yourself or Jake, do it for me. I've caused a rift in this family long enough. I can't carry the pain of that to the grave."

"The problem is between Jake and me, Susan. It has nothing to do with you."

"It has everything to do with me. You think Jake robbed me of respectability. He didn't. Like you and your brothers, he paid the price for mistakes I made before I was old enough to know what life was about. You know the truth of that now and you have to accept it."

"I accept that you make it awfully convenient for Jake to do exactly as he pleases, to play life his way, by his own self-serving rules."

"He lives life the only way he knows how, the same as you do." Her voice fell to a pain-filled whisper. "Come home, Matty. A quick visit for your father's birthday. Is that so much to ask?"

Matt shifted the phone to the other ear. His gaze cut to the front door and the darkness that was settling like a veil over his world. "Don't count on me, Susan. Not this time."

Her sigh cut through the static that was forming on the line. "I am counting on you. I need you here and so does Jake. And *you* need to be here for yourself. You're a part of this family and always will be."

Left without an argument, Matt shifted the conversation to impersonal topics, the weather, the dry spell in South Texas that was threatening to turn serious. But the tension created by Susan's pleas continued to cloud the conversation, and by the time he hung up the phone, Matt was sweating.

He walked back to the porch, this time easing to the swing beside Heather. He rubbed his clammy hands together, then wiped them on the rough denim that covered his thighs. "I'm sorry for the interruption."

"You look upset. Is something wrong?"

"Jake McQuaid's sixty-fifth birthday is approaching. I was invited to the party."

"You'll go, of course."

"I have a murderer to catch. Speaking of which, where were we?"

Heather sensed more than saw the change in Matt, although the signs were not invisible. The cocky, self-assured Ranger had drawn inside himself, leaving his shoulders to sag and his eyes and chin to drop. She longed to question him further about Susan's call, but she knew it would be a waste of time. Matt talked only when he was ready.

"We were discussing the murder of Billy Roy Lassiter," she said, dreading more than ever what she had to say.

"Billy Roy." Matt drummed his fingers against the swing's wooden armrest. "The man whose grave you discovered in the McCullough family cemetery. I asked a few questions about him today in town."

"What did you find out?"

"That the mention of his name stops conversation cold." Matt tensed, his muscles drawn and pulling at the fabric of his shirt. His face twisted into hard, unforgiving lines. He turned to face her, his eyes a frigid shade of gray. "Tell me exactly what Sylvia told you."

Heather did, wincing inside as she uttered the words of accusation.

"So Sylvia thinks Jake killed Billy Roy Lassiter," he said when she'd finished the statement. "Evidently the rest of Dry Creek does, too. Why else would they clam up so tight at the sound of his name?"

Matt didn't protest the accusation. The only sign he gave that it affected him at all was the burst of energy that pulled him from the swing and had him pacing the porch.

"I didn't want to tell you what she said about your father, Matt, but in view of Ariana's murder, I felt I had to. But Sylvia's saying it doesn't make it so. And if everyone in town believed it, why didn't someone do something before now?" She stood and walked over to him.

"Why? Because it's Jake McQuaid."

"What will you do?"

"The only thing I can. If he's innocent, I'll prove it. If he's guilty, I'll prove that, too." He turned and faced Heather, his eyes dark pools of determination. "The only thing that doesn't add up is that the law was Jake's life, part of the code of justice that ruled him. It was more important to him than even his own children. It's hard accepting that he prostituted that the way he did his women.''

Heather slid into his arms. She needed his closeness, but even that didn't give her warmth tonight. ''There are other Rangers who can take over this investigation. Give up the case, Matt. If you don't, it might destroy you.''

''I can't.'' He tilted her chin so that she had to look him in the eye. ''I told you. My father's blood runs through me. I have to do what I have to do. That's why I'm no good for you, no good for any woman.''

''Or maybe you just never met a woman who could handle you until now, Matt McQuaid.'' His arms tightened around her, but she pulled herself from his grasp. She'd just thrown down a gauntlet, and she wasn't sure that she was ready to meet her own challenge. She didn't even know where the words had come from.

''I'll finish making dinner,'' she said, pulling the screen door open. She peeked her head back out, stopping the door just before it closed behind her. ''You might want to clean up. We're dining by candlelight. Even on a ranch, a lady needs some social amenities.''

MATT SHUDDERED as Heather disappeared from sight. He felt as if he'd been turned inside out and back again in the last few minutes. The reminder that so many people apparently believed his father was a murderer had left a raw lining in his stomach—which could usually handle the hottest of chili peppers.

But he'd shower and play gentleman rancher for the lady of the Lone M if that's what she wanted. He'd play all her games, maybe even pretend for a few minutes that he was the man she thought he was. Hell, he'd ride a wild stallion for her if he thought it would make the next few days any easier.

Susan Hathaway, Kathy Warren, Billy Roy Lassiter and Jake McQuaid. Somehow, they were all tied together in a plot that someone would still kill to keep secret twenty-five years after the fact. He stuffed his hand into his pocket and ran his fingers along the jagged edge of the note that rested there. This time the warning had been delivered to Matt, stuck under the windshield wiper of his truck while it had been parked in town.

Ranger: Let the search for Kathy Warren end before the lives of good people are ruined over something that can't be changed. If you don't, you will live to regret it. You and your girlfriend.

But what were a few more regrets to a man like him?

It was Heather he was worried about now. He'd do whatever he had to in order to keep her safe, even if it meant defying the law he was sworn to protect. More of the legacy of Jake McQuaid.

As for Jake McQuaid, he prayed Sylvia was wrong, though he had suspected Jake might be involved from the first sign of missing records. If Jake were arrested on murder charges it would tear the heart out of Susan. She would never forgive Matt for digging up the past. Maybe he'd never forgive himself, though he had no choice now.

Every muscle in Matt's body ached as he headed for a hot shower. He felt like a grain of sand caught up in a dust storm, powerless to stop the events that whirled around him, powerless to dictate where it would all end.

HEATHER FISHED fresh green beans from the pot, spooning boiled potatoes around them in the serving bowl. She'd snapped the beans herself—a neighbor had brought over a gift of vegetables from her garden—and rummaged in Matt's poorly stocked pantry for seasonings.

His freezer, however, was another story. There were packages of corn, squash, carrots and other summer vegetables, all zipped neatly away in freezer bags labeled with dates and the names of one or another of his neighbors.

Evidently the women of Dry Creek took good care of their resident Texas Ranger. And he had his own supply of meat, every cut of beef imaginable. She'd made beef Stroganoff, one of her specialties.

Standing back, she admired her handiwork. The plates didn't match, but the colors of the food prettied up the table. All in the presentation, that's what the few ladies' magazines she'd found time to read said. Hot pads in hand, she added the finishing touch, a big bowl of sweet corn, still on the cob.

Funny, cooking for just herself had always seemed a chore. Scavenging around in Matt's much less modern and meagerly stocked kitchen had actually been fun. Or had the pleasure been in the anticipation of sitting across the table from him, watching him eat, and listening to him talk?

He claimed to be all wrong for her, all wrong for any woman, but every moment she spent with him convinced her differently. Yet she couldn't help but wonder if the attraction that pulled her to him would be this great if it weren't for the danger that hung over her head like an anvil about to drop.

She touched her fingers to her hair, pushing the loose wisps back in place, and then went into the bedroom to smudge a tint of color to her lips. Steam and the sound of running water beating against the plastic shower curtain seeped through the cracks around and under the door.

In her mind's eye she saw Matt, naked, streams of water

running down the angles and planes of his body, imagined the hair on his chest, wet and curled in the running water. The images churned inside her, and she leaned against the door, weak with desire. How could she want a man she barely knew this badly?

The door squeaked open and she lost her balance, falling inside far enough to catch herself on the counter. Matt peeked around the edge of the curtain. "Are you all right?"

"Yes." Her voice came out too soft, shattered by the emotion reeling inside her.

"Come here, Heather." Matt pushed the curtain aside and reached out a hand.

"The floor is getting wet."

"Let it."

He grabbed her hand and pulled her closer. The heat from the shower mingled with the fire inside her. Breathless, she tried to pull away. "You're getting my clothes wet."

"We can take care of that." His wet hands slid beneath her shirt, his fingers hot and damp on her skin as he raised her shirt and pulled it over her head. She didn't move, barely daring to breathe as he wrapped his arms around her, loosened the clasp on her bra and let it drop to the floor.

Shaking, she stepped out of her shoes, and Matt tucked his hands under her arms and lifted her into the tub, jeans and all. Water splashed around and over her breasts and face, but all she felt were Matt's lips on hers.

When she came up for air, she was trembling, her hair straggling into her face, but she still felt more sexy and desirable than ever before in her life. "I usually shower alone," she whispered, "and with all my clothes off."

"What a waste of good water. This way you can do

your laundry, make love and get clean all at the same time." He soaped his hands and rubbed them over her breasts until soft snowy peaks highlighted her nipples.

Heather returned the favor, soaping Matt's chest and then his buttocks between kisses. Laughing, he pulled on the waist of her jeans until the snap gave. Using his teeth, he unzipped her.

She nibbled his wet earlobe. "The hidden side of Matt McQuaid. Do the other Rangers know you have this knack for conserving water?"

"If they do, they know me better than I knew myself. I've never behaved like this before." He kissed her again, thoroughly, boggling her brain. "You bring out the worst in me," he whispered, peeling the wet denim from her body.

"If this is the worst, I don't know if I'm up for the best."

"We'll soon find out."

The next few minutes were a symphony of movements and feelings, of words and moans of pleasure. Heather drowned in pleasure time after time, only to come back to life with a new touch by Matt. By the time they climbed out of the shower, she was too weak to do more than wrap herself in a towel and collapse across the bed.

Matt, on the other hand, was obviously refreshed and raring to go. She heard him padding through the house, singing a country song and calling to her. "All that and you cook, too. But you better hurry. Our candles are burning out."

She struggled into a pair of dry jeans and a white shirt. "Don't tell me you have enough energy left to eat," she challenged as she fell into the chair opposite him.

"Are you kidding? I'm famished." He passed the bowl

of beans to her. "Come to think of it, I don't remember stopping for lunch today."

He settled into eating, and within moments the quiet routine snatched away the few minutes of pleasure they'd stolen in the shower. Heather could almost see the worries of the day claiming him again, dragging his spirits down and changing his eyes from black gold to dusty coal.

But nothing could steal her happiness away. She wouldn't let it. She'd learned something about Matt in the last few days. The passion that drove him wasn't all for the law that ruled him. He could feel that same passion for a woman. She'd experienced that firsthand.

Maybe this was the gift Kathy Warren had left behind for the daughter she'd never known. A meeting with Matt McQuaid. Perhaps even now her birth mother was looking down from heaven and smiling on their union. If so, she still had her work cut out for her.

There was a murder to solve before either Heather or Matt could be free to go on with their lives. And she knew Matt still had to be convinced that he could handle a long-term relationship—that even though he was his father's son, he was still his own man.

Because Heather wouldn't settle for what Susan Hathaway had. When this was over, she'd only stay in Dry Creek as Matt's wife.

THE THREE MEN HUDDLED in the back of the barn. Outside, the sun flirted with the horizon, spreading rays of red and gold across the graying sky. Inside, darkness was winning, letting mere splotches of light sneak between the shadows.

"I never meant for things to go this far." The shorter man tugged at the neck of his shirt, pulling it away from his Adam's apple. A drop of sweat worked its way down his collar.

"What are you going to do now?" The tall, lanky man ran callused fingers through his graying hair. His question was directed to the man who always took control.

"We don't have a lot of choice, do we?"

"I don't like it," the short man complained again.

"Are you willing to go to jail for life, that is, if the jury's reasonably friendly? If they're not, you could be talking the death penalty."

The tall man hooked his thumbs into the front pockets of his jeans. "I don't know. I just don't know."

"I do. I'll take care of everything tomorrow night at the party. My plan is foolproof."

"You're talking about killing innocent people." The stench of his words filled his lungs and the man moved toward the door for a breath of fresh air.

"It's no different than it was when we killed Billy Roy."

"It's a lot different. I was young, and drunk. And the victim then wasn't so innocent."

"Susan Hathaway was."

The old cowboy felt sick to his stomach. "She wasn't part of the original plan. I've always felt guilty for what we did to her. The both of you have, too. Don't tell me you haven't."

"Not a day goes by I don't regret what we done." The tall man leaned against a giant roll of feeder hay. "Maybe we should just hold off. No one's found us out for a quarter of a century. We could keep quiet and take our chances."

"And you think Matt McQuaid will pack up and go away? You know his reputation. He's tougher than nails and persistent as a hungry mosquito."

"He's Jake McQuaid's youngest son and the heart of Susan Hathaway." The shorter man backed away from the other two, suddenly loath to look at them. "I'll take no part in killing him or Heather Lombardi. It was bad enough when you hired those two ruffians that beat her up so bad. You'd promised they'd only frighten her into leaving town.''

''Even the beating didn't frighten her enough to run her off. She's not reasonable, but you'd better be. We're all in this together, and we stick together or swing together. It's the only way.'' The man stepped closer to his reluctant friend.

''Then we swing together. We done the deed. We'll pay the price if it comes to that.'' The man who spoke thought of his wife and how she'd die of grief if she knew the truth about him. ''I hope it don't,'' he said. ''I sure hope it don't, but I'll take the risk.''

The man in charge wrapped his hand around the knife in his pocket. He didn't like the spot he was in, but he'd do what had to be done. ''You might be willing to take the risk, Paul, but I'm not.''

HEATHER ROLLED THE PEN between her fingers. ''Let's try another scenario, Matt. Suppose my mother had nothing at all to do with the death of Billy Roy Lassiter or Susan's beating. Suppose she just got out of Cass Purdy's car and caught a bus to New Orleans that night.''

''That makes perfect sense except for the fact that as soon as you arrived in town asking about her, you fell into a heap of trouble.'' He wadded the sheet of paper in front of him and hurled it across the room.

''But that could be because I said she was here in mid-October, twenty-five years ago. If I'd killed Billy Roy, I wouldn't want anyone digging up the past, especially if the past correlated that closely with the time of the murder.''

''I'd buy the possibility of that scenario if we only had the threatening note. I'd give it a scrap of consideration if we added some guys roughing you up. But throw in planting explosives in your car and killing Ariana, and it blows your theory out of the corral. A man doesn't kill to cover up a murder he's gotten away with for years unless he has damn good reason to believe his secrets are about to be uncovered.''

"I just wish the man who'd gone to Cass Purdy's looking for me, the one who showed up at my apartment the day Ariana was killed, would show up again. It's possible that he's a member of Kathy Warren's family, that he could unravel this mystery."

"You're clutching at a broken rein, Heather. I've told you before, the chances of that man being a member of your family are slim to none. He's more likely a paid killer whose job is to make sure you don't get the chance to find out too much."

She stretched her legs in front of her and crossed her arms over her chest, so tired of dead ends she could scream.

Matt leaned closer. "Are you cold?"

"A little. Inside."

"I'm afraid I can't do anything about that."

"But you do help, all the time. Just being with you helps."

He shook his head. "That's only because you see in me what you choose to."

"And you see in yourself what you choose to see. I like *my* vision better." She wouldn't give in to his demons tonight, not after he'd played and made love to her the way he had in the shower. He was flesh and blood, not some inhuman clone of his father, whether he cared to admit it or not.

"Tell me about Susan Hathaway, Matt."

"What about her?"

"You told me she didn't know a soul in Dry Creek, that she was only passing through town that night, when she was beaten and left for dead, but you've never really talked about her."

Matt put down the legal pad he'd been using to scribble possible matches between the skimpy evidence he'd collected so far and every man in town. "She was quiet, loving. She laughed a lot, but sometimes I'd come in and find her crying. I never understood that until recently, when we found out who she really was."

"What do you mean by that? Who was she?"

He walked over to the counter and poured himself a double shot of whiskey, drinking it down before turning back to Heather. "Susan kept her past a secret, not even letting my brothers know about it until just recently. I don't know how much she remembered or how much she wanted to remember before that, but I've honored her wishes to keep it her secret."

Matt returned to the couch. He took the end opposite Heather, working his feet from his boots. When the last one clattered to the floor, he propped his stockinged feet on the wooden coffee table. "In light of all that's happened to you, I don't think Susan would mind your knowing her story, but it's to go no further."

"Of course not."

His gaze met Heather's "Have you ever heard of Pamela Jessup?"

"Pamela Jessup? The name sounds familiar." Heather pulled her feet up under her. "Wait, isn't that the California heiress who ran away from home and joined up with some bank robber? I saw a TV show about her once."

"That's her."

"According to the show I saw, her family never heard from her again. Her body was found in some motel in Texas. So what does that have to do with Susan?"

"Pamela Jessup *is* Susan Hathaway."

Chapter Thirteen

Matt reached for the newspaper.

"Oh, no, you don't, Matt McQuaid." Heather snatched the paper from his hands and tossed it over the arm of the sofa and to the floor. "You don't nonchalantly announce you were raised by some infamous bank robber heiress and then turn away as if you'd given me a weather report."

Matt sighed and rubbed his forehead as if his head hurt, but he went on. "My brothers and I were raised by a homeless woman we found at the side of the road. Believe me, we never had a clue the woman who cooked our oatmeal and patched our jeans was a bank robber or an heiress. No one did."

"Can you imagine, a woman wanted for bank robbery found by the sheriff's sons. It was probably a good thing no one knew who she was." Heather tapped the end of her pen against her tablet. "But I thought Pamela Jessup's body was found in some motel in Texas."

"That was all a lie concocted to keep her family from looking for her. Apparently Philip Gould lost track of her about the time we found her. When her body didn't show up, he made up his own version of her disappearance. He admitted as much when he was finally arrested. He still claimed he wasn't the one who'd attacked her."

"It has to have been all one and the same, Matt. Your dad, Pamela Jessup, Billy Roy, my mother, all involved in something someone is determined to keep secret. You tried to tell me I might not like what I found out, but I couldn't have imagined that Kathy Warren might be involved with a bank robber."

"We don't have proof of anything."

"It still doesn't make sense. I can see how my mother could have been mixed up with Pamela Jessup. We know nothing about her, but Billy Roy was just a local wrangler."

"He could have just been in the wrong place at the wrong time. It happens, especially when there are two beautiful young women about."

Heather's insides churned. All she'd wanted was to find a connection with her past, learn something about her birth mother, but the old secrets she was discovering were actually hidden crimes. She turned around so that she could face Matt. "Tell me about Susan, or should I say Pamela?"

"She'll always be Miss Susan to me." Matt's tone softened. "She was different from the women around here. Her voice had a musical quality to it, and she had funny ways of doing and saying things. We laughed at her, but she was fast as the wind on the horse Dad bought her."

"It must have been difficult for her, going from a life of luxury to being the caretaker for a poorly paid sheriff and his three sons."

"I guess so, but we never noticed. We had no idea she'd ever been rich."

Matt shifted, and a smile touched his lips. Heather sensed he was lost in his own past, this time in the good parts of it.

"Susan and I bonded right from the first," he said, continuing the story. "I suspect I was a needy child, aching for a mother like all the other boys had. She gave me more than my fair share of love and attention. Not that she let me get away with anything. She was tough as nails.''

''According to the documentary that I saw, Pamela Jessup was a wild teenager who'd gotten involved in drugs and partying, a victim of too much money and loose morals.''

''There's two sides to everything.'' Matt reached in his back pocket and pulled out his wallet. He removed a small photograph, yellowed, the edges crinkled. ''This is the woman I knew. No drugs unless you count an occasional aspirin. And I don't remember a single wild party.''

He handed the photo to Heather, a smile curving his lips. ''But she could dance. She'd play the radio and boogie with the broom or the mop or one of us boys. That was the wildest I ever saw her. Unless you count the time my brothers and I let a snake loose in the house.''

Heather held the photo so that it caught the glow of the lamp. ''She was very pretty.''

''She still is.'' Matt fingered a loose string on the throw pillow that rested between them. ''You remind me of her.''

Heather studied the photo. There *was* a resemblance. Not the hair. Not the eyes or cheekbones, either. The mouth, maybe, or the shape of the face. A sinking feeling settled in her stomach. ''Is that why you took me in, Matt, because I reminded you of Susan?''

''I took you in because you were in danger.'' He stretched his arm across the back of the couch, catching a strand of her hair between his fingers, toying with it. ''I know what you're thinking, Heather. Forget it. The attraction between us is a hell of a lot more than my looking for a lost mother figure, and you know it.''

''You're reading my mind. I'm starting to get worried.''

''I'm worried myself, but not about my mind-reading

abilities. More that I'm so comfortable having you around even after we make love." He pulled her to him, settling her in the crook of his arm. "That doesn't usually happen with me. Most of the time, I'm ready to clear out and be by myself."

"Have there been so many others?"

"Fewer than I like to admit."

The confession warmed her heart. She snuggled closer. "I'd still like to know about Susan. What made her so angry with her parents that she turned to a life of crime?"

"A lack of trust, I suspect." Matt paused, his fingers unconsciously rubbing Heather's arm. "She was raped by the son of a family friend, the same man who faked her death. Her parents refused to back her in pressing charges, saying that she would cause unnecessary embarrassment for herself and her sister, but she decided to press charges anyway."

"How sad, to have your own family turn against you after such a traumatic experience."

"It gets worse. After he raped her, Phillip Gould apparently paid one of his no-good friends to kill her. Instead, the guy kidnapped her and tried to collect a ransom."

"I remember that part from the TV show. David something or another. He was arrested later."

"David Eisman, a first-class louse. May he rot in the California jail where they stuck him."

"Wait a minute. Didn't she marry him while they were on the run?"

"Yeah. Apparently, he was a charming and very charismatic first-class louse. She was caught on the surveillance camera helping him rob a bank."

"But Pamela Jessup somehow wound up in Texas with Jake McQuaid and his three sons. This is a bizarre story." Heather slipped from the shelter of Matt's arms and picked up her pen and tablet again. The answer to the riddle of her own mother might lie somewhere in this muddle of facts. "So the notorious Pamela Jessup raised you and your brothers and none of you ever knew who she was until a few years ago."

"That's the size of it. We would probably never have known if my brothers hadn't discovered her identity while trying to solve another crime."

"Was she prosecuted then?"

"No. More than two decades after the fact, she was granted immunity and an annulment of her marriage to David Eisman. The best part was that she was able to keep her anonymity. It would have reopened the nightmare all over again if she'd been forced to become the focus of the media after all those years."

"Your father must have been thankful to have it all out in the open. Now, with her annulment and immunity from criminal prosecution, she was finally free to marry him. It's a beautiful story, Matt."

"It is the way you tell it." He rubbed the muscles behind his neck, the smile gone from his face, replaced by taut lines. "There's been no wedding."

"Maybe she doesn't need his name or a license. Maybe knowing he loves her is enough for her."

"Yeah, sure." Matt walked to the window and stared out into the murky darkness.

Heather moved over to stand behind him. She circled his waist with her arms, smoothing her hands over his chest. His muscles tightened, every nerve in his body urging him to move away, not to let her get too close, not to let her into his personal world.

"You should go back for your father's birthday. It would please Susan."

"Leave it alone, Heather. Family is a dead issue with me. I've made my life here in Texas."

"You've made an existence, not a life."

She buried her head between his shoulder blades. Part of him ached to turn and take her in his arms. Part of him longed to run like hell. He did neither.

"You told me when I first came here that I shouldn't dig up old secrets, Matt, that doing so might shatter the present."

"And I was right."

"Maybe, but it's no worse than what you're doing. You're letting the past eat away at the present, letting it make you just as afraid as your dad to show emotion."

"You've noticed. A chip off the old block, that's me. Being with you these last few days has convinced me of that more than ever. I should never have touched you in any intimate way while you were under my protective custody. Follow the rules when they suit me, ignore them when they don't. It's a family tradition."

Heather tugged him around to face her, rose up on tiptoe and met his gaze straight on. "Don't give your father blame or credit for what's happened between us these last few days. It was what we both wanted, and no matter what happens after this, I'll never be sorry we made love."

"Don't count on that."

Heather touched her lips to his, and seemingly unable to stop himself he wrapped his arms around her. The kiss this time was softer, sweeter than ever before. She shuddered, sensing instinctively that their relationship had moved beyond the savage sensual hunger that had driven them initially.

There was no denying the signs. She had fallen in love with Matt McQuaid, a man whose destiny remained chained to his past. A man who would never be able to

love completely until he could learn to forgive his father
and accept that he was his own man.

The phone rang then, and the next round of bad news
hit home. Paul Ridgely's wife had come home and found
him unconscious in the barn behind their house. He had
been stabbed twice, once in the back, once in the chest.
The good news was that even though he'd lost a lot of
blood, he was still alive.

HEATHER STOOD in the waiting room of the small hospital.
It was a good forty-five-minute drive from Dry Creek, but
the room was filled with Paul Ridgely's friends and neighbors. John Billinger and his wife, Gabby, Rube and Edna,
the pastor from his church, even Logan Trenton had shown
up. There were others as well, some Heather had seen before, but she couldn't put names to the faces.

Most of the men were grumbling about the fact that a
man wasn't safe on his own land anymore. Most of the
women were consoling Mrs. Ridgely. She was dry-eyed
now, but her red, swollen eyelids made it clear that she'd
shed her share of tears.

"I hope Matt finds out who did this soon," Edna said,
walking up behind Heather. "None us are safe with a murderer roaming the area."

"He's doing everything he can, Edna."

"I know. He's a good man, just like his dad was. Where
is he now?"

"He's in the room with Paul."

"I hope Paul lives, I truly do." Edna shredded the tissue
in her hands into tiny pieces. "But even if he doesn't, I
pray he regains consciousness long enough to tell who did
this to him. I haven't had a minute's peace since Ariana
was killed. And Rube's as worried as I am. He's hardly
eaten since he found Ariana's body, and I wake up in the

night to find him walking the floor or staring out the window.''

Heather turned as Matt stepped into the room. A group of men circled around him, all asking the same question. Did Paul give him a name?

Matt put his hand up to silence the anxious questions. ''Paul is still unconscious. The doctor promised to call me when he's able to talk. In the meantime, we have a guard at his door to make sure the man who stabbed him doesn't come back to finish the job. Believe me, the problems in Dry Creek are top priority. Go home and get some sleep, but keep your doors locked.''

''And your shotguns loaded,'' John Billinger muttered. There was a rumbling of agreement among the men.

''Just watch out who you shoot,'' Matt warned. ''Nervous fingers on the trigger can get a man in a lot of trouble.'' He motioned for Heather to meet him at the door. She did, and he wasted no time in hustling her outside.

''Do you think Paul will live?'' she asked, as they hurried down the corridor and to the car.

''He has a good chance.''

''But he didn't tell you who stabbed him?''

''No, he was muttering, but not coherently. The only name I recognized was Billy Roy Lassiter.''

Dread filled Heather, thick as smoke from a smoldering fire that refused to die. It burned her lungs and rolled in her stomach. The secrets that had lain hidden for a quarter of a century were ripping Dry Creek apart. She had been the catalyst for reawakening the terror.

And the end wasn't even in sight.

STANDING under a tree a few yards from the back door of Logan Trenton's sprawling house, Heather surveyed the scene, and marveled, "So this is how they throw a party in Texas!"

"It's how the wealthier ranchers do it." Matt grabbed a couple of glasses of champagne from the tray of a passing waiter. He handed one of the crystal flutes to Heather.

"I propose a toast," she said.

Matt's eyebrows rose inquiringly. He lifted his glass and waited.

"To finding answers to all of our questions so that we can go on with our lives."

Matt clinked his glass with hers. "I'll drink to that," he announced, "and I propose another toast."

"What to this time?"

"To Lady Luck, for setting me up with the prettiest lady at the ball."

A blush heated Heather's cheeks. "I'm sure there are a lot of men here tonight who'd argue that with you."

"Let them. My eyes don't lie."

They clinked their glasses again, but when Heather looked into Matt's eyes, it was more than desire she read there. "Do you think there'll be trouble tonight?"

"Could be. I plan to keep my eyes and ears open. That's why we're here, to try to find a few more pieces to the puzzle."

Heather made a full turn, taking in the entire front lawn and the grassy area to the side of the house. Tables laden with food were sheltered from the late afternoon sun by huge white awnings. Brightly colored streamers and white lights hung from the branches of trees, and waiters in white shirts and black bow ties mingled with the festive crowd, passing out drinks and hors d'oeuvres.

"Even music," she said, as a trio of strolling mariachis stopped nearby to serenade a young couple.

"And more people than you can shake a stick at. Let

me know if you see John Billinger. I'd like to catch him away from his wife and ask him a few questions.''

"So, that's why everyone's avoiding you tonight. You've been harassing them with questions."

"I hope they keep on avoiding me. I can work better that way. Are you up for a little snooping?"

Heather's heart beat a little faster. "I'm up for anything that might produce results. What do you have in mind?"

"I don't see Logan, but I'm sure he's occupied now doing what he does best, schmoozing with people with money and power. It's a good time to take an exploratory look around his office."

"Without asking him?"

"That's the general idea. You can stand outside the door, let me know if he's coming."

"What do you expect to find?"

"I don't know. That's why it's exploratory."

Excitement battled with doubt. "Isn't breaking into someone's office illegal?"

"We're not breaking in. We're invited guests. If someone asks me what we're doing in that part of the house, I'll explain that we were looking for a little privacy." His eyes danced with devilment. "I'll tell them you couldn't keep your hands off me."

"You'll do no such thing."

"Why not? It's half true."

"It's you who can't keep your hands off me."

"That's the other half. Now take my arm and smile a lot. We'll go in the back door and take the hall off the den. Don't worry. Most of the people are outside where the food is."

Heather followed his instructions, the adrenaline rush making it easy to smile but hard to speak intelligently when Ben Wright stopped them to ask about Paul Ridgely and whether or not Matt was close to arresting a suspect in the stabbing incident.

Matt gave him a quick update on Paul's condition, but dodged the rest of the questions in his easy cowboy manner, short sentences that sounded friendly but said nothing. She followed him to the back of the house where a fiddler was tuning his instrument and a tall, skinny guitarist was adjusting a microphone.

"The dance band is warming up," Matt announced, pushing through the back door and into the cool interior of the house. "That should keep Logan busy. He loves to show off his fancy two-steppin'."

A couple of teenaged girls were giggling in the den. They didn't give Matt or Heather a second look. The hall was empty. Matt stopped at the door to the office and jiggled the knob. The door opened, and Matt stepped inside. His gaze traveled and settled on a window. He walked over and unlocked it, sliding it up a few inches and then shutting it again.

"An escape hatch in case I need it," Matt explained, walking back to the door. "Hang out in the hall. If you see Logan, call to him, loudly, so that I know he's around. Then keep him talking long enough for me to climb out the window."

"What if someone sees you?"

"I'll chance it, but it's not likely. The window's on the east side, and there aren't any tables of food set up there. Besides, we're not breaking and entering. We're invited guests. Now, are you clear on everything?"

"All clear." Heather swallowed a lump of fear. "This is my first lookout."

"Watch it. It gets in your blood. You might want to give up your job and become a Ranger."

"Not likely. *My* associates don't carry guns."

"You've got a point." Matt kissed her on the tip of her nose. "I'm counting on you, partner." He steered her away from the door with a hand on the back of her waist and then shut himself inside the office.

Apprehension balled inside Heather the first dozen or more times the back door opened. After that, she grew lax and weary of waiting. She tapped on the door. "Matt."

The door squeaked open. "What is it?"

"You've been in there so long I was starting to get worried."

"Look at this."

Heather scanned the file he stuck in front of her. "It's an insurance claim on Logan's wife."

"Right. The insurance company demanded an autopsy to prove the cause of death was accidental. Logan refused the autopsy, even though it meant losing two hundred thousand dollars."

"That seems strange."

"It got my attention. I need a few more minutes in here. If Logan shows up, stall him."

"How?"

"I don't know. Flirt. Ask questions. Do whatever you have to. Just buy me enough time to check the rest of these files."

Matt disappeared behind the closed door again. Heather paced nervously. It was clear she had the least exciting part of this mission. She had half a mind to forget Logan and go help Matt.

What would Logan do if he did find them inside? Shoot them? At the thought, images of Ariana's dead body filtered through her mind. *Someone* in this town would shoot to keep their secrets. But Logan? Not likely. He just seemed too much the gentleman.

She leaned against the wall, her toe tapping to the music

that drifted in from the band stand. Suddenly, the back door swung open and Logan Trenton stepped inside. Unlike the others who'd come in, he noticed her immediately.

"Logan, I've been looking for you." She said his name extra loudly so that her voice would carry through the closed door. Her breath caught in her throat as he hurried toward her, the smile on his face not hiding his surprise at seeing her there.

"Well, you've found me, or I've found you. Now how can I be of service?"

"I wanted to tell you how much I'm enjoying the party. And—" she moved closer, the skirt she'd bought at Ridgely's store swishing about her legs "—I'd hoped to persuade you to dance with me. I heard you're terrific at the Texas two-step, and I've never danced it with a real cowboy."

He tipped his hat and smiled. "I'd like nothing better, but first I have to get something out of my office."

"Surely you wouldn't put me off to take care of business. Not at such a great party." Heather batted her eyes in what she hoped was a coquettish manner. Flagrant flirting wasn't part of her usual repertoire, but desperate times called for desperate measures.

"It flatters me to think you're that anxious. I'll take care of business quick." His stepped toward the door.

Faint, yell fire, throw myself into his arms. The options flashed through her brain. Instead she grabbed his arm. "Please, Logan, that's my favorite song. I'd hate to miss it."

He stared at her, his eyebrows at angles that indicated she was overplaying her role. "'Deep in the Heart of Texas' isn't much of a dance number. Besides, it's almost over. We'll request a much better tune when I'm finished." He pushed the door open and walked inside.

Heather took a deep breath and waited. A minute later, Logan was back at her side, sliding a slender envelope into the inside pocket of his Western-cut jacket. She glimpsed the silver handle of a pistol peeking from a shoulder holster.

He took her arm. "Now, shall we dance?"

"Yes." It was all the answer she could manage, and it came out in a shaky whisper. Evidently Matt had made a quick, unnoticed escape through the window. Her relief was short-lived. Logan was leading her the wrong way, down the hall, away from the back door.

She stopped walking. "The band is outside."

He circled her waist with his arm. "Don't worry, the party will be going strong for hours. I have something I'd like to show you."

"No." She tried unsuccessfully to pull from his grasp.

"Logan, *there* you are."

He whirled around. Heather breathed a sigh of relief as she spied Sylvia rushing down the hallway.

"I've been looking all over for you."

"I'm a very popular man tonight."

"I wouldn't know about that." Anger burned in Sylvia's eyes, her muscles drawn tight in her face and neck. "I was at the cemetery a few minutes ago. Someone has dug up the area around my mother's grave. I'd like to know why."

"Probably just vandalism—but we'll talk later, Sylvia. This is a party, in your honor I might add. And right now Miss Lombardi has asked me to dance." He took Heather's arm again, practically dragging her down the hall, but at least this time they were going in the right direction.

The afternoon sun had vanished, leaving the yard in dusky shades of twilight. The air was still filled with laughter, music, tinkling glasses, and the odor of barbecue. Logan took her hand, leading her to the center of the sawdust-covered dance floor. She searched the crowd for Matt, but there was no sign of him.

The music started, and Logan fell into perfect step. He made her look good, leading her into twirls and guiding her around the floor with practiced steps. His boots seemed to only brush the ground, and he whispered in her ear that had he known she was such a wonderful partner, he wouldn't have even stopped at his office, much less considered wasting time showing her a painting he'd just purchased in Santa Fe.

He was charming, the perfect gentleman. Heather wondered how she could have imagined that he had been luring her to the back of the house for sinister purposes. Had the events of the last few days made her see danger in innocent events, made her think everyone she saw was a potential murderer?

For a brief second she wished she was back in Atlanta in her cool, gray office of glass and polished wood. Wished she'd never come to Dry Creek at all. Wished she'd never tried to find anyone from her distant past.

The next second, Matt was making his way through the field of dancers toward them. His light blue yoked shirt was open at the neck, his dark hair rumpled by the wind, his smile devastating. And all Heather's wishes to be back in Georgia evaporated the moment his gaze met hers.

He tapped Logan on the shoulder. "You can't hog *all* the beautiful women. You have to give us poor lawmen a chance."

Logan faked a grimace. "Don't you have crimes to solve?"

"Not when there's a party."

Heather slid into his arms. The tempo picked up, an upbeat country song. Matt took over where Logan left off, never missing a beat. If he had less expertise than her previous partner, he made up for it in charm. Every young woman they danced by turned positively green with envy.

"I thought you told me you didn't like 'boot scooting.'"

"I never said I couldn't do it. Miss Susan insisted all her boys learn to dance."

"I like Miss Susan better all the time. So, did you get what you needed from Logan's office before you made the fast getaway?"

Matt twirled her around and gathered her in his arms. "More than I expected. Are you ready to get out of here? I'll tell you all about it on the way to the cemetery."

Heather missed her step, scraping her foot against Matt's boot. She might have imagined Logan's motivation a few minutes ago, but the figure she'd glimpsed in the bushes behind the cemetery yesterday had been all too real.

To go back there now, on a dark, moonless night... Her stomach grew queasy, her pulse rapid. "What is it you expect to find in the cemetery? It's too dark to see anything."

"I have a flashlight. We'll see what I need to see."

"What's that?" She fought to keep the dread that churned inside her out of her voice.

"I just talked to Sylvia. I have a hunch that her mother's grave is either empty now or will be soon."

HEATHER PRESSED CLOSER to Matt as the truck skidded and bumped along the dirt trail. A shovel, borrowed from the back of a pickup truck belonging to one of Logan's unsuspecting guests, was bouncing around in the bed of the truck.

"You are surely *not* going to dig up the grave of Logan's late wife tonight."

"No, I'd just like to check the condition of the soil. According to Sylvia, it was rock-hard when the two of you were there yesterday. She said it's loose now, and that the spotty grass covering has been upturned."

"Why would someone dig up that grave?"

"For the same reason Logan refused to have an autopsy done, to keep anyone from finding out the true cause of death."

Heather looked up as they approached the narrow bridge that had sent her into spasms the day before. She shuddered and crossed her arms in front of her chest.

Matt circled an arm about her shoulders. "What's the matter? You're not getting scared on me now, are you?"

"No, I've been scared ever since you saved me from the attackers last week." She took his hand and placed it back on the wheel. "You need both hands to handle this bridge."

"Nothing to it. I cross bridges like this all the time. This one will hold several tons more than my truck weighs."

"So I've heard." She closed her eyes as they left the dirt for the rumbling wooden ties. She opened them as the truck came to a jolting stop. "What happened?"

"A few boards must have worked loose. I didn't see that they were missing in time, and I think both front wheels are stuck in the hole."

"I thought this bridge could hold tons."

"Ordinarily it can. Open the door slowly and step out. But watch your step. There's quite a drop-off."

"You want me to get out of the truck in the middle of this horrible bridge?"

"That's the idea." Matt opened his door and stepped out. Before Heather could follow, the crack of a bullet shattered the night air. Instinctively, she ducked. When she looked up, Matt was nowhere in sight.

Chapter Fourteen

Panic jangled Heather's thoughts. *Do something. Get out.* Her mind shouted orders, but her body refused to obey. Finally she slid over to the driver's side of the door and peered through the window.

Another shot came, this one crashing into the windshield, sending fragments of glass flying into her face and hair. She crouched, brushing away the glass, scrambling to the other side of the car. The passenger door eased open, and her heart jumped to her throat, then plunged in relief. It was Matt.

"Don't panic." His voice was surprisingly calm.

"I already have." Her voice was shaky and high. "What are we going to do?"

"Get out of the car." He tugged on her arm. "And stay down."

She managed to climb out the door without getting her head above the roof line and without drawing another shot. She stooped on the wooden bridge, and her gaze settled on the murky waters below. "Now what?"

"We jump."

"Oh, no. Not me. I'll just creep back across the bridge."

"The second you get out from behind this truck, you're a target for whoever ambushed us."

"Then let's stay here. You have a gun. Shoot them."

"When I count three, we jump." He took her hand.

"No, I don't swim."

"You won't have to. You can wade out. Heather, you've got to. It's jump or be shot."

"I don't like the choices."

"One, two, three."

Heather felt herself toppling over the edge, falling too fast to think. The next second she was gasping for breath, water in her face and mouth and nose. Pain shot through her right elbow, and when she tried to get up, she stepped on a sharp rock and slipped back into the creek.

Matt found her floundering in the water. "Are you hurt?"

"Yes, no, I don't know."

"You're not dead, so keep low, and keep moving. We have to get out of here fast."

He pulled her along, and she trudged to the shore, water filling her boots and soaking into her full skirt, weighing her down. Once her boot cleared the last gushing hold of the mud, she dropped to the bank.

Matt yanked her back to her feet. "We can't stay in the open. You'll have to make it to that cluster of mesquite."

She forced her legs to keep moving, but evidently not fast enough. A bullet whizzed by her head.

"Run," Matt yelled, "and don't look back."

Gunfire cracked through the air, and Heather's breath came in sputtering, burning gasps. Finally, she made it to the mesquite and dived under the branches. Matt wasn't behind her. He was still at the bank of the creek, half hidden behind one of the supporting beams, firing into the dark. He'd stayed behind intentionally, made a target of himself to save her.

The chorus of gunfire ceased for a few seconds, and

Matt was on the run, climbing the bank and heading toward her. She wrapped her arms around her own shaking body, fighting the urge to scream until he'd dived in beside her.

He cradled her in his arms, and she held on extra tight. "What do we do now?" she whispered.

"*You* stay out of sight. *I'm* going to try and work around, get behind the filthy cowards, see if I can identify anyone."

"You can't. That's too dangerous. "

"Heather, this is what I do. I fight the bad guys. It's my job."

"Not like this. I feel as if I'm trapped in a poor imitation of some spaghetti Western. Those men have guns."

He kissed her, more to stop her talking than anything else, she imagined. Then he left her there to wait for him to return. A few minutes later, crashing timbers startled her to attention. She looked up just in time to see Matt's truck plunge from the bridge into the water.

A second later he was by her side.

"Did you see anyone?"

"No, they drove away before I could get close enough. I saw the beam of their headlights on the dirt." Matt gathered her in his arms, and for a few minutes they sat in a silence broken only by the hooting of an owl and the sounds of Matt's truck sinking deeper into the mud beneath the shallow creek.

She leaned into him. "Tell me again how safe that bridge is."

"It wasn't the fault of the bridge. This was a planned ambush. Someone cut those ties loose."

"That couldn't have been planned for us. No one knew we were leaving the party and going to the cemetery."

"One person did."

"Who?"

"The good sheriff. Always helpful. Always insisting he be included in every aspect of this investigation. If I find out that he's responsible…" Matt picked up a stick and broke it fiercely.

"Gabby couldn't have done it, Matt. Not by himself. Not in the dark. Not so fast. You only decided to come up here a few minutes ago."

"Actually, I didn't just decide to come out here. Gabby and I had already discussed my paying a visit to the cemetery tonight. I wanted to check out why someone was stalking you there yesterday."

"You told him about that? I haven't mentioned it to anyone but you, not after the wrangler practically convinced me it was my imagination."

"No, Gabby knew about it already. Apparently the man who checked out your story told Gabby about it. Gabby followed up on it and found a couple of Logan's hired hands digging up a grave. Logan showed up about then, and he wasn't pleased to find the sheriff observing the scene. He put a stop to everything, telling the guys doing the digging that there had been a mistake."

Heather wrapped her arms about her chest, suddenly chilled.

"I hate thinking Gabby could be responsible for all that's happened in the last few days, Matt."

"I don't think he is. But I have to consider that he might be in on it, either as an innocent pawn or a player. He's the only person I told we'd be on this road tonight."

"Pamela Jessup, Kathy Warren, Billy Roy Lassiter, Paul Ridgely and now Gabby." She pushed dripping strands of hair from her face. "Will it ever end?"

"Oh, yeah. It's going to end, and damn soon. And before this case is closed, more than one person is going to take up residence behind bars."

''We can't solve it out here.'' She shivered again as a gust of wind whipped at her wet hair and clothes. ''So, Ranger McQuaid, how do we get back to civilization?''

''My lines of communication all went down with the truck, and I don't think we could yell louder than the music from the party even if we weren't waterlogged.'' His arm circled about her shoulders. ''That leaves only one option. We walk.''

Her head flew up. ''In wet boots? Through thick brush inhabited by rattlesnakes and coyotes? In my soaking skirt and ridiculously thin wet blouse?'' She groaned.

''A piece of cake,'' he promised, standing and tugging her to her shaky legs.

''You saved me for *this*. And I actually thanked you!''

''You can always count on a Texas Ranger.''

THE DAYBREAK PARTY at the collapsed bridge was anything but festive. A tow-truck team worked at hauling Matt's truck from the creek. Logan, Gabby, and Matt watched, circling each other like a pack of wild dogs.

Heather stood in the background, the memory of last night's dive into the creek and the game of dodge the bullets destroying any objectivity she might have otherwise mustered.

''You had no call to go snooping around my land, Matt McQuaid. You slink around like a skunk in the night and then have the nerve to accuse me of destroying my own damn bridge and having you ambushed.'' Logan stuck his nose in the sheriff's face, including him in his angry tirade. ''You, too, Gabby. I know you started this, messing around where you have no business. I'll have you *both* investigated for improper procedures.''

Matt stepped between Logan and Gabby. ''You do what you like, Logan, but unless you come up with a fast explanation for why a section of this bridge was cut, and some ties removed, you'll be filing your complaints from a jail cell.''

"I told you, I had no idea the bridge had been vandalized.'' Logan waved his arms in frustration. "Hell, my own daughter travels this road sometimes. And I sure have no reason to hire gunmen.''

"Your *step*daughter.'' Matt's eyes took on a frightening sheen, cold as death. "Someone around here attempted to murder Heather and me last night, and I know you well enough to know that nothing goes on around this ranch without you knowing about it.''

Logan's hands knotted into fists, and his chin jutted defiantly. His accusing glare moved from Matt to Heather. "If you want to find the real roots of all the problems we've been having around here, Ranger, I suggest you let your brain—not some other part of your body—do your thinking.''

"Say what you mean, Logan. Forget the sarcasm. A man in the position you're in now shouldn't waste energy.''

"I'm saying you need to look a little closer to home. We didn't have any problems in this town until Heather Lombardi showed up, prancing around in her short skirts, asking questions, pretending to be looking for her mother.''

"I wasn't pretending, Logan. And I didn't ask for trouble. It came looking for me.'' Heather jumped into the fray.

"All I know is you drove into town, and trouble rode in right behind you. You made your moves on the Ranger, and he got sucked right in. You turned him against all of us.''

At that, Matt's face twisted into hard lines. "You've said enough, Logan.''

"No, not nearly enough. If you weren't such a brown-nosing coward, Gabby, you'd tell Matt yourself.''

"Tell me what?"

"That the whole town's talking about how you're just like your old man. The minute Susan Hathaway dropped into his life, he forgot the law he lived by, forgot his friends, forgot everything except protecting some skirt passing through town."

Gabby stepped backward. "You're about to say too much, Logan."

"No, just what needs to be said. Jake McQuaid took up with some tramp and forgot who put him where he was. He turned against the honest citizens of Dry Creek, the same way Matt is doing."

Tramp. The word stuck in Matt's gut, and every muscle in his body knotted. He lunged for Logan, pinning him against the trunk of the only tree in the area.

"You say what you want about me, Logan. You say what you want about my dad. We can take it, might even deserve it. But if I ever hear you say another word about Susan *or* Heather, your face will be mincemeat. Do you understand?"

"Yeah. I understand everything. I understand it all too well."

Logan met Matt's gaze, and Heather trembled at the rage that passed between them. She knew the fight was far from over. It would be continued some place, some time, and the results might be deadly.

Logan wiped sweaty hands on his jeans. "You better have a damn good case if you have me arrested, McQuaid. My lawyers will walk over you like..."

"Like your wife's horse walked over her."

"You sonofa—"

This time it was Logan who raised his fist. Gabby grabbed his arms. "That's enough, the both of you. This ain't how the law around here operates."

"What does any of this have to do with my mother?"

They all spun around at the sound of Sylvia's voice. She was mounted on a magnificent horse, the two of them rising like a centaur above a cluster of thorny cactus.

"What are you doing out here?" Logan demanded. "I told you to stay at the house."

"I'm not a little girl, Logan. You can't order me around any longer, especially not here. In three years, half the ranch will belong to me."

"Fine, then you stay out here with these sorry excuses for lawmen. I'm going back to work, and I'd suggest the sheriff and the Ranger do the same. One person has been killed in Dry Creek in the last week, and one stabbed nearly to death. Shots were fired again last night. And the best they can come up with is some damn fool notion that I'm involved in this."

Matt pulled his hat low. "Oh, it's more than a notion, Logan."

Logan headed toward his horse. "If you have evidence against me, spit it out now, Matt, like a man."

"I'll spit it out when the time comes. Like a *lawman*."

Logan climbed on his horse and turned it around, leaving at a fast gallop and not looking back.

"I'm sorry you had to hear any of this, Sylvia." Matt walked toward his friend.

She threw her head back, as a gust of wind caught her long black hair and flung it across her face. "What were you saying about my mother?"

Heather saw the defeated shrug of Matt's shoulders. He put a hand to Sylvia's horse, running his fingers through the flowing mane. "I have reason to suspect your mother's death may not have been an accident. I'm sorry. I know it's going to be hard on you, but I have to reopen the case."

"If you know something, Matt, tell me. I have a right to know."

"I can't say anything yet."

"Because you're a *lawman*."

She spit the word at him, and Heather saw him wince. But he held his head high.

"Because I'm a lawman, and because I'm your friend."

"I can tell which carries the most weight." Sylvia turned her horse and galloped away, but not before Heather saw the glint of tears in her eyes.

The weight of the world appeared to settle on Matt's shoulders. He pulled his hat low over his forehead. "Let's get out of here. I've got work to do."

He yanked open the passenger-side door of the truck he'd borrowed from John Billinger. Heather touched her hand to his shoulder. "You did what you had to, Matt."

"Thanks. I'm glad somebody believes that."

"You wouldn't be a good Ranger if you didn't do what has to be done. You know that."

He took her hand and squeezed it. "Most of the time I know it, but it's a damn hard job when you have to hurt your friends."

"When it's all over, Sylvia will understand and be thankful to know the truth."

"Maybe, but what about the rest of the town? How will they react when I hang all their dirty laundry up for public inspection? And will my own family be thankful if I have to drag the name of Jake McQuaid through the dirt in order to find justice?"

"Let's hope that doesn't happen."

"Hope isn't in my job description." He jerked the truck into gear and revved the engine. In minutes they were heading back into town.

IT WAS LATE AFTERNOON before Matt finished up his business in town and he and Heather started back to the ranch. Nothing was settled yet, but they were miles ahead of where they'd been yesterday. The paperwork was in process.

By tomorrow they'd have the insurance records on the death of Logan's wife, and legal permission to dig up her grave. If the body was there, an autopsy would be conducted to see if evidence indicated the death might not have been an accident. If the body was missing, that in itself still implicated Logan.

Not only that, but Paul Ridgely had regained consciousness for a few minutes and spoken for the first time since the stabbing. By tomorrow, the doctors had said he might be coherent enough for Matt to ask him a few questions.

Heather adjusted her visor, warding off the blinding glare of the sun. Watching her, Matt felt a crazy urge to stop the truck and take her in his arms, and realized how drastically the focus of his life had changed in the last few days.

He'd driven down this same road eight days ago, needing nothing but time alone at his ranch to satisfy his every need. It would never be that way again.

Now days at the ranch would be colored by the memory of Heather sitting at his breakfast table, her hair rumpled from sleep, her face bruised and battered and still so tempting. He'd see her in the swing, sipping lemonade, her lips wet and pink.

But the nights would be the worst. He'd be forever haunted by the moments they'd spent making love. He'd feel her beneath him, smell her fragrance, all flowery and intoxicating. He'd taste her lips and long to run his fingers across her velvety skin.

Damn. How had he let this happen? Even if she wanted

to, he couldn't ask her to stay. His dad's blood ran too pure in his veins. The art of small talk, of cuddling, of making a woman feel loved and wanted, was as foreign to his makeup as branding cattle was to Heather's. He'd never be able to satisfy her, not over the long haul.

Or was he just unwilling to give it a try, because he was too afraid of failing?

Surprising himself, he made a sharp left turn, swerving onto a dirt road he hadn't been down in years. So much of the past had crashed down around him the last few days, a side trip to the scene of it couldn't make things any worse.

"Where are we going?"

He reached across the seat and took Heather's hand, tangling his fingers with hers. "To the old home place, the house where we lived before Jake pulled up stakes and moved us to Colorado."

"I'm glad. I'd like to see it."

"It's not much to look at—crumbling walls, broken windows, a leaky roof."

"Does the property still belong to your dad?"

"No, he sold it to Logan Trenton for less than it was worth, but I guess he was anxious to put Dry Creek behind him."

"I wouldn't put much stock in what Logan said about your father. Everything I've heard since I've been in this town indicates that the people thought your father was a saint."

"Yeah, most of them did."

"Give your dad a chance, Matt. He deserves that much from you." She slid closer as he pulled into an overgrown dirt drive and stopped in front of a dilapidated old house.

Matt opened the door and climbed out. She followed

him, jumping from the truck to the hard ground. "Is this where you found Susan, out by this old drive?"

"No, it was down the fence line, close to that lean-to that's half gone." He pointed to what looked like a pile of boards a quarter of a mile down the road. "The grass was high then, the way it is now. She'd been thrown out of a car and somehow managed to roll under the fence and into that cluster of mesquite and hackberry, just west of the lean-to."

"Why don't we walk down there before we go inside? I could use the exercise."

"If you want. There's nothing there to see."

They walked in companionable silence for a few minutes. Heather was mulling over the events of the last several days. "I don't understand about Logan," she said at last, turning to Matt. "If his wife owned such a big ranch, why was he a deputy under your father? Why did he want your dad's job of sheriff when Jake left for Colorado?"

"Talk is Logan's wife didn't give him much say in running the ranch while she was alive. He gave up the job of sheriff a few months after she died," Matt explained.

"But not so soon that he couldn't squelch an investigation into her death."

"Exactly, and from the time the new sheriff took over, there are no missing records."

Heather shivered. "Death, murders, cover-ups. Even the possibility of Logan killing his own wife. I pray we find out that's not true."

"Me too, for Sylvia's sake. But men have killed for far less than a ranch the size of Trenton's place, not to mention the enormous cash inheritance that provided the power he so enjoys."

"Let's go back, Matt. I've seen enough out here, and

I'd like to see the inside of the house before it's totally dark.''

Quietly, hand in hand, they retraced their steps. Heather had never felt closer to the rugged Ranger at her side. She wasn't sure why, except that he had once run this land as a boy, played chase with his brothers around this brush. She could almost see him now, a smaller, less assured image of the man beside her.

He was opening up to her more and more. The trip here today was proof of that. For most men, taking a woman to see the home they grew up in might not mean so much. But Heather knew Matt well enough now to know that this was as intimate as making love, perhaps more so. He was tearing down another of his defensive walls and letting her peek inside. She knew this was a rare revelation.

"Go on inside," he said, when they'd reached the back steps. "I'll get a couple of soft drinks out of the cooler in the truck. I'm dryer than dust."

Heather started to wait, then changed her mind. Darkness was setting in fast now that a few clouds had blown in. If she wanted to get any kind of feel for the house Matt was born in, she'd better get moving.

She stepped inside. The door slammed behind her. And even before she felt the barrel of the gun boring into her back, she knew she was not alone.

Chapter Fifteen

"Logan!"

"Don't tell me you're surprised to see me."

Her mind struggled to accept the reality. Somehow she and Matt had stumbled into another trap. "Put the gun away. Matt's just outside."

"Put the gun away?" He poked the pistol harder into her flesh. "Why would I do a thing like that after I followed you all the way out here to kill you?" He grabbed her arm and twisted it painfully behind her back, shoving her against the rickety counter that housed the rusted kitchen sink.

"I didn't see your truck."

"You *do* take me for a moron, don't you? You and that damn fool boy of Jake McQuaid's. I knew where Matt was going the minute he turned off the main road. I came the back way, cut across my own land and left my truck parked out of sight. The better to surprise you."

Panic skittered along Heather's every nerve. She had to warn Matt. Her gaze roamed to the door. If she could see him coming, she could yell out to him.

Logan ran a finger across her cheek. "You're a pretty woman, Heather. I didn't want to hurt you. I sent you a note and warned you to get out of town, but you just wouldn't listen." He slid the gun from her back and nestled it against her right temple. "Now call your Ranger lover in here so I can get this over with."

She didn't have to. The footsteps on the back porch were heavy and quick. "Matt..."

Logan's hand slammed across her mouth, muffling her voice. She kicked at him and bit into his fingers, but his hold never loosened. Sick and shivering with fear, she watched Matt's face turn ashen as he walked through the back door and caught sight of the gun at her head.

"Hands out to the side, Matt. One rash move on your part and Heather Lombardi's brains will spray the room."

Matt did as Logan said, standing quietly while Logan reached over and yanked his gun from the holster, tossing it across the room. The sound of metal on wood echoed like thunder in Heather's brain, her senses soaking in each sound, each movement, as if it were her last.

Matt's eyes turned black as coal, his stance rock-steady. Only the perspiration dotting his brow hinted at the fear that had to be churning inside him.

"You won't get away with this, Logan."

"What makes you think that, Ranger?"

"Because too many people know what you've done. There's Paul, and Gabby."

"Paul hasn't told you anything."

"How do you know that?"

"I know Paul. And he knows what I'm capable of."

"We all know you're capable of murder."

Logan's grip on Heather's arm tightened. She fought the pain, determined not to give him the satisfaction of hearing her cry out. And she wouldn't keep quiet any longer. "You killed Billy Roy Lassiter, didn't you, Logan?"

"Smart little woman you have here, Matt. Too bad you won't get to enjoy her after tonight." He twisted the barrel of the pistol into her temple. "Billy Roy got what he deserved. He was messing around with my wife, no-good tramp that she was. She'd already had Sylvia out of wedlock, and still she had to have her men."

Matt eased closer. "Is that why you killed her, too, Logan, because she wanted to dump you for another man?"

"She didn't want to dump me for another man. She was scared of me. That's why she wanted a divorce. But there was no way I was going to stand by while she cut me out of her will. She left me no choice but to kill her."

Matt stepped closer. "But you made it look like an accident."

"That part was easy. I delivered the killing blow to her head and then threw her under the feet of a horse that I drove to kick and buck."

"And Jake protected you."

"Jake McQuaid would have arrested his own mother for jaywalking. Only one person ever spit crosswise of the law and escaped his punishment."

"Susan Hathaway." Heather didn't realize she'd spoken the name out loud until she heard her own voice.

"Yeah. Jake worshiped her, though she never told him the truth. If she had, it would have saved Heather a lot of trouble. She wouldn't have gone looking for a woman you and your brothers had already found."

Heather swallowed past the lump in her throat. "What are you saying, Logan?"

"Do I have to spell it out for you?"

Matt eased closer. "Tell Heather all of it, Logan. Susan and Kathy Warren were the same woman. You stole Susan's ID after you and your buddies had beaten her and left her for dead."

"Double jeopardy. I wonder how well you'd do in the lightning round. Too bad we don't have time to find out."

He pulled back the hammer, cocking the pistol. "But you're right so far, on all counts. Kathy Warren—or should I say Susan—wandered from the bus stop crying. She stumbled behind the building and right into a little beating that turned real ugly."

"And the good sheriff never bothered to find out that you were the one responsible?"

"Jake's priorities had changed by then. It wasn't me or Billy Roy or even my wife your dad was worried about."

"Who was he worried about?"

"Susan Hathaway. He'd have killed to keep her safe, if it had come to that. Instead he took her and her secrets and left town. I don't think she remembered what she'd seen or even who she was at first. All Jake knew was that she was running away from something."

"But why did you kill Ariana?" Matt asked, inching still closer. "You didn't mistake her for Heather."

Logan sidestepped, moving so he could see out the window. Heather held her breath. The gun was cocked and ready to fire. One slip of his finger, and she'd be dead.

"Ariana's killing was none of my doing. She didn't know anything. No one does, except me and Rube and Paul. That's how you get people to keep secrets, Matt. You involve them in the crime."

"Evidently Paul changed his mind about keeping quiet."

"No more talking, Ranger. It's over. You first, then your pretty woman."

Something rumbled above them and a rotten piece of lumber crashed through the ceiling and onto the floor. Heather ducked just as the pistol in Logan's hand fired, the bullet skimming the top of her head.

Matt lunged for Logan, grabbing his hand. Heather spun around, looking for something, anything, to slam into Logan's head. The gun. Matt's gun. Her gaze swept the room and then back to Matt and Logan.

One second they were scuffling. The next the gun had gone off. A horrible cracking noise thundered in her head as she stared at the dark crimson stain darkening Matt's shirt.

Heather swayed dizzily, her stomach churning wildly. She fell to the floor and placed her hand over the wound. "Matt, I'm here. Don't die on me. Please, don't die." Tears rolled down her cheek mingling with the blood as he stared at her through glazed eyes.

"No need to worry, Heather. You're going with him."

"No, Logan, please. Call an ambulance. You'll never get away with this, but if you get help for Matt..."

"No one will blame me for this tragedy. The stranger in town, the one whose car you found the other day, will make a perfect scapegoat. Folks around here will blame a stranger long before they'll blame mc. I'm one of the good-ole-boys."

This time when the gun fired, Heather clung all the tighter to Matt's hand. At least they'd die together. She waited for the pain. It didn't come. She felt nothing but emptiness and the sting of the foul curses from Logan's mouth.

She turned and watched him sink to the floor beside her, his hands clutching his chest. And then she looked up and into the eyes of the man who'd just dropped from the attic and saved her life.

"So, we finally meet," he said, moving to stand beside her. "I'll say this for you. You're just as much trouble as your mother." The man kicked Logan's body, rolling it over.

Relief surged through her. "I don't know who you are, but I'm glad you're here. Get the cellular phone from the truck in front and call 911. And hurry. Please hurry.'' She bent back over Matt, feeling desperately for a pulse, whispering assurances in his ear.

"We'll call on the way out. I'd like to keep the Ranger alive myself. It would make life easier on me. Now get up. We're getting out of here.''

"I can't leave Matt. He's been shot.''

"You'll do as *I* say.'' He kicked her in the thigh to prove his point. "Get up and start walking.'' He yanked her to a standing position.

Confusion dulled her senses. She wiped away tears and stood, holding on to Matt's limp hand until the man forced her toward the door.

Middle-aged, thin blond hair. Edna's description of the man she'd seen in Heather's motel room rattled through her mind.

"Who are you?'' The words stuck in her throat, scratchy and hoarse when they finally worked their way clear.

"David Eisman. Your dear mother's ex-husband. Now keep walking. I want you breathing, but I don't care what shape you're in, so make it easy or hard on yourself. It doesn't matter a bit to me.''

"What do you want from me?''

"The ransom your grandparents should have paid years ago for your mother. But don't worry, I'll get the money this time. Pamela will see to that. She'll make the Jessups pay to keep her precious daughter alive. The baby she carried inside her bulging belly was the only thing I ever saw her care about.''

Heather stumbled to the truck, David Eisman beside her, leaving a shot and bleeding Matt behind her. She'd finally come face to face with her past and discovered a horrifying nightmare. She no longer cared what happened to her, but, *please, God,* she begged silently, *don't let Matt die.*

GABBY STOOD OVER Matt's hospital bed. "Too bad we didn't ID the fingerprints on that deserted car a little sooner. Then we'd have known they matched the ones we found in Heather's motel room."

"Too bad we didn't know a little sooner that the ones in the motel room belonged to David Eisman." Matt's hands knotted into fists, his nerves ragged and raw. "David Eisman, out of prison early on good behavior. And now the filthy scum has Heather." Anger and frustration tore at his voice.

"I'm doing what I can to find her, Matt. Me and half the men in town have combed the area around your old home place looking for her, and the Rangers are sending help."

"All this and I'm lying up here useless. Did you find the truck I'd borrowed from Billinger?"

"No, I guess Eisman still has it. There's no telling where he's gone with Heather."

Matt wrung the sheet into a tight knot. "I just hope I get my hands on him. I'd like to tear him apart, limb by sorry limb."

"You better get a sight healthier than you are now before you tangle with anybody. You're lucky to be alive."

"I'm healthy enough. What I need's a vehicle. Get Heather's car for me."

"You're not going anywhere."

"I'll decide that. I want the car brought to the hospital. Do you understand?"

"You're not the only one who can find Eisman, Matt."

"No one else has done it yet. Just get me the car."

"I'll have it brought over first thing in the morning."

"I want it tonight. Now find my clothes. I'm tired of wearing this gown."

The sheriff backed toward the door. "The nurse said not to let you con me into anything."

"In that case, I'll get up and find them myself." Matt slid his legs over the side of the bed, and the room spun dizzily around him, round and round until the world went black.

Gabby lifted Matt's feet and laid them back across the bed. Then he pushed the emergency button and waited for the nurse.

HEATHER PICKED AT the sandwich of dry bread and smelly luncheon meat David Eisman had given her for lunch. For two days, they'd been holed up in a rattrap of a cabin. She had no idea where it was, except that they hadn't driven more than a few miles. At least Eisman had told her Matt was alive and recovering. To be stuck here without knowing whether he was dead or alive would have been unbearable.

She forced a bite of the sandwich down her parched throat. Eisman gave her little enough food or water, and she had to try to keep her strength up. Given half a chance, she'd run.

"Just a few more days, Heather," Eisman commented, sitting on a bale of hay and whittling on a stick of wood. "As soon as your Ranger friend gets out of the hospital, I have a message for him. He's the perfect emissary to deliver the ransom note. Matt McQuaid, the kid Pamela raised like her own son."

A low, sinister laugh rolled from Eisman's lips, and he dropped the piece of wood to the floor and walked over to stand in front of her. "The irony of all of this appeals to my twisted sense of justice."

"It would."

"You sound awful high-and-mighty. But you're nothing

but the offspring of rich garbage. Your mom was no good, and your dad was worse."

"Who was my dad?"

His eyebrows shot up. "Don't you know?"

"I wouldn't have asked if I'd known. I only hope it's not *you.*"

"You'd be a sight luckier if I was your father, but I'm not."

"I doubt you know who my father was."

"Oh, I know all right. Haven't you heard of the famous rape? No, I guess not. You wouldn't have been looking for your mom if you'd known how black your past really was."

His gaze walked across Heather and her skin crawled under his slimy assessment.

"Or maybe you would," he continued, picking strands of hair from her shoulder and releasing them to fall back about her face. "Maybe you're in it for the money, too."

Heather swallowed past a choking lump in her throat. Pamela Jessup and Phillip Gould. Her birth parents. No, Pamela Jessup no longer existed. Her mother was Susan Hathaway, the woman who'd loved and cared for Matt. A good woman, Matt had said so over and over. She wouldn't let herself think about Phillip Gould.

"Are you the one who went to the orphanage and told them Kathy Warren had died?"

"No, that was your loving father, protecting his own hide, as usual. Not that he didn't get it in the end. He's in jail now on other charges. Once rotten, always rotten."

Heather rubbed her hand along the cuts on her wrist. Her hands were free now, but they'd be in ropes again soon. Her legs as well. That was the way Eisman made sure she'd always be there when he got back. Wherever it was he went, he left her behind, with only the spiders and

the wail of the coyotes for company. Still, they were better
company than he'd ever be.

MATT WAITED UNTIL the nurse left the room and then spit
the sleeping pill into a paper napkin. He raised himself to
a sitting position, swallowing his moans and curses as pain
shot through his body. He had to get out of this place, had
to find Heather. He'd tried to leave yesterday when Gabby
was here, but his body had refused to function.

Stretching, he grabbed his shirt from the hanger and
shoved his arms through the sleeves. He didn't bother tuck-
ing it into his pants or buttoning it over the bandage that
covered his chest. A second later he shuffled out the door
and down the hall before anyone could notice and stop
him.

MATT STUDIED the ransom note. It had been waiting for
him when he'd gotten home from the hospital. Tucked under the front mat, one white edge stuck out so that he
couldn't miss it.

*I have Heather. I'll exchange her for a million dollars
of Jessup money or I'll leave her dead. No tricks, Ranger
McQuaid. I'm through playing games. Have the money
ready before I call.*

Eisman had to be the one who'd delivered the note. That
meant he was somewhere in Dry Creek, waiting for the
money. But where? Matt went to the sink and let the water
trickle from the tap until it ran cool before filling a glass
and drinking it down.

David Eisman had been in town for a while. Thinking
back, Matt realized he'd probably been on the Lone M the
night the horses acted up. He was probably the one who'd
fooled with the ax. Perhaps it had been in his hand, a
planned weapon for the middle of the night. The thought

released a new surge of adrenaline, and Matt paced the
floor of his small house.

Eisman had also been at the motel. And Matt and
Heather had found his car deserted on the road between
here and town. Matt scribbled a series of meaningless doo-
dles on the pad at his fingertips, then began drawing a
rough map. Here, the motel, the highway…

And Logan Trenton's ranch. Heather thought she had
seen someone watching her when she visited Lassiter's
grave the day before the party.

Matt's mind swung into overdrive. There was an old
shack out there, between the cemetery and the stables. He
and his brothers had played in it one time when they'd
been out at the ranch with Jake. The shack, a former bunk-
house, hadn't been used in decades except by rats, snakes,
and scorpions.

Matt grabbed a couple of guns and headed for his truck.
He'd call Gabby on the way.

A COYOTE HOWLED outside the cabin, too close for comfort. Eisman pointed his shotgun in the direction. "I don't
know why anybody in their right mind would choose to
live in this godforsaken dust pit," he muttered.

"Some people like it."

"They can have it—soon. I'll give McQuaid twenty-four
hours after he gets out of the hospital to get the money."

"Does he know that?"

"Not yet. He'll find out when the time comes."

"Will you be delivering the instructions for the
exchange in person?"

"No. I'll call from a pay phone. He can meet me at the
edge of town with a small plane and the money. Then he
can come back here and find your body."

Her body. She'd known all along he planned to kill her,

but hearing it said gave it a finality that left her nauseous. "Did you plant that bomb in my car, Eisman?"

"Yes, my only mistake, but it worked out in my favor. It was supposed to explode while you were in it."

"You couldn't have gotten a ransom if you'd killed me then."

"I know. The ransom idea didn't hit me till later, but it was choice, don't you think? At first I only planned to kill you to get back at Pamela. The bitch walked away scot-free while I rotted in jail. A sorrier wife never lived, but I liked imagining her face when she opened a box with little pieces of her long-lost daughter inside."

The image turned Heather's blood icy cold. Still, she needed to keep Eisman talking, find out what she could, just in case she did get out of this alive. "You killed Ariana, didn't you? You just stood there and put a bullet through her chest at close range."

"The woman in your motel room? Yeah. I killed her. She was strutting around in your clothes. I guess the temptation of dressing up in nice things was too great for her to pass up. I came in and saw her preening in front of the mirror. I thought I was killing you. Imagine my disappointment when I realized my mistake."

"You poor guy."

"You're Pamela's daughter all right. Sassy like her. Pretty like her, too."

He ran his rough fingers down Heather's arm. She jerked away.

"You think you're too good for me, don't you?"

"I think *everyone's* too good for you."

He raised his hand and slapped her across the face. She reeled from the pain, but held her ground. If she was going to die anyway, she'd do it without his filthy hands on her body.

"I should have ruined you that night in your car, sliced you up so badly the Ranger would have gotten sick just looking at you."

"That was you!" She should have known. "But why, if you'd already planted a bomb in my car?"

"I ran into Logan Trenton at a bar outside of town right after the bomb didn't blow. My reputation was already spreading, thanks to the two-bit cowboy I'd roughed up the night before. Logan paid me and one of his cowardly hired hands to beat you up. Imagine getting paid for something that brought me so much pleasure."

He chuckled, and the sinister sound of it sent shivers up Heather's spine. "If Matt hadn't come along when he did, you would have killed me?"

"Lucky for me he did. Now I'll get my million and have my fun, too." Eisman jerked to face the door. "What was that?"

"A coyote. Why don't you go out and keep him company?"

"Not the coyote. The other noise."

"I didn't hear anything." She hadn't, but still, hope swelled in her chest. People would be looking for her by now. Matt would see to that. "Are you scared, Eisman?"

"Keep quiet."

"No, let's make noise." She grabbed a loose board and hurled it against the wall.

Eisman was on her in a second, wrestling her to the floor and pinning her under him while he tied her hands. "One more peep out of you and I'll feed you to the coyotes."

He pulled a pistol from his belt just as the door burst open and a bright light flooded the room. Heather squinted, barely making out Matt's form behind the light. She rolled away from Eisman as a shot rang out.

She closed her eyes. She couldn't bear to see Matt shot

again, but this time it was Eisman's voice she heard yelping curses. When she looked up, he was on the floor, a few feet away from her, clutching a bloody wrist.

Heather jumped to her feet. Matt stood over Eisman, his gun pointed at the wounded man's head.

"You won't shoot me," Eisman taunted. "That badge you wear won't let you."

Matt kept the gun pointed. He could pull the trigger so easily. "Are you all right, Heather?"

"Yes, Matt. He didn't hurt me."

"I should have killed you. The tramp daughter of a slut."

Matt's hand tightened on the trigger. With one movement he could shut David Eisman up forever. His hand shook. Was this what it was like for Jake McQuaid? he wondered. Had he turned his back on the law for Susan the way Matt longed to do now?

Finally, he regained control. "You're right, Eisman. The badge won't let me kill you unless you make one foolish move. Just one, and I can pull this trigger with a clear conscience."

He reached for Heather, and she moved beneath the shelter of his outstretched arm, burying her head in his chest, holding on tight, breathing in the very essence of him. She fought a losing battle with the tears that stung the back of her eyelids.

Matt rocked her against him and then wiped her tears away with the tips of his fingers. "I thought I might never see you again."

"I wasn't worried for a minute," she lied. "I knew you'd come." She was still in his arms, his pistol still pointed at Eisman's head when Gabby led a team of Texas Rangers through the cabin door.

SUSAN HATHAWAY SCURRIED about the Colorado ranch house, feeling more lively than she had in months. Matty had called. He was coming home for his father's sixty-fifth birthday, and he was bringing a guest, a female guest.

Jake's middle son Cameron stamped into the room and reached past her to run his finger around the rim of the frosting bowl.

She tapped his fingers with her hand. "You'll spoil your dinner."

"It would take more than one bite of chocolate to spoil my appetite for your pot roast."

"Where's Cy? He and Amy should have been here by now."

"Relax. They're on the way. He'll be here before Matt and his new sweetie arrive." Cameron dragged a kitchen chair away from the table and dropped into it. "So what did you do to get Matt to show up for Dad's birthday?"

"I didn't do anything but invite him. He's part of this family. I don't know why you McQuaids are so suspicious."

"I'm not suspicious. I just know how you are about my kid brother. We all know he's your favorite."

Cameron was teasing, but Susan had to admit there was a bit of truth in what he said. She loved all three of Jake's boys as if they were her own, but Matt was different. He'd been so young when she'd come to live with them, so in need of the mothering he'd never known. She'd showered her love on him, praying that some woman somewhere was doing the same for her little Heather.

"I don't have favorites. I just want the day to be nice for Jake. But Matt did say he had a surprise for me. I think he's going to announce his engagement to the woman he's bringing home with him."

"More likely his surprise is a picture of a new horse he bought."

"We'll see. We'll just see. Is that a car I hear pulling up? Look out the door and see if it's Cy."

Cameron stopped at the screen. "No. It's Matt."

Susan fumbled with the ties on her apron, dropping it to the back of the kitchen chair and then smoothing her hair. Her pulse raced as she walked to the door. Matty was home at last.

Chapter Sixteen

Heather's heart pounded furiously as she climbed out of the car and got her first look at the woman who'd given birth to her. Susan was smaller than she'd looked in Matt's picture of her, delicate, but not frail. And even though she was smiling, Heather caught the gleam of moisture in her eyes as she hurried toward them.

Susan held Matt for a long time. When she finally let go, she turned to Heather and held out her hand. Heather took it, realizing that her own hands were shaking. She murmured a hello, her mouth so dry the greeting sounded strained and way too formal. Part of her longed to blurt out the truth, to hurl herself into her mother's arms, but another part shuddered in fear that Susan might not want her in her life.

The introductions went the way she'd asked Matt to handle them. For now she was just Matt's guest. When she told Susan who she really was, she wanted more privacy than the porch provided, more intimacy. It would be as much of a shock for Susan as it had been for her.

It would be different if Heather had been a love child, but she was the result of a traumatic rape, a tragedy that had changed Pamela Jessup's life forever, stolen her very identity.

Matt was joking with his brother Cameron, but he eased a reassuring arm around Heather's shoulders as they climbed the porch steps. His nearness helped steady her nerves, but now that she was here, she was anxious to finish what she'd come for, anxious to tell Susan Hathaway that she was the daughter she'd given up so many years ago.

But she would have to wait a while longer. Matt's brother Cy and his wife drove up, and a new round of hugs and greetings got under way.

THE BIRTHDAY PARTY was primarily a family affair—Matt's two brothers and their wives, Jake and Susan and a few close friends. Heather had barely tasted the food, managing to eat just enough not to call attention to herself while the men wolfed down more than one helping of pot roast, creamy potatoes, fresh butter beans, sliced tomatoes from Susan's garden and huge portions of chocolate birthday cake and hand-churned ice cream.

They had laughed and visited at the kitchen table, lingering over coffee, everybody talking at once. If anyone noticed Heather's nervousness, noticed that her breathing all but stopped when Susan's gaze focused on her, they'd been too polite to say so.

Finally, the guests and family members had said their goodbyes. Now it was only the four of them left in the den of the massive ranch house—Susan and Jake, Matt and Heather. Heather's pulse raced, her stomach a knot of nerves. She took a deep breath and signaled to Matt with an uneasy glance that she was ready.

Matt reached over and cradled Heather's clammy hands in his. "I told you I was bringing a surprise for you, Susan. Actually, it's Heather who has the surprise."

Susan leaned forward in the chair, her hands crossed in

her lap. "I hope you didn't do anything special for me, Heather. Just having you and Matt here is treat enough for us."

"No, I didn't do anything." Her voice cracked, shattering into a whisper. "This is about something you did for me. Twenty-five years ago."

The color drained from Susan's face. "What are you saying?"

Moisture burned at the corners of Heather's eyes. She bit back the tears, and plunged ahead, afraid to say more, but knowing she couldn't rest until she'd said the words that tore at her heart. "I'm your daughter."

Silence filled the room, tension as thick as fog wrapping around them. Heather sat still, her insides trembling, but she met Susan's gaze head-on.

"No, this can't be happening." It was Susan who broke the deafening silence. Her voice faltered, and she wiped a tear from her cheek with the back of her hand. "All these years. All this time."

"It's true," Heather whispered, her fingers digging into her sweaty palms. "I'm the child you gave up for adoption."

Susan tried to stand, but her legs seemed to give way beneath her. Jake was at her side in a split second, his big work-scarred hand around her shoulder as she staggered across the floor and took her daughter in her arms.

"Heather. My own little Heather. Let me look at you." She cradled Heather's face in her trembling hands. "You can't know how many nights I lay awake thinking about you, wondering if you were happy, praying you were safe."

Heather quit fighting the tears, quit fighting anything but the unfamiliar emotions churning inside her. "I was always safe, and usually happy. My adopted parents loved me very much, and I loved them.''

"You were so tiny when I was forced to leave you, so helpless.''

Susan's breathing was ragged, her face pale. Heather held on to her as if she might dissolve in front of her, as if this might all be only a dream.

"You should have no regrets about leaving me at the orphanage. My new parents gave me everything I needed to grow into the woman I am today.''

"The things that I could never give you, even though I loved you more than life itself.''

Susan's eyes shone like diamonds in a mist, full of a love so strong Heather could feel it wrapping around her, warming her heart. If she lived to be a hundred, she'd never forget this night, this moment. It was as if Susan's spirit had bonded with hers, mother and daughter, joined for all time.

Finally, Susan pulled away, though she never let go of Heather's hands. Shoulders drooping, she dropped her head and stared at the rug beneath their feet. "I don't know how much you know about my life, Heather. I made so many mistakes.''

"I know all I need to know about your past. It doesn't change the fact that you gave birth to me, that I'm part of you and always will be.''

"Always.'' Susan's voice broke on the simple word. Tears spilled from her eyes again, this time running unchallenged down her sun-bronzed cheeks.

"Always, *Mother*. I've come home.''

A knot the size of Texas welled in Matt's throat. He swallowed hard, emotion pummeling his gut, dissolving the tough shell he used as a shield. The two women he loved the most in the world were both crying and talking all at once, pouring out their hearts.

Jake touched his arm. "I think we may be in the way here, son."

Matt stared at his father in amazement. If he didn't know better he'd think that was the glint of a tear in Jake McQuaid's eye.

MATT STEPPED into the kitchen and poured himself a cup of coffee. He and Heather had been in Colorado two days now, long enough for the events of the last few weeks to come out and be discussed in detail. And it was all the time either he or Heather could spare. She'd already extended her vacation long enough to see him through the touch-and-go days after Logan's bullet had torn through layers of flesh and muscle.

"You're up awfully early," Susan said, hurrying through the door. "Couldn't you sleep?"

"I slept fine, but my body's on Texas time now. Besides, I'm all grown up. I get up without being prodded, most of the time, anyway." He kissed her on the cheek. "Where's Jake?"

"Your *father* is in the shower. He'll be down soon. He doesn't move as fast as he used to."

"You're a saint, Susan, to live with that man all these years. You know my biggest fear in life is that I'm just like him, that I'll make some woman as miserable as he's made you."

"Miserable? Is that what you think, Matt, that I've been miserable living with Jake McQuaid?"

"Haven't you been? He grumbles and gives orders and does little else. If a compliment ever fell from his lips, we'd all expect the world to come to an end."

"Grumbling is not what this is about, Matt. Say it out

loud. You're still angry with your dad because your mother left him.''

"No, I was for a long time, but not anymore. Deserting me was her choice, and I can't blame him for that.''

"You shouldn't blame her, either. You can't know a person's heart. You certainly don't know Jake's.''

"You're right. How could I?''

Matt took his coffee to the table and sat down. Susan wiped her hands on her apron and dropped into the chair beside him. "Look at me, Matt, and listen to what I say. Jake never wanted things to be the way they were. He followed my wishes. I couldn't take his name legally, and I wouldn't take it any other way. If I was ever found out, I didn't want him dragged into it. He'd done enough already.''

"It seems to me *you* did all the doing. You took care of us, cleaned the house, canned food from the garden. How is it you figure Jake had done enough?''

"Your father gave up his job as a lawman because he couldn't keep it and me, too, and that was practically the same as giving up his soul. He was too much a man to live a lie, to hide a woman wanted for bank robbery under his roof while he wore a badge. Besides, even before he knew about the bank robbery, he knew I needed protecting. He just didn't know who from.''

Matt finished his coffee and pushed away from the table. Susan grabbed his arm. "I'm not through, Matt. It's time you faced things the way they are. Your father bore the brunt of his sons' resentment for years, just so that he could protect my secrets and so that he wouldn't destroy the bond I shared with each of you. He all but gave up his life for me. So don't tell me he doesn't know how to love. And don't tell me you're worried about being too much like him. You are like him, and you should thank your lucky stars every day that you are.''

''What's all the racket down here? You sound like a bunch of clucking hens.'' Jake's boots clacked on the kitchen floor as he made his entrance.

''Just a friendly discussion,'' Matt answered, carrying his cup to the sink.

''Well, since you're talking anyway, you might as well fill me in on the rest of the details. What's the latest on Rube and Paul?''

''They're both out on bail. The district attorney has offered them a plea-bargaining agreement. I'm sure they'll take it. Just having people know what they did to Billy Roy and Susan has been tough punishment for them, and no judge in the country is going to think they're dangerous.''

''What about Logan?''

''That's another story altogether. I talked to Sylvia yesterday. She said they're going for murder one for killing her mother. She wasn't as upset as I thought she'd be. I guess we've all grown up over the years. Now she just wants closure and to go on with her life.''

''And that leaves David Eisman,'' Susan said. ''It's hard to imagine I was ever married, even under duress, to a man as evil as he is. If he'd killed Heather or Matt...'' Her voice trailed off into a sigh. ''I can't even bear to think about it.''

''Well, he won't be on the streets again for a long, long, time, if ever,'' Matt assured her. ''Not only did he shoot me and kidnap Heather, but he killed Ariana Walker in cold blood and never showed a second's remorse.''

Susan trembled. ''I brought so much on all of you. I don't know how you keep on forgiving me.''

Matt kissed her on the cheek. ''Because we love you.''

"Yeah, we do," Jake seconded. "But we can't spend all day standing around talking. I've got a corral that needs some repair work. You can help me with it, Matt, if you don't have anything better to do."

Matt stood and stared at Jake, really seeing him for the first time since he and Heather had arrived in Colorado. The lines in his face were much deeper than Matt remembered them, his shoulders bent a little with age. "I think I could make time to help with the corral."

"Good." Jake poured himself a cup of coffee. "I'm glad you're home, son."

"Me, too, *Dad*. And no one is more surprised about that than I am."

MATT TOSSED in the twin-sized bed he'd slept in as a kid, a million thoughts galloping around in his mind. Things still weren't perfect between him and his father, but some of the resentment had eased. It was easy to see things in black and white, much more difficult to deal with shades of gray.

His father and Susan had dealt with the shades of gray and made a new life for themselves the best way they knew how. He understood that now. They'd found something in each other to hold on to, and years later, they were still together and happy. Who was he to argue with that? They were even talking about a wedding, a quarter of a century after the fact.

Matt had always loved Susan, just as much as if she had been his real mother. At some level he'd probably always loved Jake, too, but he was just now coming to terms with it. Hopefully, in time, the bond would strengthen between them, but it wouldn't happen in an instant, not the way it had with Susan and Heather. But then neither he nor his dad had ever been able to open up so freely.

Tomorrow he and Heather would leave Colorado. He'd go back to Texas, and Heather would go back to Atlanta. It would kill him to watch her walk away. She'd invaded every part of his life, every corner of his heart.

He knew she'd stay if he asked her, but how long would she be happy? He couldn't believe she wouldn't miss the city, expect him to be more romantic, to be someone he wasn't. He closed his eyes and tried counting cattle. He gave up as his bedroom door squeaked open.

"Are you awake, Matt?"

"Yeah. I can't sleep. I guess you're having the same problem."

Heather pushed his sheet aside and sat beside him. "I don't see it as a problem. My mind's just so full. I've never been so happy."

"I'm glad."

"My mother never wanted to give me away. It's nice to know that. She did what she had to do to keep me safe and to keep my life from being tainted with her past." She kicked off her slippers and pulled her feet onto the bed. "I think she needs me even more than I need her."

Matt tousled her hair. "You're easy to need."

"Do you need me, Matt?"

There was no missing the seriousness of her tone. He swallowed hard. "Not me. You're much too bossy for my style." He pulled her close, and his lips found hers, the need inside him eating away at his control. He struggled to keep the moment light. "Not to mention that you're a city girl and I'm a sh...a manure-kicking cowboy lawman."

"Since when did you launder your language so closely?"

"Since I stepped back inside Miss Susan's house. The

taste of soap forever lingers on my tongue when she's around.''

Heather ran her fingernails across his bare chest, and desire pitted inside him, hot and aching.

"You know, Matt, I may be a city girl, but I have boots now. A hat, too. It would be a shame to waste them."

"Whoa, hold on a minute." His insides tightened. "You're not getting caught up in the emotion of meeting your mom, and going off half-cocked, are you?"

"No, I know exactly what I'm doing." She dropped to the pillow and pulled him down beside her. "I want to sleep with you, Matt."

A strange mixture of relief and pain flashed through him. If that's all she wanted, he could definitely oblige. "Under your mother's roof? You are brazen." He started to kiss her again, but she rolled away from him.

"I want to sleep with you, but not just tonight. I want to do it forever. I want to sit across the breakfast table from you. I want to share your problems and tell you mine. I want to have your children."

"I doubt you know what you're asking for."

"I know. The question is do you want me, Matt? Do you love me?"

He buried his head in her breast. "You know how I feel about you. It's the *us* part that worries me. You'll stay a while, but what's to hold you forever? I'll get used to having you around, used to needing you, then you'll up and disappear."

"No one can promise forever, Matt, but I'm not your mother. I'm Heather, the same woman who has stood with you and by you. And I love you."

"What if I'm no good at being a husband?"

"You'll make a wonderful husband, maybe not for everyone, but for me."

Matt held her close. All his life, he'd been convinced he was too much like Jake McQuaid to ever make a woman happy. Susan had forced him to rethink that theory this week. Now Heather was in his arms, asking to be his wife. How could he say no to that? Why would he ever want to?

"You won't be getting much of a bargain. Just a cowboy lawman."

"I'll be getting the man I love."

Matt released his hold on her, his heart beating fast, as if it were already reaching out for the happiness she was offering. "If this is going to be it, I guess I'd better do it right." He rolled from the bed and fell to his knees.

Heather sat on the edge of the bed, her nightshirt brushing her shoulders, her hair tumbling about her face. He studied the image, knowing the sight of her at this moment would live inside him forever. "Heather Lombardi Hathaway…Jessup…whoever you are, will you marry me?"

"Yes, I'll marry you, but you forgot the 'I love you' part."

He crawled into bed beside her. "I didn't forget anything. I'm a man of action, remember? And I'm about to show you exactly how I feel." He skimmed her body with his hands as his mouth claimed hers.

She moaned and squirmed beneath him. "Matt McQuaid, are you sure you want to do this in Miss Susan's house?"

He kissed her again, soundly, his body screaming its need for her.

"What Miss Susan doesn't know won't hurt her."

"I love you," she whispered.

"And I love you."

"You did say it."

"Of course. You can always count on a Texas Ranger."